THE WATANABE NAME

SAKURA NOBEYAMA

Black Rose Writing | Texas

ISBN: 978-1-68433-290-8
PUBLISHED BY BLACK ROSE WRITING
www.blackrosewriting.com

Printed in the United States of America
Suggested Retail Price (SRP) $19.95

The Watanabe Name is printed in Calluna
Edited by Katrina Haritos
Cover painting by Akitomo Tsuchiya

The Watanabe Name is for my best friend and partner M,
and her four handsome boys.

ACKNOWLEDGMENTS

In writing this book, I was assisted by many friends. I would like to thank Karen Schneider, Sharon Browning, Dr. David Zmijewski, Julie Rice, and everyone else who contributed their invaluable advice and encouragement in the creative process and editing of this project. To all of you, I express my heartfelt gratitude.

I would also like to thank MJ Wang for her assistance with all things Chinese and the fine people at the Naka-Karuizawa Library and Blue Sky English School for their support and counsel. Many thanks to all.

THE WATANABE NAME

Up until 2004 in Japan, a fifteen-year statute of limitations existed. If the perpetrator of a crime, even murder, could elude capture or prosecution for that period, he or she was free to live a normal life.

PROLOGUE

New Year's Eve was supposed to be a peaceful day spent alone at Kenji's cabin, tucked away snug in the mountains. After a walk in the woods and an *onsen* bath, perhaps he would cozy up by the fire with a bottle of *sake* and watch mindless comedy on TV or, better yet, search the shelves for a good old book he hadn't read in years.

Though the temperature was still well below freezing, Kenji took his steaming mug of green tea out onto the front deck to enjoy the nature and tranquility of his private retreat, far removed from his chaotic daily routine in Tokyo. He wrapped both hands around the cup, taking advantage of the warmth it provided, as he sipped in leisure and took in the splendor of the surrounding forest. If any stranger had happened to chance upon the old man that morning, clothed in his warm cotton pajamas, housecoat, and slippers, they would have had no idea from the looks of him the unique struggles and painful episodes that had befallen such a well-to-do and well-known gentleman who was now eighty years old. There are always intimate thoughts and experiences below the surface of people which we don't know about, even those as intimate as our spouses or best friends – a secret past, veiled ambitions, unexpressed prejudices, hidden desires to name a few – that everyone keeps to themselves; and so it was with Kenji.

To all outward appearances, Kenji Watanabe was like many other successful men; he had a family, a business, friends, enemies, and the usual secrets that typically accrue to all such relationships. But there existed in his past one monumental event that he had painstakingly concealed, more to shield the others involved than for his own benefit. And, up until now, he had been successful in that endeavor.

And then the phone rang.

He didn't move right away as he presumed the caller to be his wife checking to see that he had arrived and to inquire about the condition of their log cabin after an extended absence. After a few rings, he began making his way back into the house, but before he reached the phone, the answering machine clicked on and played the recorded message informing the caller that no one was home and asking them to leave a message. The caller, a man to whom Kenji had not spoken for many years, left a message that sent a chill through his veins and halted him on the spot.

"Mr. Watanabe, this is Captain Miyabe. I have some urgent news that I am eager to share with you. I believe I may have finally solved the mystery surrounding your father's death, or at the very least, I have discovered information that would have given someone a strong motive to have killed him – something we never uncovered in our original investigation. A person of interest has been discovered but refuses to cooperate. I need to speak with you to verify a few details. Please contact me as soon as you receive this message."

Kenji stared at the phone and listened to the disconnecting click and hum of the dial tone. He had dreaded this moment for many years. It had all been set into motion on the fateful day back when he was still a young man, when his naivety had been exposed, and all he had been taught about honor was swept away. In a sense, life as he knew it had already ended because his view of the world had changed.

The murder the detective had spoken about had been committed many years after that day on August 15, 1967 at a festival in honor of his father's lifetime achievements. It had nearly ruined the Watanabe family name because Kenji had been the prime suspect both in the eyes of Captain Miyabe and the public. Kenji had hoped the matter had been laid to rest all those years ago, but it now appeared the family demons were poised for resurrection unless he took immediate action.

Kenji knew the *person of interest* well, and that this person had indeed been involved in the murder.

Kenji also knew why his father was killed.

But he had never told a soul.

And he never would.

The detective's message confirmed what Kenji had known for years – that he was the only person, other than the guilty, who could explain who killed his father and why, something Kenji desired to keep hidden from the world at all cost. Without Kenji's assistance and confirmation of details, Captain Miyabe would have no means to investigate the cold case.

He considered the alternatives one last time and resolved to take it all to the grave. The police would never be able to make a case without him. Now all he needed to do was find a way to sneak away and, somehow, die.

BOOK 1

1967

CHAPTER 1

Thursday, August 10th: Afternoon
Toumi – Village near Karuizawa, Nagano

There were days when the war and China seemed little more than a distant dream, and then there were days like today. Kenji sat naked on the smooth stones of the outdoor hot spring bath high above a mellow green valley deep in the mountains of Japan and marveled at the serenity. He took in the scenery through the rising steam swirling above the fountain. Views such as this, abounding in the magnificence of nature, had always been uniquely spiritual for him. This was the land where he had spent his summers as a youth away from Tokyo's stifling heat, horizon-blocking skyscrapers, punctual trains every four minutes, and the anonymity that came with living in the largest city in the world.

Out on the plateau far below, he spotted a train meandering down a track and a few scattered specks of automobiles ambling about unhurriedly. The terrain brought back bittersweet memories of the days he had spent in Manchuria serving in the Imperial Japanese Army during World War II. He closed his eyes and listened to the breeze lifting and lowering the branches of the many cedars beside the bath and inhaled the scents of summers past.

It was a time and place to ponder, and Kenji was a man who loved to reminisce.

If he could just go back to those days of youth – of simplicity and freedom from the complexities of life that now dogged him daily. A sudden gust of wind caused him to open his eyes, and he resolved that he would begin living life differently from today, a promise he made to himself and broke on a regular basis. He had one last soak in the hot spring, dried and dressed, and went out to the lobby to meet his companion.

As was her custom, Ai sat in a provocative pose on one of the many sofas in the spacious lobby, her slender legs drawn up under her petite frame, smoking a cigarette, and thumbing through a magazine. She wore a red silk pantsuit embroidered with fearsome golden dragons. Her hair was held in a bun on the back of her head with a few inviting strands falling about her face and neck. She had a natural beauty that required little effort to maintain. Few women smoked in public, but Ai lit up in defiance of social norms. It was her protest to the world and all its inequities. As Kenji strode through the empty lobby toward her, she smiled at him – a smile that still thrilled Kenji after all the years they had been together.

"You had a nice bath?" she said in Japanese, but with a Chinese accent that Kenji found captivating. Ai had come to Japan from China after the war with her baby girl, Kayo. Her Japanese was far from perfect, but with her sense of style and elegance, it was impossible to detect anything other than grace in her delivery. Her slight mispronunciations merely added to her considerable feminine charm.

Her name, Ai, was one of the few words that held a common meaning in both Chinese and Japanese: love. Kenji had helped her name her daughter Kayo, a Japanese name meaning forgiveness.

"Wonderful. And you?" Kenji replied, holding out his hand to help her up.

"The view here is so beautiful. It reminds me of home." She placed her fingers in his hand and stood, sliding her feet into gold sandals.

"Are you homesick?"

"Sometimes," she said as she put her hands on his chest. She looked into his eyes and asked, "Will you go away with me? We could have such a peaceful life together."

Ai loved to play the seductress, and it took all of Kenji's powers of restraint to keep her at bay in public. He hated the thought of cheating on his wife, but there was no doubt that Ai held a bewitching sway over his sensibilities. To her credit, Ai didn't enjoy torturing Kenji in any sadistic sense; she just thought he deserved better. She thought his family – his wife, mother, and father – caused him pain, and she hated anything that made Kenji unhappy. She loved Kenji, truly.

"If only that were possible," he said as he touched the hair about her cheek.

"Because you love her more than you love me," she teased.

The thought of his wife snapped him back to reality and caused him to become self-conscious. He glanced around, fearing that someone might be watching even though he didn't know anyone in the small town.

"Let's get out of here," he said as he took his hands away from her and began moving toward the exit, "I'll get the car." He pushed through the door and walked out into the parking lot.

Ai frowned as she moved even though there was no one to watch her, and Kenji knew that she would be pouting even though he couldn't see her. This was not the first time they had had this conversation.

He pulled to the front in his new Corvette convertible which he had just picked up in Tokyo the previous week. The family wealth afforded him many luxuries, and like most kids who grow up pampered, he took it all for granted. With a smile, he leaned over and pushed her door open, but she stood and stared for a moment before sliding in beside him. He wheeled through the parking lot and out onto the wandering mountain road.

"Can you stay tonight?" she said over the whine of the engine.

"I've got to be at the office first thing tomorrow," he said, trying to give a better excuse than the fact that he didn't want to have to go to all the trouble of making up lies for his wife as to why he wasn't coming home. "I'd better get back to Tokyo tonight."

"But I told you I have something important that I need to speak with you about."

Kenji shifted and downshifted through the sharp turns and could only glance at her occasionally. Ai sat with one foot pulled up on the seat under her thigh, staring at Kenji with an unlit cigarette between her fingers. The free strands of her hair were pressed by the wind against the sharp features of her face. Kenji had to make a conscious effort not to look at her.

"Let's talk now. What is it?" he asked.

"It's about Kayo," said Ai reluctantly, trying to decide how to discuss the topic in such a way that Kenji would be forced to stay the night to finish the necessary deliberations. "She's become bored living in the country like this," she said, waving her hand at the forest, "and wants to attend a university in Tokyo. She's interested in the arts and may want to pursue acting as a career."

"That's fantastic," Kenji said, looking over at her with a laugh that he tried to cut off as it was leaving his mouth. He didn't want to appear condescending and laugh off the prospect as the ludicrous idea of a star-struck young girl. "She's so beautiful. She'd make a wonderful movie star," he said with a straight face.

"And so that's it? You can just decide on our..." she hesitated. "I mean, you can just decide Kayo's future while flying down the road without a second thought." Kenji knew that Ai had almost said *our daughter's future*, and that was a phrase which was strictly forbidden.

"Well, Ai," he stammered, "I was just saying that it sounds like a good idea. That is, of course, it will require a great deal of thought and discussion, but if that's what Kayo has decided to do, then she'll have my full support."

"So, just let her move to the city alone? Is that how much she means to you, Kenji Watanabe?"

"Well she certainly isn't going to find a top-notch acting school here in the sticks of Nagano, now is she?" he said, allowing himself the laugh he had checked earlier. "You may think I'm lying, but I've always thought she was gifted. I believe that she'll be successful at anything she sets her mind to, and honestly, when I think about it, yeah, she could be an amazing actress."

"And I'll make such a fine, lonely, old spinster – how did you say it – *here in the sticks of Nagano*," Ai repeated.

Kenji stared straight ahead for a moment as they wound their way under the overreaching arches of the forest toward Ai's hideaway. A fisherman in hip boots just off the roadway fishing a rocky stream turned with a sneer as their car sped by, kicking up a torrent of dirt and pebbles.

"Ai, you know how I feel," he said as he glanced over to meet her gaze. "As much as I would like to move away somewhere and never come back...I just can't. My wife – my children – it wouldn't be right."

They pulled to a red light, giving Ai the opportunity to light her cigarette. She inhaled, tilted her head back, and let the smoke out through pursed lips as Kenji watched, thinking how she made anything she did look erotic. The heat of the day had been sweltering, and a welcome, cool breeze blew along the peaceful mountain road. A car behind them honked to break Kenji's reverie, letting him know that the light had changed.

"How is your dad?" asked Ai in a way that made it clear she didn't like the man.

Kenji's father, General Tatsurou Watanabe, had been diagnosed with lung cancer the previous year. Japanese doctors always kept such diagnoses from their patients so as not to place additional stress on an already difficult medical situation. They had only notified Kenji, as the eldest son, and his mother. He had confided in Ai because she was the one person he trusted not to spread the information. After discussing all of the possible treatment options, and the dangers of each, Kenji and his mother had decided to forego any treatment and let the old man enjoy whatever time he had left.

"Not bad. Little signs of slowing down, but he still doesn't know."

"That's good," she said. "We wouldn't want to see the great General Watanabe suffer, would we? He's such a wonderful human."

Kenji decided to let the comment go.

Chapter 2

Friday, August 11th: Morning
Tokyo

Kenji had been no match for Ai's powers of persuasion and had stayed until she decided to release him in the wee hours of the morning. The drive back to Tokyo was normally a good three hours, but Kenji had made it in half that, managing to get back a little before daybreak and lay down on his futon next to his wife, Ami. The *kanji* her parents had chosen for her name meant elegant beauty, and she had not disappointed.

Kenji had just dozed off when the alarm rang, which he slapped off before rolling over and going back to sleep. Ami woke him again at eight o'clock and asked why he hadn't gotten up earlier. He explained that he lost track of time on his test drive to Nagano the previous evening and had decided to take a nap in their summerhouse before returning early this morning. Following the standard protocol, she phoned and let his office know he would be getting in late, and he slept until ten. When he went downstairs his breakfast plate was on the dining room table covered with a napkin along with a glass of orange juice. Ami was outside in their front yard weeding the soil around the lavender and morning glory in her flower garden.

Kenji squinted, his eyes not yet adjusted to the light of day, and called out to her through the open sliding doors: "Did you call the office for me?"

"Of course – first thing this morning," came the chipper reply. "I told them you'd be in this afternoon and to call if they had anything urgent. Your secretary laughed when I said to call if she had anything urgent," she plodded on somewhat absentmindedly. "She said she couldn't remember anything urgent in all the time she's been there. Is that true? With such a large and important company, I told her there must be urgent matters sometimes. Don't you find it odd that she would say that?"

"Can't you ever just answer yes or no?" Kenji mumbled, turning away from the yard and the light.

"What did you say, dear? I can't hear you with all these bees buzzing around."

"Thank you," he said a bit louder as he sat down to eat.

Ami was not a bad wife, and she was actually quite an efficient and prudent mother. She was charming and attractive; she had been faithful; she kept house exquisitely; and, most importantly as far as Kenji was concerned, she always kept a cheerful, though at times insincere, disposition. But for many years now it had been as if he tolerated her rather than having any genuine feelings toward her – nothing like the desire he felt for Ai. Both the apathy and the passion troubled him.

Many things had begun to trouble Kenji.

"Did you have a chance to ask your father about the money?" she said as she came in, dropping her gardening gloves in a basket and moving to the sink to wash her hands. She had found a new house in the mountains which had caught her fancy, and since they had not purchased a new property in several years, she reasoned they were due for a new place. They already had their principal residence, a very spacious modern home in the high-rent district of Tokyo, and two other houses – a beach bungalow in Hawaii, and a log cabin in the mountains. But she had been after Kenji to talk his father into buying the new house for them because their mountain home was getting too old for the likes of a noble family such as theirs.

"He said he'd think about it," Kenji lied. He knew he could easily persuade his father to purchase the house but felt a bit disgusted at his wife's greed. Between new cars, private school tuition, new homes here and there, this favor and that *loan*, it seemed as if he was hitting his father up for money five or six times a year. And he already earned a ridiculous salary in the family business.

"Tell me again why it is that we need a new house," he said with a hint of sarcasm that eluded Ami.

"You know we can't continue to entertain guests in that little old house forever. The insects in summer are unbearable, and the wood on the deck is simply embarrassing," she replied.

"So why don't we sell it?"

"Well we can't do that," she said as she turned off the spigot and dried her hands. She brought a pail of boiling water from the stove, sat down beside Kenji, and poured over a strainer full of green tea leaves into a cast iron teapot. "We have so many wonderful memories there, and I was planning to let the boys use it in the future."

"I suppose the insects won't bother them at all, huh?" Kenji said as he pried open his salmon with chopsticks.

"Stop toying with me, Mr. Watanabe," she said, playfully slapping him on the arm.

"And I suppose this has absolutely nothing to do with your friend buying that new house in the same snooty neighborhood."

"Why would you say such a thing?" she replied. "Do you think me that shallow?"

"Of course not, dear. You are the epitome of moral integrity," he said with a straight face. "Salt of the earth – that's what I always say about you."

Ami gave him a cold stare, angry that he dared to hold her in ridicule, but knowing that there was no honest reply to be made. She knew, and she knew that Kenji knew, that her tennis mate's boasting about her new house in the snobbish, over-priced neighborhood where *anybody that was somebody* had to have an address had indeed influenced her. Ami had rehearsed her announcement to be made over lunch at the tennis club with the entire haughty-bitch populace present – the same way the impudent Miki had cockily regaled the women of the club some months prior. Maybe she would even invite the handsome young instructor to dine with them to add to the humiliation. *"Oh Miki,* she would begin, *Kenji and I drove by your new house. It is so cute! You had the right idea – keep it small and simple. That's what I wanted to do as well, but Kenji insisted we buy that mansion just up the street from you. You may not have seen it yet since it's located in the center of several acres of forest, not out on the street like yours. We've had to hire a team of caretakers year-round to oversee the place for us even though we're only there a couple of weeks during the year, whereas you can probably take care of that place of yours all by yourself, can't you?"* She couldn't wait to see the reaction on Miki's face.

Kenji knew that he should stop while he was still on the moral high ground, but he couldn't resist the temptation to further his assault on his wife's susceptible character. He had never known when to let well enough alone.

"And, by the way, you were asking the other day about my father's will," he said with apparent sincerity. The mention of the sacred topic lassoed Ami by the neck and brought her immediately out of her trance at the tennis club.

"Yes. Yes. Did you have a chance to speak with him?"

"I know it's because you're concerned for his well-being and peace of mind, of course," he began. "I asked him and, indeed, he did prepare a will several years ago," he said, pausing to see her reaction.

"Well, go on," Ami entreated. "Please, go on, Kenji."

"He's leaving everything to charity – Buddhist monks," he said without cracking a smile. "He wants us all to make our own way just as he's done."

Ami stood abruptly upon realizing the ruse and tossed the towel she had been holding toward the kitchen sink and started out of the room. "I'm glad my concern for our family's future provides you with such amusement," she said.

Kenji broke into laughter, choking on his breakfast. "Wait, I'm not finished. He says we can keep the money if we join," he said as he banged his fist on the table. "Come here. I want to see what you'd look like without any hair."

When she came back into the room in tears, Kenji felt ashamed for not stopping as he knew he should have. Although he still couldn't stop laughing, he wished he hadn't been quite so contemptuous of his wife's feelings.

"I'm sorry," he said as he stretched out his hand. She shied away, so he stood and took her into his arms. "Now come on, you know you want to laugh. That's pretty funny – you and I shaving our heads and becoming Buddhist monks, according to my father's wishes no less."

She attempted to pull away, but Kenji could tell that it wasn't a sincere effort. This was Ami's chance to gain sympathy, and she knew how to play this game like a pro. Kenji held her from behind and kissed her on her nape like he had often done when they were newlyweds. Years ago, he would have taken this opportune moment to carry her upstairs and spend an hour alone with her, but those days and those feelings were as dead as the samurai to Kenji now; although, not to Ami.

"Dad said he's taking care of Mom and then leaving everything to the three of us in equal shares, but that I can take over the business and buy them out."

"You've *got* to be kidding me," she said as she spun to face him. "Why should those useless brats get *anything*, much less a share equal to yours? That means they'll get some of his land and houses?"

"Look now, I didn't ask him to go into detail. I find it revolting to discuss what will happen to his property after he's dead. One-third of all his money is a heck of a lot, you know. And besides, Yumi and Taro need it a lot more than I do."

"Need has nothing to do with it," Ami snapped. "We deserve it. I mean – you deserve it. You've done everything your father has ever asked of you. You joined the army and served with honor and distinction while those little good-for-nothing leeches lounged in luxury. You took over the family business and caused it to thrive while they wined and dined and wasted whatever share they might have deserved. He's asked them both a thousand times to take a job with the company to earn their keep, and they've had nothing but excuses all their lives."

"I think he realizes that it's his fault that they've been spoiled and feels a need to take care of them after he's gone. In fact, he asked me to do just that."

Seeing a break in the clouds, Ami said, "That's fine. Of course we can look after them. Just tell your father to leave everything to you so they don't blow it all. We can see to it that they receive a yearly allowance of whatever he thinks they need – within reason of course."

Kenji sat back down to finish his breakfast, and Ami, sensing that she was gaining momentum, sat down with him and refilled his teacup. He eyed her with a grin expressing a mixture of suspicion and admiration. He thought of his father's cancer and realized Ami had a good point, although she knew nothing about it.

"Maybe you're right. I'll speak with him sometime today. Speaking of the family business, I'd better get to work – urgent matters or not."

"You know I'm right," she said. She placed her hands on his cheeks while gazing into his eyes. "What would you do without me?"

Without considering the question in the least, Kenji stood up and said, "Where are the boys? I haven't seen or heard them all morning."

She sighed, knowing she was being ignored, and pushed him toward the door. "They're studying. Don't worry about them, we can talk about them later. You need to focus on your father and make sure he gets that will right before something happens to him. I'll tell you what; you get him over here for dinner tonight, and I'll pick up some of his favorite sushi on the way home from the club this evening."

"I don't know about that. You know what condition he leaves everyone in every time he visits," Kenji said, stopping in the bathroom to brush his teeth.

"It'll be okay – I promise. We'll all have some *sake* and relax."

Kenji received the idea reluctantly knowing how his father stirred and stoked the ire of his family whenever he visited. Kenji was oblivious to his father's insults and condescension, but his wife and children took each barb into their psyche where they were stacked and stored alongside countless others for posterity. The result was that his wife and children hated his father, but, of course, Ami showed nothing but respect and admiration for purely ulterior motives.

He grabbed his coat and necktie by the front *genkan* and slipped on his shoes. Ami gave him a quick shoulder massage before he set out for the station.

"I'll take care of everything. You'll see," she called out after him.

He waved his hand without turning around and walked down the hill and out of sight. He knew it was a bad idea but decided to make up for the Buddhist-monk joke by letting Ami have her way.

CHAPTER 3

Friday, August 11th: Early Evening
Tokyo Ginza

After an uneventful afternoon, Kenji walked out of his office onto the bustling sidewalk of the Tokyo Ginza, home to some of the most exorbitant rates per square meter on the planet. He stopped at a corner market, bought a pack of Lucky Strikes, tore off the wrapper, and tossed one into his mouth – an actual toss and catch, like a kid catching pieces of popcorn. Smoking was an enjoyable habit for him, and part of the fun was lighting up. He had an unusual method of popping his Zippo lighter open with a downstroke on his thigh and striking the flint with a quick reverse stroke.

Every time he did it, he thought it looked cool. That thought was followed by the realization that he was hopelessly spoiled and had way too much free time on his hands.

He lit up and stood on the corner, watching herds of faceless men and women flow by, and tried to think of an excuse to get out of dinner with his family tonight. There was a payphone on the corner, so he picked up the receiver, dropped in a 10-yen coin, and pulled the digits of his home number on the rotary dial.

"*Moshi, moshi,*" was the answer from the other end.

"Masa, it's Dad."

"Hey, Dad. What're you doing?"

"I'm still downtown waiting for a contractor. I need to buy him a few drinks and talk over a deal."

"I thought we were having dinner with the tyrant tonight," replied his son.

"Come on, Masa; don't be so judgmental – that's your grandpa you're talking about."

"Yeah, you're right. I should be more factual and precise, as Grandfather points out every chance he gets. Let me try again. I thought we were having dinner with that annoying, verbose, control-freak who knows everything about everything and never has one kind word to say for the rest of humanity tonight."

"You can be truly entertaining at times, Masa – especially when you're not trying. Anyway, try to be nice – Grandfather won't be around forever, you know."

"Thanks for the uplifting thought," Masa replied. "Anything I can do to speed up the process?"

"Seriously now, you be nice. And tell your mother I might be running a little late. He'll be there around seven. You guys go ahead and get started if I'm not there."

"Actually, I was serious. And speaking of hastening death, Mom is going to kill you if you're not here on time. She can't stand him any more than the rest of us."

"Take it easy, Masa. Tell her I'm sorry. It came up at the last minute. I'll get there as quickly as I can. I promise." An expression between a cringe and a smile appeared on his face as he uttered the last word.

"Just between you and me, Dad, I know you're lying. And Mom's going to know it, too. I'll be sure to pass on your message, but she's going to be ticked off if we have to deal with that man all by ourselves."

"Be a good kid and try to be convincing."

Masa was the eldest of Kenji's two sons. He was a twenty-one-year-old college student, reasonably bright, but not ambitious; at least, not ambitious in the way his grandfather thought he should be. Yoshi, his youngest son, was eighteen and had entered a small music college after graduating high school. There had been a time not so long ago when both of his sons worshipped their grandfather – true hero worship, a general in the Imperial Japanese Army, revered and known by all – but somewhere around adolescence their relationships had spiraled downward. The grandfather had decided that the only suitable careers for his progeny other than the military, which had been replaced with an impotent self-defense force after World War II, were either in the fields of law or medicine. Masa had inherited his grandfather's strong will but was in all other respects very different. He was interested in becoming an artist, a painter, while Yoshi dreamed of becoming a concert violinist. Their grandfather, however, had belittled both *hobbies* at every opportunity since learning of their interests. This was one of the few areas where Kenji's wife and his father were in agreement, and it had driven an irrevocable wedge into the bond they had once shared.

Kenji hung up the phone, flicked his cigarette butt on the sidewalk, and snuffed it out with the toe of his Bruno Magli. He went back into the same store where he had bought the cigarettes minutes earlier and seemed to notice the shopkeeper for the first time. He selected a small, but expensive, bottle of *sake* just because he liked the cherry blossom tree on the label and placed it on the counter.

"Fifty yen, sir," the merchant said as he placed the bottle in a brown paper bag.

What a life, Kenji mused as he watched the man, about his own age, make change and place it in his hand. *Inside this little shit hole all day, every day, and can't even afford a trip to the dentist's office,* he thought as he regarded the numerous gaps in the man's smile.

"Thank you for your bi'ness, sir. Please come again," said the shopkeeper.

What the hell could you possibly be so happy about? "Thanks to you, my friend. Have a nice day," he said as he picked up his bottle and headed back out onto the crowded street. The sun was going down, leaving streaks of pink and light blue on the evening horizon in the few spots where the sky was visible between buildings. He struggled with the choice of going home straight away or procrastinating as long as possible. After a minute's deliberation, he resolved to make his way directly, but if he was going to be subjected to an evening of his wife's ass kissing, his father's abuse, and his children's slow torment, he was going to have a stiff buzz doing it. And, although he assured himself it was not his intended purpose, there was a definite possibility that the trip home might take longer than usual.

After a leisurely stroll, stopping twice to glance at newspaper headlines, Kenji reached the train station at 7:30 but decided to take a taxi instead. It was quite a bit more expensive, but roomier and easier to drink and smoke. He walked to the cab at the front of the line and hopped in the back seat as the driver, wearing a white hat with black brim and white gloves, held the door open. He gave his address and told the driver to stop at the nearest liquor shop, then lit another Lucky as he pulled his bottle of *sake* out of the paper bag. He finished it off just as the driver pulled to a stop on the side of the street and opened his door. Within a minute, he was climbing back in with two large cans of Sapporo Beer and a bag of rice crackers.

"Sadaharu Oh is having a hell of a season," said the driver who was listening to the Tokyo Giants baseball game on the radio.

"Yeah. He'll be setting the home run record someday without a doubt," replied Kenji. He popped open one of his beers, drank it down, and started to feel pretty good despite the dreaded dinner engagement.

"Were you in the war?" Kenji asked the driver out of the blue, knowing that many men of his age had been. The driver studied him in the rear-view mirror.

"Lost three brothers and my father – two brothers on Iwo Jima. I was lucky. I was in China. What about you, Captain?"

Kenji knew that many soldiers had had worse experiences than he in the war – obviously, as he had been fortunate to survive – but he had never heard anyone use the expression *lucky* in connection with their time in China. "I guess I was lucky, too. I was also in Manchuria." Kenji looked back at the driver through the same mirror. "I suppose, compared to some places, life was good there, huh?"

The driver smiled and nodded his head with delight. "You know, I wish I had one yen for every Chink I poked over there. Those young Chinese girls used to put up a good fight before we held them down and showed them who was boss," he said, letting out a laugh that, along with the subject matter, brought an abrupt end to Kenji's festive buzz. "You're right, Captain. Life sure was good there."

The carefree mood he had achieved with the alcohol was replaced by indignation and contempt. Memories of Manchuria came flooding back.

"Just drive the fucking taxi," he said.

"Hey buddy, you're the one who started this conversation," the driver said. "If you don't want to talk, maybe you shouldn't ask questions," he said as he shook his head and turned up the volume of the ballgame.

Kenji opened his last beer and played with his lighter. His house was a few short blocks away now, and he wondered what hell was playing out in his unexcused absence. Then his mind drifted back to China.

Life sure was good there.

What a sickening thought.

CHAPTER 4

Friday, August 11th: Evening
Tokyo

Kenji entered the front door and announced that he was home. Ami hurried down the hall toward him wearing a kimono, a definite sign that she was playing a role tonight. She concealed her irritation at his tardiness admirably, as she had other fish to fry at the moment.

"I take it no one has strangled him yet," Kenji said, stumbling out of his shoes.

"Stop that," she whispered. "What if he hears you? You didn't mention anything at all about having a business meeting tonight. I thought you and your father were coming together," she continued in a low voice.

"It came up at the last minute. A very important city councilor stopped by the office and asked me to join him for drinks. There was no way out of it," he said, forgetting which lie he had told his son.

"That's funny. Masa said you were waiting to meet a contractor." After a short pause as he slid his feet into his house slippers, he smiled, adding, "Oh yeah, him too."

Not wishing to waste precious time on meaningless squabbling, she pulled his arm, stopping him in the hallway that led from the entrance to the dining room. He swayed noticeably as he peered down into her sober eyes.

"Before we go in, I want you to know that we've been talking about the importance of maintaining our family image, and he agrees that buying a new house in Nagano would be an excellent idea."

"Let me guess," he said as he placed a hand on her shoulder for balance. "The poor sucker just doesn't know that the plan is for *him* to pay for said abode yet, right?"

"Listen. He's in a very good mood. He loved the meal, and he's on his second bottle of *sake*. Just say something along the lines that you like the idea of a new place, but you're not sure that it will fit into our budget at the moment. You know he'll offer to pay for it if you act like you want it."

"Where is the mark?" said Kenji slurring his words.

"I told you to stop joking like that," Ami implored in a loud whisper before catching herself and lowering the tone. "Are you drunk, Kenji? I hope you realize how important this is for us. I've set this up perfectly; all you have to do is finish it off."

Ami motioned the way and then followed along behind him subserviently to further impress her father-in-law, demonstrating that she was a traditional, obedient wife.

There was a long, hardwood corridor that ran the length of the front of the house on the first floor with traditional *shoji* doors to the left. They opened to a stone garden with *bonsai,* but Ami had shut them all for additional privacy tonight. On the right were three rooms precisely the same size but of very different styles and furnishings. The first was a western-style parlor filled with European furniture and paintings, maroon velvet curtains on the rear wall, and an ebony grand piano that Ami used to impress her club friends to show how enlightened and modern they were. However, she was careful to keep the doors of this room closed whenever more traditional, conservative guests were visiting. The doors were closed tonight.

The next room was dedicated to paying homage to the family ancestry and contained a two-meter high Buddhist shrine. An extensive gallery of portraits of the superior Watanabe lineage lined the walls, beginning with Kenji's father on the right as one entered the room, and, in reverse chronological order, the patriarchs of each generation wound around the room going back ten generations. Ami had placed fresh fruit, rice, pastries, and *sake* on the altar, and lit several sticks of incense as an offering to the gods and ancestors. The doors to this room were wide open.

The third room along the corridor was a traditional Japanese *tatami* room with one low, black lacquer table running perpendicularly to the hallway at which Kenji's father now sat at the far end at the head of the table wearing a summer kimono with Kenji's two sons on either side. Masa, seated on the left, and Yoshi, across from him were both in a visible state of displeasure when Kenji entered and took his seat nearest the door facing his father.

"Ah, Kenji, how was your business meeting?" asked the old man.

"Fantastic," said Kenji. "Everything is working out perfectly for the new golf course project. I think we'll be breaking ground by next spring if all goes according to plan."

"You see how your father gets things done?" began the old man's castigation of his grandsons. "I'm guessing that this project will bring the corporation more than a hundred million yen per month if it's managed competently." He picked up his cup of *sake* with his left hand, his elbow resting on the table, and took a long drink while pointing the index finger of his right hand at his young audience. "Now," he began, "playing a violin in an orchestra will *never* bring in even a million *per year*. In fact, it's a damn good way to lead your family straight to the poor house. And painters, even *if* they're good, don't make any money until they're dead. And I believe there's a general consensus on this point; namely, that this is not a particularly good time to amass your fortune. It's high time you boys give up this foolishness and let me get you into a reputable law program. After graduation, I guarantee I can get you into any political seat your heart desires."

General Watanabe was not a large man, but his presence in a room, any room, was impressive and formidable. Every word he uttered seemed to be in someone's face, as if he had his shoulders pulled back and his head thrust nose-to-nose with an adversary. With his white hair still in a military-style crew cut, his head held high, and his strong bass voice booming at full volume, he had a most intimidating nature, even while sitting cross-legged and speaking to his grandchildren.

"Yoshi was just elevated to first chair in his college orchestra," said Masa proudly, and in defiance of his grandfather's predilection. "I think he should be commended for this accomplishment, especially in his first year. Are you not at all proud of him, Grandfather?" he said as he stared at the old man with what Kenji feared was a look of veiled contempt. Ami rushed and knelt behind the grandfather ready to refill his cup as soon as was prudent.

The general turned up his cubical wooden cup and drank the remainder, then slammed it down on the table for emphasis and slid it over so that Ami could refill without disturbing him. Ami took the bottle and poured, trying not to make a sound. The old soldier leaned back, assuming a pose of strength and authority, a knowing smirk creasing the lines of his hard, weathered face.

"You know," he said, pausing for effect so that everyone knew to listen for the wisdom he was about to impart, "I suppose a man at this," he hesitated again and with condescension added, "*college* you attend, who is promoted to head janitor might feel some sense of pride when he goes home and announces to his wife and children, in their dilapidated one-room apartment, that he's been elevated to chief toilet scrubber and will be rewarded with an additional 500 yen to his measly monthly pay. But the fact is, he is still nothing more than a janitor, now isn't he?"

Yoshi sat staring straight ahead at nothing, trying not to show any emotion, but his lips and eyes were beginning to betray him. Ami sat obediently quiet. She dared not interfere. Kenji looked at his sons with empathy but also said nothing, happy that he had decided to guzzle as much booze as possible on the ride home.

Masa, however, was unable to hold his tongue after such an affront to his brother's dignity.

"That is unfair on so many levels I hardly know where to begin," he said in a voice that was beginning to tremble.

"And lest you risk the penalty of impertinence, I suggest you do *not* begin anywhere," their grandfather said.

"Not the least of which," Masa continued, disregarding his grandfather's warning, "depending on his birthright, or lack thereof, his upbringing and station in life, and his mental acuity, it is most likely unfair to your hypothetical janitor. It may be that one born to unfortunate circumstances, or with limited means or opportunities, may well be justified in taking pride in such advancement. And regarding my brother," he said as his speech slowed to emphasize each word, "he worked very hard to get that promotion."

Kenji could see that Masa was struggling to keep control of his emotions and maintain proper decorum and respect for his elder. He feared his son was in danger of losing the battle.

"Working hard is not the issue at hand," said the old man. "Working hard is a given for anyone in my family. The *goal* for which you strive is the measure of a Watanabe. And your goals and ambitions are about to change. Kenji, Ami, you will cancel their enrollments at these vocational jokes that pass themselves off as colleges at once and apply to the University of Tokyo. I have already spoken to the dean of admissions, and they will matriculate at the beginning of the next term." He turned up his cup and drank without taking his eyes off of his grandson. Masa stared back with an expression that, while blank, still had the effect of conveying detestation. Yoshi had recovered and continued to stare straight ahead, as if he were a marble statue, revealing nothing.

"I think it best for the two of you to go upstairs and let me discuss this with your grandfather," said Kenji.

They stood, and Masa looked away from the old man. "*Gochiso sama deshita*," they said in unison with a formal bow. Even with the excess of hostility, the boys still turned and bowed to their grandfather again before leaving the room. The three adults sat, not looking at one another, as they heard the boys climb the stairs and shut the doors to their rooms.

•   •   •

After a few minutes, the old man said, "I know you think I'm being too hard on them, but I'm speaking from experience. I was away during the war and spent very little time with Yumi and Taro. Their mother babied them, and before I knew it, they were ruined as far as being productive members of the family, or even society in general," he said, raising his hand in a gesture of disbelief. "Unlike you, Kenji, they were pampered, placated, not just as children, but through their teenage years and into adulthood. They were spoiled, and I know full well that it is beyond my powers to ever change them. When I just said that working hard is a given for anyone in my family, I know that I'm being hypocritical. But your boys are still young, so I think it wise to alter their course before it's too late. Trust me; this will be best for them in the long run."

The old man had been talking as if he were still trying to convince himself as much as Kenji and Ami. The way he talked, looking at nothing in particular as he spoke, was atypical of the old soldier. They listened to his thoughts without interruption, neither agreeing nor disagreeing with the sentiments. When he finished, they sat in silence for several minutes of meditation on the subject with the men having occasional drinks to lubricate their minds. The only sounds to be heard were those which ordinarily went unnoticed: the tick-tock of the grandfather clock in the corridor, the occasional shift in position of the old man, or the mesmerizing drop and swirl of *sake* as Ami poured.

"And by the way, I've been thinking about what you mentioned earlier today," the general started again. "Of course, I thought all these things over when I wrote my original will, but I think you may be right. Perhaps I should leave Yumi and Taro a home, enough money that they'll not be destitute, and leave everything else to you with the understanding that you agree to see to the welfare of your little brother and sister and their families. I assume you can both give me your word of honor on that."

The subject seemed to have materialized from thin air. Kenji looked up at his father and saw Ami, urging eyes wide open staring at him, nodding her head up and down, from where she knelt at the side of the table. Reasoning that it would be best to display restraint rather than blurting out immediate assent, he paused before nodding.

"Yes, I feel that this will truly be in their best interests. This will be best for them in the long run," Kenji said without realizing that he had just repeated, verbatim, his father's words regarding Masa and Yoshi minutes earlier.

Ami excused herself, tiptoed out, and returned with a tray of crackers, caviar, and a new bottle of *sake*. She spooned the delicacy onto crackers and slid them before the men, mindful to keep both cups full while they discussed various business matters. To the untrained eye, she was a dutiful, well-trained wife and daughter-in-law, performing menial tasks for her masters. In reality, she was a cunning manipulator who was playing the old man like a well-tuned Stradivarius. And, of course, both Kenji and his father knew her schemes but were willing to let her have her way as long as she continued to play by the rules.

"Bring some beer, Ami," commanded the old man as the mood in the room appeared to be coming out of the doldrums. She sprang to her feet without a word. Her kimono was wrapped tightly, but she moved as swiftly as the garment would allow. She returned with two large bottles of beer, two small, clear glasses, and a bottle opener. She opened one of the bottles and poured for them, first for the general and then for her husband.

Kenji held his glass out toward his father for a toast.

"Wait. Ami, bring another glass," the old man said.

Ami attempted her best blush and shy smile, which she concealed behind a hand over her mouth, as she stood and did as instructed. When she returned and placed the glass on the table with both hands, the old man picked up the bottle and poured for her, something he had never done before.

"Now," he said, "*Kanpai*!" They all lifted their glasses and drank to good fortune. Kenji picked up the bottle and poured his father's glass full again.

Then he waited for Ami to finish and filled hers. The glasses were purposefully small to give them many opportunities to pour for each other – a Japanese custom to allow friendly gestures during the drinking ritual. Ami soon slipped out, taking her glass away so as not to push her luck.

"Ami tells me you've found a nice, new place in Karuizawa," his father commented.

"Not me," said Kenji. "Ami has found a place *she* likes in Karuizawa. I just don't think it's wise to lay out that kind of money for another vacation house at this time with all the college tuition we'll be paying. Did she happen to tell you how much they want for that place?" Ami reappeared and took up her duties, pretending not to have heard a word of the men's conversation, when, in reality, she had not missed a syllable.

"That's of no consequence. Give me the name and number of the listing agent in the morning, and I'll see to it that we get it for far less than the asking price."

"Yes sir, but even if you do get it at a good price, I don't have the liquid cash to pay right now, and I don't want to have a loan payment to worry about."

Everyone knew that a game was being played, and they thought they knew the others' motives. The old man had money and was using it to control their lives. If he was to speak the truth, he would just tell them that he was a spoiled rich man, accustomed to getting his way, and here was the money if they promised to make their sons go to the school of his choice and follow the career path he chose for them, regardless of what they wish to do in life, because he's a selfish SOB. He played the game instead. If Ami were to receive a dose of sodium pentothal, she would admit that she hated the general, that her only true loves were money and her own vanity, that she wished the old man would drop dead and leave everything to her; but she, too, played the game instead. If Kenji were honest, he would tell them both that he found their greed and love of money revolting, and that he wished to be done with them forever so that he could spend the rest of his life with Ai, but like the others, he played the game instead.

"I'd love to buy it for her, Dad, but I think we'd better stick with the places we have for now."

"Let's call it a celebration gift in honor of my grandsons' acceptance into the finest university in Japan. Knowing that they will carry on the Watanabe name with pride and distinction gives me peace of mind, and, in return, I would like to reward you."

With the strings having appropriately been attached, the grandfather knew that his diligent and obedient daughter-in-law would ensure the enrollment he desired. He knew she would rather sever a limb than lose out on a house such as this: a home to be showcased, and upon which there would be no end to her boasting. He had them all exactly where he wanted. Kenji and Ami bowed with appreciation.

One small detail had eluded the party's notice. One of the young gentlemen had come back downstairs and hidden behind the Buddhist shrine in the adjoining room, listening to them plan his future.

"Did you come by train tonight?" Kenji asked. "I didn't see your car outside."

"No. Kazu dropped me off and I sent him on a few errands. I'm sure he's outside waiting by now."

"Kaz is here and you didn't tell me?" said Kenji. "Ami, go tell Kaz to come in and have some dinner."

"You'll do nothing of the sort," said his father with disgust. "Kenji, for all your superior breeding and good sense, you've never been able to distinguish what is proper for family and what is proper for the treatment of a servant."

"Kaz is family as far as I'm concerned," said Kenji.

Kazu Ishii was the general's driver and had been one of Kenji's favorite people since he was a boy. Kazu's father and mother had also worked for the Watanabe family many years earlier, and Kazu had been a friend of Kenji's father long before he became a general. He had served in the Imperial Japanese Army in China as General Watanabe's personal assistant. Kazu was a hefty, handsome, gregarious man about the same age as General Watanabe. He had been a handsome young man also, popular with the ladies even though he was a member of Japan's lower class. The general had enjoyed his company, both for the personal interaction and for the endless stream of young ladies that seemed to follow in his wake. And if there was one person on earth who Kenji held in higher regard than Kazu himself, it would be Kazu's wife, Mrs. Ishii.

Instead of dragging him into the house and causing a scene, Kenji excused himself under the pretense of checking on the boys upstairs and headed in the direction of his old friend. The young man who had been eavesdropping from the adjoining room moments earlier had vanished. Kenji stopped by the kitchen and grabbed a plate of sushi and some sandwiches, a bottle of beer, and a paper cup, all of which he piled on a silver serving tray. He went out the back door with his hands full, kicking the door shut with his foot. He snuck around the house and into the carport behind the large Cadillac where he saw Kazu, sitting behind the wheel, paging through a magazine of scantily clad young women. He crept up to the open window on the driver's side and spoke out: "What are you looking at there, Kaz?"

Kazu jerked and shoved the magazine between the seats. A friendly smile flashed across his face when he realized it was just Kenji giving him a hard time.

"Dammit, Kenji, I nearly pissed all over myself. Why do you want to scare an old man like that?" He opened the long, heavy door and stepped out.

"I thought I'd bring you a snack and have a chat," said Kenji, placing the tray on a metal storage cabinet on the side of the carport. "You're looking good, Kaz. Must be those magazines you read that keep you looking so young." For as long as Kenji could remember, Kazu had always had a few girly magazines stashed in his glove box. It had been a treat as a youngster to sneak into Kazu's car with his friends and look at the forbidden pictures.

"Wow, how did you know I was starving out here? Boy, this looks great!" Kenji loved the sound of Kazu's voice. It was clear that he was not pretentious, and that was one of the things Kenji adored about him. The uneducated, childlike qualities of his nature and speech set him apart from everyone Kenji had to deal with on a daily basis.

Kenji pulled some chopsticks from his pocket and handed them to him. Kazu was a big man with a big appetite. When he was hungry, he could put away large helpings of sushi without the necessity of chewing. He tossed down the first few pieces in a matter of seconds while Kenji opened the beer and poured him a cup.

"Thanks, Kenji," he said holding up a hand in noble protest, "but you know I can't drink while I'm on duty."

"Yeah, right," said Kenji. "I know this isn't nearly as strong as the *juice* you keep in the trunk, but I think you'll be alright as long as we hold it to just one bottle."

Kazu smiled, took the cup of beer, threw it back like a shot of whiskey, and held it out for a refill. In all his days, Kenji could never remember seeing Kazu drunk, but he always had a flask of *shouchuu* handy for extended waits.

"Say, what are you doing out here anyway?" Kazu asked. "I thought you and the old man had some serious business to discuss tonight."

"I just couldn't take it anymore, Kaz. Between Dad and Ami, I'm not sure who disgusts me more. You know how they are; all they've ever cared about is money and prestige. I swear I think if I dropped dead here on the spot, their only regret would be that I wasn't around to further their money-making schemes."

Kazu gave a disapproving frown and lowered his head at the young man to signify that Kenji was about to receive a reprimand. "Come on now, you know that's not true. You should hear your dad talking about you everywhere he goes, 'Kenji did this, and Kenji did that,' and, well I've just never seen a prouder father in all my days." The idea of Kazu trying to scold was comical. His smile was back before he finished the first sentence.

"That's my Kaz. All you can see is the good in people. I guess that's how you landed that beautiful wife of yours. I wish I could have been lucky enough to find someone like Mrs. Ishii. She's the last of a dying breed. Speaking of which, how is she?"

Kazu was about to pop another piece of sushi into his mouth but stopped with the mention of his wife. His ubiquitous smile vanished. He stood leaning against the door of the car staring at the food held between the chopsticks. Kenji could see that there was a problem.

"Kaz. Is something wrong?"

"Yeah," he said, "I guess your dad wouldn't tell you something like that – to spare your feelings, you know."

"What," said Kenji, trying to enunciate clearly, "did he not tell me?"

Kazu took a deep breath as he returned the food to the plate. "Doc says she's got something called leukenia."

"You mean leukemia?"

"Isn't that what I said? Got it pretty bad." Kenji could see that Kazu was giving a speech that he had given before. It was practiced, and there was little emotion where Kenji would have expected it. "Poor thing's lost all her weight, always cold, even in the middle of summer. Doc says I'll be lucky to have her another six months."

The words came to Kenji, but instead of the sympathy he sought, it was the more base, coarse emotion – the one he could rely on in times of crisis – anger.

"Dad knew about this," he said, "and didn't tell me? Why the hell does he have you out working tonight? Damn, how can a man be so cold?"

Kazu shook his head. "Hold on there, Kenji. Don't blame it on him," he said as he wiped his mouth with the back of his hand. "I know you're upset, but this is just a part of life. He can't get used to a new driver while he has all this important business to tend to. Think about it, Kenji, you guys have that new golf course to worry about."

Kenji stared in amazement as he reflected on the words. He wondered if it were possible that Kazu could believe so lowly of him to think that he considered a golf course to hold greater value and importance than Mrs. Ishii's life. Ami and his father? Of course, but did people like Kazu really think of him the same way?

"Besides, I can't stand to sit and watch her waste away like that all day, and if I stay home, she'll figure something's up." He fidgeted with his chopsticks and stared at the food, unable to look Kenji in the face. "We've got plenty of friends who stop by and make sure she's okay, and the kids try to help out when they can."

"Damn, Kaz, I'm sorry. I want to go see her. Is that okay?"

"Of course," Kazu said, his smile back in a flash. "You know she loves you like her own son. But Kenji," he reached out and put his hand on Kenji's shoulder, a gesture he often used to show sincerity, "no word of this leukenia. She doesn't know. Doc thinks it'll take time off her clock if she finds out."

"I promise not to mention a thing about it. I just want to see her. Can you tell her I'll be stopping by tomorrow?"

"She'll be thrilled," said Kazu, patting Kenji on the shoulder with his bear claw of a hand. "Too bad there aren't more young men like you in the world these days."

Kenji waved off the compliment as he started walking back around the house.

"I'll kick Dad out so you can get back home to your beautiful wife."

"No need to rush him, Kenji. And thanks for the feast," he shouted out after Kenji turned the corner.

CHAPTER 5

Friday, August 11ᵗʰ: Night
Tokyo

The American hit song "San Francisco" played on the radio upstairs in Yoshi's room while he did his math homework and Masa threw darts. Masa often visited his little brother's room in times of family friction and sought the stoic and calming influence the latter could bring.

Be sure to wear some flowers in your hair, flowed into the room. The excitable older brother could never understand how Yoshi could keep his cool in stressful situations but admired him for it all the same. He felt a bit embarrassed that his younger brother played the role of soothing counselor typically reserved for the elder sibling.

"Why can't we ever be left alone to make our own decisions?" said Masa rhetorically as he threw. And then turning to his brother added: "Aren't we capable of deciding what we want to do with our futures?"

There was no answer as Yoshi continued solving a problem. The younger brother had learned long ago that the best way for Masa to work through his troubles was to vent unimpeded by anyone else's input. Masa knew the answers to his questions before he asked them, and any answer in contradiction of his opinion was flat wrong. He never wanted to discuss alternative viewpoints; he just wanted confirmation that his judgment was the only sane and rational way to think – not at all unlike the character of the grandfather he railed against.

"Times have changed," he said, unaware that his mantra was that of countless generations of similarly situated young adults for time immemorial. *There's a whole generation, with a new explanation. People in motion...* "Why can't he get that through his thick head? There's more to life than trying to weasel everything you can into the sacred Watanabe Corporation coffers. Why should he care if we choose to live our lives differently than he and Dad have done? Don't just sit there scribbling – say something."

Yoshi looked up from his book and closed his eyes. He considered his options. Number one was to join Masa in the revolt, even though he knew the futility of the campaign. Number two was to point out the uselessness of said revolt, but that would lead to a bitter argument in which he had no desire to participate. Or, number three, he could try to find a way to be Swiss and pass it back to his brother to handle.

"What do you think we should do?" said the pacifist.

Masa shook his head and threw his darts harder than was prudent for accuracy. Physical exertion was his principal medium of stress relief.

"We can't openly disobey him if he's made up his mind," offered Yoshi. "Is there any chance we could talk him out of this? Convince him that we have no interest in becoming politicians or lawyers?"

"You know the answer to that as well as I do. Grandfather *never* changes his mind. He's going to try to control us until the day he dies." Masa stopped throwing, and Yoshi turned around to look at him and saw that he was deep in thought.

"What?" said Yoshi.

"Nothing."

"Why did you stop throwing?"

"Just thinking."

"Thinking about what?"

"Well, just that when he dies, you know, things will be better."

"You shouldn't think things like that."

"I didn't say I wished he was dead."

"Well, you should get it out of your mind."

"I didn't try to think it. It just popped into my head. Sometimes my mind has a mind of its own."

"You should think of something else."

Masa sat down cross-legged on the floor and put the darts down beside him. He said, "I'm not saying I wish it or anything, Yoshi, but it's just a fact that he treats us and everyone else like a bunch of puppets; and when he dies, I don't plan on shedding one single tear for that man."

Yoshi turned back around to his desk and said, "He's our grandfather. No matter what, you have to be more respectful."

"How can you talk like that?" Masa said with a baffled expression. "Do you want to quit your college and go to the University of Tokyo and become some stiff-necked lawyer wearing a suit every day for the rest of your life? Because I sure as hell don't."

Yoshi turned back around once Masa began to speak reasonably and said, "No, of course not, but then again, there could be worse things to have to do in life. Have you ever considered that just maybe Grandfather could be right? Maybe he's seen more of life than we have and thinks we'll be better off this way. I mean, it is the University of Tokyo, you know. Some people would give anything to get into that school, and here we are griping about it."

Masa shook his head as he considered the point.

"If we keep our mouths shut," said Yoshi, "you can still pursue art, and I can still pursue music. We just have to change our majors to law, but we don't have to give up our ambitions."

"You don't see it yet, Yoshi, but he's guiding us in like a shepherd guiding sheep. And once he gets us into that pen, we're never getting out."

The two sat in silence for several minutes, Masa seated on the floor and Yoshi at his desk, pondering the uncertainties and contemplating what seemed to them the most significant decision of their lives. So many choices were made every day which had significant implications, but they knew that the course about to be chosen would have a profound impact on their futures.

From Masa's perspective, there was the fundamental belief, common to strong-minded young men, that he knew what he wanted for his future more than anyone else and that he had the right, as an adult, to choose for himself. But equally compelling for him was the antipathy he had, not only for his grandfather, but also for the idea of letting a man such as that make his decisions for him. He loathed the man, his determination, the audacity in trying to usurp his independence, and if he allowed it, his cowardice – his emasculation. But there was also the other side of the coin – Yoshi's idea that perhaps Grandfather knew best. Although hard to conceive, he had to admit it was possible that he might look back one day and regret ignoring his grandfather's advice.

Yoshi's thoughts were on an entirely different plane. Grandfather had spoken, and that was the end of the discussion. Dissension was not a plausible consideration. It was *shoo ga nai*, or as they said in Spanish *que sera, sera* – whatever will be, will be. Although unpleasant, it could not be avoided, and, therefore, one mustn't fret over things that cannot be helped.

There was nothing else to be said on the subject. Case closed. So, all that was left to be decided was how best to move forward. Yoshi knew that for him, the answer was clear. Just as Masa had said in his analogy, he would walk freely into the pen and accept his fate. He wished that Masa would do the same, but knew from experience that his older brother would struggle mightily before giving in to the inevitable.

"It might not be that bad," said Yoshi.

"You being a lawyer is about as ridiculous as me being a sumo wrestler. You have no desire to do it. You have no aptitude for it. You hate those people. The only reason you would ever do it is because Grandfather asked you – told you, to be more specific. This should not be his decision to make."

"But it seems important to him."

"Damn," Masa said. "You are as blind as a bat. This is not about him. He's downstairs right now promising to buy Mom a new house if she makes us go to the University of Tokyo. There is nothing he won't do to control our lives. You just don't get it." Masa stood up and hurled all of the darts against the wall.

"Yeah, I guess," muttered Yoshi.

Masa walked out, went to his room, and slammed the door without another word.

"All You Need Is Love" was playing on Yoshi's Sony transistor radio on the windowsill, but the irony of the lyrics was lost in translation. He put his books away, unfolded his futon, lay down, and went to sleep. *Shoo ga nai.*

Across the hall, Masa lay on his futon staring at the ceiling, thinking of schemes to thwart his grandfather's demands. But a small, nagging voice deep in his head was telling him that he couldn't win – *shoo ga nai.*

The sheep were on two paths: one smooth and direct, the other treacherous and long, but both ended in the same pasture. Masa knew his grandfather would get what he wanted.

Unless, of course, Grandfather was no longer around.

CHAPTER 6

Saturday, August 12th: Morning
Rural Village on Outskirts of Tokyo

Kazu and his wife lived in a modest country home within a cluster of similar houses, all of which were inhabited by relatives. They never felt any lack of privacy, nor did they ever consider any other way of living. Generation after generation had lived in the same houses and farmed the same fields. Primogeniture was as natural a thought as the sun rising daily in the east. All the homes were identical wooden structures with thatch roofs because they had all been built or rebuilt by the same members of the community. The road leading into the neighborhood, and all of the streets within, had never been paved. It was impossible to find anything along the streets or among the houses that did not conform to the predominant shades of gray or brown.

And as a result, Kenji's yellow convertible cruising through the narrow roads stuck out like a flashing neon banana as he made his way to the Ishii home. All the way from his house Kenji had been trying to decide what he wanted to say, what he could say, what to avoid, and *how* to say what was permissible. It was complex.

There was a night from his childhood that was etched in his mind when he had lain awake on the couch reading a book. Many a night he had fallen asleep just so, and his parents would cover him with a blanket. But on one particular night, his parents came home arguing, and he had feigned sleep to listen surreptitiously to what it was all about. Although he never knew all the details, from what he had overheard it appeared that his parents had been to a company party and his father had made unwelcome passes toward Mrs. Ishii. The general had been drunk that night, not an uncommon occurrence, and his mother had been embarrassed and outraged, which was rare. Kenji had always had a desire to apologize for his father's behavior toward Mrs. Ishii and indirectly toward Kazu but could never think of a way to broach the subject tactfully.

There was also the problem of her sickness. Kenji had struggled in his father's case with the Japanese custom of doctors withholding the information from patients and lying to them about their condition. It was understandable, he could agree, that knowing the truth would bring a great deal of stress, but there was also an excellent argument to be made that a person had the right to know they had a disease which would soon end their life. But in this case, the matter was out of his hands as Kazu had already made the decision, and Kenji had promised to keep the secret.

He parked on the street in front of their house and strolled through the yard remembering the visits of his youth fondly. Although by no means wealthy, Kazu kept a beautiful yard and garden complete with a pond full of carp. Kazu had given all of the fish colorful names that had been entertaining to Kenji as a youngster – *Golden Galileo, Yangtze Yellow,* and *Witchy White* he remembered. Kazu had always promised Kenji that *Bodacious Blue* would soon arrive (which it never did), so Kenji felt obliged to stop and have a peek to see if the elusive fish had been found. Apparently not. Kenji walked to the front door and went in without knocking.

"Well hello, Mr. Kenji Watanabe," came the warm, familiar voice with the distinct country dialect. "Kazu told me I'd be blessed by one of your rare visits today."

Mrs. Ishii was seated at a low table in a *tatami* room just off the entranceway, holding a cup of tea in her fragile hands. Kenji had been afraid of what he might see upon encountering his old friend, imagining she would be pale and cold on her deathbed. When he heard her voice and saw her face, he thought it possible that the doctor had made some horrible mistake. Mrs. Ishii was the type of woman who one could see, even now, must have been ravishing in her prime. Her gray and black hair was neatly combed and pulled back into a girlish ponytail. Like her husband, she was rarely seen without a smile. Her face had somehow avoided many of the telltale signs of age, owing no doubt to the fact that she had lived a virtuous, low-stress life, allowing Kenji to see her radiance much the same as when he was just a child. She still wore a kimono, old but somehow elegant on her, even though most women had converted to western-style clothing. Over her kimono, she wore a crocheted wool shawl.

"Come sit down and let me make you some tea. We didn't have any good tea, so I had Kazu go to town and pick up something special from Kyoto this morning when I heard you were coming."

"Oh, Mrs. Ishii," said Kenji, his first minute in the house and already feeling like a spoiled brat, "you needn't have done that at all. You shouldn't have gone out of your way for me. I love the tea you normally serve. Besides, I only came to see you and have a nice chat. It's been far too long."

"Sit down, sit down," she said while gesturing toward a cushion. Kenji sat and looked around the old house, observing the cornucopia of objects holding all-but-forgotten memories of childhood. The *tatami* room was just a small rectangular section of a much larger room. It was situated near the entrance and had a window which overlooked the front yard, the space just large enough to hold the coffee table and four cushions. The remainder of the room was a large, open space that contained the kitchen and a spacious living area with a new Sony television, one of the first in the neighborhood.

Mrs. Ishii stood and walked to the edge of the *tatami*, slid her feet into her house slippers, and went to a cabinet in the kitchen area, pulling out one of her best china cups, a saucer, a teapot with a strainer, and the tea leaves purchased that morning. She placed all of the items on a wooden serving tray and returned to the table with Kenji, slipping out of her house slippers at the edge of the *tatami*. She opened the bag of tea and poured some into the strainer, then she went back to the kitchen, following the same slipper etiquette, took a kettle off the stove, and picked up a round piece of wood she used as a coaster. She returned to the table, poured the boiling water over the tea leaves, and placed the coaster and kettle on the table before kneeling on her cushion.

Although Kenji thought she looked remarkably well for her age and condition, he noticed that she moved much more deliberately than he remembered. She spoke throughout the rituals regarding a variety of mundane events – doctor visits, caring for Kazu and her children, the nosy lady who works at the post office – all in her tiny, delightful, rural Japanese accent which had a hypnotic effect. He listened to her as one would listen to background music: the words had little meaning, but the cadence and melody allowed his mind to roam as he took in sight after memorable sight around the room. He recognized the china, recalling that she had been using the same cups and teapots for the last forty years. He smiled when he saw the chips and scratches, some of which he had no doubt inflicted himself as a boy.

Kenji remembered Kazu's ancient mother whom he had never been able to understand because she had no teeth. How he had feared her in this very room when she stalked him with incoherent commands, how corpse-like she had looked with sunken eyes and jawbones, amphibian skin, and stringy gray hair. When he had forewarning, he had been able to elude her grasp, but she had managed to lay her cold, bony fingers on him a few times when he was off his guard, and he recalled with vivid terror the chill in his spine when he had been alone with her on those occasions. It was in this room, exactly where he now sat, that her body had been lain for viewing after her death. He recalled approaching her as she lay in repose, dressed in a black and gray kimono, hands folded on her stomach, and fearing that she would reach out and seize him if he got too close. Mrs. Ishii had served tea with the same teapot and cups at the old woman's wake.

"How are your parents, Kenji?"

"Fine. Thanks for asking."

"They're such nice people," she said as she filled his cup.

Kenji snickered at the comment. "Not so sure about that, but it's nice of you to say so anyway. Actually, don't tell anyone, but I used to wish that you and Kaz were my parents."

"You'll stop that foolishness right now, young man," she said with a voice that might have been fearful to anyone who didn't know her. "You wished no such thing. I assure you that Kazu and I could have never bought you that car parked in front of the house. In fact, that car probably cost more than this house."

"That may be, but as they say, money isn't everything. I was always just a little jealous at how you and Kaz could dote on your children and raise them without using money as leverage."

"Now you listen to me," she said, with a voice he remembered, but with an elderly tremble that had not been there when they last spoke, "your mother and father love you just as much; they've simply been saddled with wealth all their lives. While I'm sure it must be nice to have a lot of money, I'm also convinced that it brings its fair share of difficulty – even downright misery. Their feelings are just as genuine. Now stop talking nonsense. How do you like the tea?" she said, changing the topic.

"It's delicious, but please don't ever do that again. I honestly prefer the tea you normally serve. It takes me back to better times. Let me reimburse you for this."

"Well, now I am insulted."

"Don't get upset," said Kenji. "I didn't mean it like that. But unfortunately, I know how little my father pays Kaz, and I'm sure there can't be a whole lot left over after you pay the bills for such frivolities as green tea from Kyoto for the likes of me."

The comment caused Mrs. Ishii to smile.

"Perhaps you're too presumptuous, young man." She was unable to keep herself from glowing as she shifted, prolonging the anticipation she knew she had created. "I'll share a little secret with you if you'll promise not to tell."

He nodded.

"This just goes to show you how people can often be mistaken in their judgments of others; this regards finances, but the same applies to judgments about character." She looked around the room to be sure they were alone before she began. She leaned over the table and whispered, "I've had a dream since I was a little girl. I've always wanted to visit Egypt to see the Sphinx and the pyramids. I remember seeing picture books as a little girl and thinking how fascinating and mysterious a country it was. But we were so poor in those days, and I feared that it would always be just a dream; I would never set foot in those historical deserts. But when I met Kazu, he was such a talker," she said as she made herself giggle. "He was so charming and cocky at the same time – never mind that he didn't have two coins to rub together. Mind you, this was before he went off to war, when he was still carefree. He carried on about how we would travel to Italy someday, and we would ride through the Grand Canal of Venice on one of those gondola boats with crushed velvet upholstery, how the driver would serenade us with romantic Italian love songs. We would stop at a restaurant and eat pasta and drink a bottle of their finest wine as we watched other young lovers glide past."

Kenji watched her and saw that she was indeed in Italy in her mind. She was staring into a point in space above where she had been transformed, no longer sitting with Kenji at a table in Japan. Then, just as quickly as she had left, she came back and looked him in the eye.

"You must promise that you'll not mention a word of this to Kazu, but I've been saving what I could for fifteen years so that we could take a trip to both places. The lady at the travel agency arranged the whole thing – twelve glorious days – to be spent half in Egypt, half in Italy. And I've got enough left over so that we don't have to watch every cent during the trip. I arranged it so that we'll be flying out on Kazu's birthday. Don't you think that'll be a grand present?" she said, finishing with a beautiful smile.

Doc says I'll be lucky to have her another six months, Kenji remembered hearing Kazu say the night before. Kazu's birthday was May 16th. He did the math.

He felt a tear forming in his eye and turned to look out the window. He was the confidant of secrets kept between husband and wife, one of which would negate the other. If the doctor was accurate in his prediction, there was a damn good chance that Mrs. Ishii wouldn't be alive in May, and even if she were, she wouldn't be fit for world travel.

"So, you see, you don't know as much as you think you do," she gloated.

The irony was painfully conspicuous; she had scrimped and saved and kept a secret for fifteen years but was about to die never having seen the promised land. He remembered his mother and father returning from a trip to Europe last summer, bitching about the heat and the flight. *Youth is wasted on the young, and wealth is wasted on the rich,* he thought.

Kenji remembered that he had come to speak with Mrs. Ishii on a touchy matter and decided that now might be an appropriate time to change the subject.

"I guess you're right; things aren't always as they seem, are they?" He paused as she smiled in triumph. "There's something else I've been meaning to talk with you about if you don't mind," Kenji said.

"By all means. I hope nothing's wrong."

Kenji twisted on his cushion wondering if he should indeed continue on this path. He knew he could still change the subject and guide the conversation back into friendly waters.

"Well, uh, as I was saying, you and Kaz have been pretty special to me all my life, and, uh…"

"You're not sick are you, Kenji?"

"Me? No, I just…"

"I'm beginning to worry that something is wrong with you."

"No. No. Nothing like that. I'm fine. It's just that, well, what I wanted to say is that I wish my dad would have treated you both better all these years."

Kenji paused to see her reaction and to give him time to think.

"Is that what this is all about?" she said with relief. "I wish you'd look at yourself, Kenji," she said with a charming chortle. "Here you are tying yourself up into a knot, not to mention worrying the daylights out of me, over something that has absolutely nothing to do with you. Your father has given Kazu a nice job for many years, and we are quite thankful for that."

"Well yes, he has given him a job, but there's a difference between giving someone a job and being a good employer. That's all I want to say, is that I wish my dad had been a better employer – a better person."

"Kenji, I have a secret for you. None of us are perfect – not Kazu, not me, not anyone else in this big, wide world. You just see your father's faults because you're so close to him. Trust me, Kazu has faults you would never believe." Kenji thought of the girly magazines and smiled, wondering if that was what she was referring to.

Kenji stared at her smiling face and realized that it was going to be impossible to get his point across. "Somehow, I have a hard time imagining your faults or Kaz's faults on the same level as my father's, but let's change the subject shall we?"

"Here," she said, pushing snacks in front of him, "have some peanuts and rice crackers."

"So, you're going to Egypt and Italy?"

"That's right," she said. Kenji saw a flash of delight on her face with the change of conversation. "Can you believe I've never been on an airplane at my age?"

"Trust me, you haven't missed a thing."

"The travel agent has arranged for us to go to Italy first for six days and then fly to Egypt. Isn't that unbelievably romantic? I have no idea how we're going to communicate with them, but the travel agent said everything will be fine."

She rambled on like a schoolgirl, alternating between how fantastic it was going to be and how nervous she was. Kenji enjoyed every word and every minute, trying to preserve her talking face and voice in his memory because he knew the time was coming soon that she would be forever silent. It saddened him in so many ways. Of course, he was sorry for her. He was sorry for Kazu and their children. He was sorry for himself, that he wouldn't have many more visits like this. He was sorry that this small community would lose such a kind friend. And he felt that her passing would bring him one giant step closer to his own end.

He remembered her when she was younger than he was now. He considered the possibility that some little girl he knew now could be sitting with him as an old man, concealing the fact that he was about to die.

Mrs. Ishii had been such an integral part of his childhood, such a vibrant young woman. She had gone from that young, energetic, beautiful mother to this in what seemed like no time at all. He realized that although he had loved this lady all his life, he had never fully appreciated her as much as he did at that moment.

CHAPTER 7

Sunday, August 13th: Morning
Tokyo

General Watanabe's home was located in Azabu, one of the wealthiest districts in downtown Tokyo, two kilometers away from the main thoroughfare in a quiet section of the busy city. A moss-covered wall of volcanic granite two-meters high surrounded the property, with one pedestrian gate and one automobile gate adjoining the street, the rest of his land being bordered by the yards of neighbors. It was his rule that the gates should remain locked at all times when not in use. Numerous white pines and Japanese yew bushes were strategically located around the yard to block any view of the house from officious meddlers. There were over four acres of land on the lot which dwarfed all other properties in the area. Everyone with a residence in Azabu was considered the upper crust of Tokyo, but even a casual observer would be left with no doubt as to who was the wealthiest of the wealthy after a brief stroll through the general's neighborhood. From the street, the wall and grounds had the look and feel of a miniature Japanese castle.

As this was the *Obon* holiday in Japan when many people returned to their hometowns to commemorate and honor their ancestors, whose spirits return once a year according to Buddhist lore, the general had given leave to most of his staff. And as it was a Sunday, Ms. Tanaka, his housekeeper, left through the front pedestrian gate as she did every week at precisely 9:00 a.m. after preparing the general's breakfast. She had been given the week off since the general was leaving town for a few days, and a watchman was to arrive at noon to keep an eye on the house while everyone was gone. Mrs. Watanabe, the general's wife, had left the previous week to spend time at their summer home in the country, which left the general all alone this morning.

The Watanabe family had employed Ms. Tanaka for six months, which was about the average period servants lasted in the general's employ. Whether it was physical and verbal abuse at the hands of Mrs. Watanabe or sexual harassment from the general, domestic staff seldom lasted a full year. Ms. Tanaka was in her early forties, thin, quite plain, dressed modestly, and wore black horn-rimmed glasses. She was not a provocative woman, but that little deficiency would not be enough to deter the exalted General Watanabe. It was all about power to him, and he believed that women who worked for him were duty-bound to submit to his desires. And given the pervasive nature of the male-dominated society of the time, Ms. Tanaka accepted her lot without protest.

Mrs. Watanabe was well aware of her husband's philandering but had given up trying to stop him many years ago. If she had cared for him, it would have mattered, but she did not. She viewed him as a necessary evil to maintain her pampered lifestyle. Mrs. Watanabe certainly had no interest in satisfying his prurient longings, so it was just as well that he indulged himself with the domestic staff – at least he wasn't out embarrassing her in public. On this day, however, Ms. Tanaka had made it safely out of the house unmolested and wasted no time distancing herself from the home to keep it that way.

Even if she had not been in a hurry to get away, it is doubtful that she would have spotted the bystander. Since she was trying her best to get away from the house as quickly as possible, however, the figure lurking in dark clothing in the shade of a weeping willow at the edge of the stone wall along the street, watching her lock the gate and scamper away, completely escaped her notice.

The general, in his silk pajamas and housecoat, sat at a table on the veranda outside the kitchen and dining room at the back of the house. As he sat sipping juice and reading the day's headlines, the anonymous intruder was entering the pedestrian gate with a key and a nefarious purpose. Unbeknownst to the general, who thought he had a couple hours of privacy, the unannounced visitor walked from the gate to the front of the house, placed an empty guitar case just outside the door, and put on a pair of gloves. Entry was achieved, again with a key, and the age-old custom of removing shoes before entering the house was ignored. There was a stairway just inside leading to the second floor, a hallway which went through the center of the house to the kitchen and dining areas in the rear, a formal Buddhist shrine room to the right, and a living room to the left. The burglar moved through the hallway to a point where the general could be seen reading his newspaper, then silently returned down the hall and into the living room. The general's sword, the one he had worn throughout his military career, including his service during World Wars 1 and 11, had been displayed prominently above the mantel on a hand-carved ornamental rack since the day he retired from the army in 1945.

The *katana* was a masterpiece with a Masamune blade, crafted in the 14th century, one of the few signed by the renowned sword smith, which had been handed down in his family for generations. The red and gold tassels, denoting his rank of general, hung from the hilt. The weapon, still in its scabbard, was removed from the mount, but the sound of the door opening in the kitchen and the general's footsteps inside halted the orderly process.

The sword was unsheathed silently, the scabbard placed on the carpet, and the burglar moved to the living room entrance and pressed against the wall to hide any shadow, raising the sword overhead in position to strike if necessary. The general moved about in the kitchen and then began down the hallway toward the living room and staircase. Before he reached the living room where the intruder lay in wait, the telephone in the kitchen rang. The general returned and picked up the receiver.

"Hello...Yes, I'm about to take a shower and then I need to stop by the office before 1 leave...How's the weather? 1 need to know what to pack...Okay, I'll call you from the office before 1 leave." He hung up and began walking back to the staircase.

He passed by the living room entrance, a mere meter from the tip of his own sword, then labored up the steps at a pace befitting an old man. Soon, the sound of running water in the shower could be heard, and the burglar put the sword on the floor and tiptoed up the steps and into the general's bedroom where his pajamas and housecoat lay across the bed. The door to the bathroom where the general was showering was shut. The intruder produced a dagger and a typed letter, and pinned the note to the bathroom door with the weapon.

The noise startled the general who called out to ask who was there. "Tanaka, is that you?" No answer. "Who's out there?"

The trespasser went back down the steps, retrieved the sword and scabbard from the living room floor, and left the house, leaving the front door open as an added insult to the general's omnipotence. The thief then opened the guitar case, placed the sheathed weapon inside, and left the premises.

The general toweled off, opened the door and saw the note. This was not the first mysterious message the old man had received, though it was the first time the menace had been brazen enough to leave it in his house. He didn't scare easily, but as he stood in the doorway with nothing but a towel, he was acutely aware that someone had gained the upper hand on him. He no longer felt untouchable. He scanned the room and listened to see if someone might still be in the house, and then his eyes returned to the note and dagger. He pulled the weapon out of the door, held the letter up, and read:

He who lives by the sword, dies by the sword. I hope your will is in order – it will be necessary to divide your estate very, VERY soon.

The general went to his bureau, dressed, and then went downstairs and out to the street but saw no one. He returned to the house to look for any clues and discovered that his war sword was missing. The police chief was a close friend and frequent golf partner, so he went to the kitchen and called him and asked him to come to the house with one of his men. After hanging up with him, he called Kenji.

"Kenji, I need to talk with you. Don't leave the office. I'll be there by noon."

•   •   •

At 1:30 p.m. the general burst through the door in Kenji's office, swearing and fuming hotter than the stogie with which he was gesticulating, and slapped the note on Kenji's desk. Kenji picked it up and began perusing as the general paced in front of the window overlooking downtown Tokyo, cursing the individual who had the nerve to break into his house, with him in it no less.

Kenji's office was an absurd extravagance on the corner of the top floor of Watanabe Tower. It was large enough for Kenji's sprawling mahogany desk and four visitor's chairs, a boardroom table which could seat up to twenty – although it was seldom used – and a sizeable area reserved for chipping and putting, which was used daily. The office took up a quarter of the entire floor and could have fetched a fortune if they leased it out. Since they owned the whole building, however, they charged themselves triple the going rate to increase their business expenses and lower their taxable income. They kept six full-time accountants on their payroll – six of the best and shadiest in all of Japan.

Their company brought in pharaonic revenue each year but did precious little to justify the earnings. Ostensibly, it was a construction company capable of building roads, bridges, apartment buildings, high rise office towers, golf courses, or most anything that construction companies construct, but there was no one on their monthly payroll who held any of the necessary licenses to do these things. The old man knew the fair market value of the government contracts on which he bid, and then he turned in bids fifty percent or more above that. The trick was that he was in tight with all the cronies and politicians who oversaw the bidding processes and voted for the successful bids. He greased their palms generously, and, in return, was granted the contracts. Then, he hired the suckers who had put in honest proposals to do the work at a fair price and filled the company coffers with the rest. It was a hell of a racket, and he did it all with impunity.

Kenji pulled a decanter of Macallan single malt and a crystal whiskey tumbler from a credenza behind his desk and poured a double to calm his father's nerves. "Sit down and have a drink. I can't concentrate with you on the warpath."

The old man sat down in one of the leather guest chairs and drank as Kenji re-read the note. Between huffing on the cigar and gulping the alcohol, the general drummed his fingers on the arm of the chair and cursed. "Son-of-a-bitch had the nerve to break into my own damn house while I was taking a shower and steal my sword. I tell you he's a dead man when I get my hands around his neck."

Kenji stared, knitting his brows and shaking his head as he pored over the note trying to pinpoint critical words and decipher possible meanings, and also tried to catch the relevant parts of the old man's vociferation at the same time. The general lasted less than a minute in the chair before he pushed himself up and continued threatening and cursing around the conference table. "I called Chief Yokoyama and had him come over with an assistant. Didn't find a damn thing – front door and gate wide-open. Yokoyama said that either the doors were unlocked, or someone had a key. I called Tanaka, and she swears she locked them both."

"How many people have keys?"

"I gave Yokoyama a list of everyone I could think of. You, your mother, Taro and Yumi, Kazu, Tanaka – hell all of the servants have had keys at one time or another. Those locks have never been changed, so I have no idea who has a key or could've made copies."

"To the front door and the gate?"

"To the front door and the gate. Hell, I don't know. Who the hell keeps up with these things? How was I supposed to know somebody was going to break in and steal my damn sword?"

"Okay," said Kenji, "let's review the information we have here and see if we can come up with some possible suspects. First of all, do you have any bitter enemies?"

The general stopped pacing and stared at Kenji as though he had suggested a game of gin rummy. "Kenji, you do realize that the list of people who hate my guts could fill a phone book, don't you? How the hell am I supposed to answer that?"

"Let's see if we can use what they say here to help. I don't know what this reference to the sword is all about, but since the thief stole it, I suppose it could have something to do with their beef with you. Does that give you any ideas?

The general put the cigar in his mouth, stopped pacing, and looked out the window. Then, he jammed his hands into his pants pockets and started tapping his foot.

"Is there something you want to say?" said Kenji.

"Well, it's like this," said the general, pulling one hand out of his pocket and grabbing the cigar from his mouth while still looking out. "I was thinking about that on the way over here." There was a pause, and it was clear that he was having difficulty expressing whatever thought he had. "Of course, I know that Masa or Yoshi would never do anything to harm me, but do you think they might have just gotten upset about some of the things I said the other night; maybe one of them was just letting off some steam?"

Kenji winced and almost laughed at the preposterous suggestion, but he could see that his father was earnest. Rather than irk him by trivializing his thoughts as foolish, he decided to give it serious consideration but to also throw in another scenario.

"I seriously doubt Masa or Yoshi could have pulled this off. First of all, I don't believe it's in their nature to make such a threat, and, second, Ami or I would've noticed if they were up to something like this." He paused and raised his index finger as if a light were coming on. "Tell me, have Taro and Yumi found out that you're changing your will?"

The old man turned from the window with a look of disgust. "Come now, Kenji, surely you don't suspect your own brother and sister. I could never believe my own children had something to do with this."

"I didn't say I think they're responsible, but if we're going to consider all the possibilities, I suppose that would be at least as likely as suspecting *my* children."

"Well, whoever it was, was trying to scare me, and I'm not scared. If the son-of-a-bitch had the courage to do something, they would have already done it. Let's just forget about it."

"No. You were right to call me. We need to think this over because someone went to a lot of trouble to leave that note and steal your sword. We have to take it seriously," said Kenji as he pulled out a Lucky and lit up. "Who else would have a motive to either kill you or scare you into thinking someone was trying to kill you?"

The old man was busy mangling his cigar between his teeth. "As you well know, the list of people who don't care for me is long indeed. Now, as to who hates me enough to kill me or pull a stunt like this, I have no idea."

"Let's run through the things we know – or at least think we know. First, someone out there has a serious grudge against you. For what, we don't know exactly, but it may have something to do with your sword. Next, they sound as if they intend to kill you, but I suppose they may simply wish to frighten you. The note also mentions your will. So, it could be someone who feels slighted, someone who knows – or thinks they know – what's in your will. They know where you live, and it looks like they have a key to your house. Have I missed anything?"

"They were in my house in Tokyo today, and they're walking around with my damn sword," added the old man.

A concerned frown flashed across Kenji's face.

"What is it? Do you have something?" said the old man moving back over and sitting in the chair.

"No, it's nothing," he said as he forced a laugh. "I guess that means we can rule out Mom."

"Quit kidding around dammit. I thought you said we should take this seriously."

"It was just that when you mentioned Tokyo, I thought of Mom in Karuizawa. Anyway, you're probably right. It's just some kind of prank. Go ahead and have Kaz drive you home to pack, and I'll be over there as soon as

I can finish up here."

The old man snuffed out his stogie and stood up. Kenji was lost in thought – and his father could see it.

"Now look, Kenji, you're holding something back on me."

"No. I was thinking about what I need to pack is all. Kaz is taking us, isn't he?" said Kenji, changing the subject.

"Yeah, and I want to get the hell out of here, so hurry up with whatever it is you need to do and get to the house as soon as possible."

Kenji walked him out to the reception area, said goodbye, and hurried back to his office where he shut and locked the door before taking a seat at his desk. He leaned back in his chair as his mind raced through the possibilities. He picked up the phone and dialed, but there was no answer. The questions he wanted to ask were going to have to wait for now. He had a suspicion as to who the culprit might be, but he was far from certain.

After packing some files into a briefcase, he walked out and gave instructions to his secretary. She was young and beautiful, but bereft of any common secretarial skills, which was just fine with Kenji because he was bereft of any common business needs. She could smile, serve coffee, and pleasantly take numbers on the phone. Her greatest asset, as far as he was concerned though, was that she endured the incessant fondling by the general without the slightest complaint. After informing her where he would be and how he could be reached for the next ten days, he headed for the train station.

The whole way home he combed through the events of the day as his father had relayed them. He tinkered with several different scenarios and continued to return to one prime suspect, but there were doubts there as well. This caper had required some serious intelligence, reconnaissance, and planning.

It was rare to find a seat on the train in the afternoon, but he got lucky. The gentle rocking and bumping, starting and stopping, and the warm afternoon air flowing in through open windows provided too much of a temptation to refuse a good nap.

It was late afternoon when he reached his house. He packed two bags of clothes for the vacation, had a quick shower and shave, grabbed a few snacks, and tossed everything into the passenger seat of the convertible. Ami had left for Nagano earlier in the day, and Masa and Yoshi would be coming tonight. He locked up and made the short drive to his father's house.

Kazu was sitting in the Cadillac in the driveway looking at one of his magazines when Kenji arrived. He had already packed the general's bags into the trunk and got to work with Kenji's as soon as he parked.

"It's about time," said Kazu. "Your dad has been wearing me out every two minutes. 'Is he here yet? Is he here yet?' That old man has all the patience of a dog in heat."

"It's about time," said the general coming out of the house. "Did I not mention I wanted to get an early start?"

"We're all packed and ready now, General," said Kazu. "Just hop in, and we're off."

"Wait a minute. Let me back in the house to make a call. I have to tell Masa I'm leaving the car here."

Kenji went inside to the phone, dialed his home number, and got the answering machine.

"Masa, Dad here. I'm leaving my car at Grandfather's house so that you and Yoshi can use it to come to Karuizawa tonight. Just take a train over here and don't forget the keys. No speeding. My spare set of keys is hanging in the kitchen. There are keys for the front gates here on the ring also. Be careful."

They went back out and climbed into the general's car. Kazu pulled into the street and stopped, got out, closed and locked the driveway gate, and also checked to see that the pedestrian gate was locked. He was back in the car and flying down the street in less than thirty seconds.

Kazu was a great driver. He had a lead foot but never seemed to make anyone uncomfortable. The police had stopped him countless times for speeding, failing to come to a complete stop, parking in the street, and about every other possible traffic infraction, but he never received a ticket. He was a smooth talker by nature, and everyone he met was his best friend. He had a way of schmoozing people without being phony about it.

"Wow, Kenji, your dad was telling me about what happened at the house this morning. He's lucky he wasn't killed!"

"I'm sure it was just a prank," said Kenji. "Hell, Kaz, you probably did it. Say, where were you at nine o'clock this morning?"

"Oh, cut it out," Kazu said. "I was at home, but what makes you so sure that this was a prank? It doesn't sound like any joking matter to me."

Kenji was alone in the back seat observing the neon lights filling the streets as the sun sank below the horizon. He thought about how differently the streets had looked when he was a child riding around with his dad and best friend, Kaz.

"Well, think about it, Kaz. If they had really wanted to kill him, don't you think they would have done it today? They had the perfect opportunity. They were all alone with no one around, they had a weapon, and Dad was obviously unarmed. I'm sure it was just a one-time thing."

"What are you talking about?" said Kazu with his infectious laugh. "This has to be the fourth or fifth letter, right General?" he said as he turned to the old man.

The general had been staring straight ahead puffing on his cigar, disinterested in the topic until Kazu shared this information without permission. There was a slow turn of the head, and a *you-dumbass* stare directed at the driver. Kenji refocused his attention from the streets outside and leaned forward near Kazu's ear.

"What other letters, Kaz?" he said.

Kazu kept his eyes uncharacteristically on the road, throwing occasional apologetic glances toward his boss, which the general ignored. There was a plea in his eye for the general to give him some direction, but none was forthcoming. The old man looked away and shook his head.

"I've told you a thousand times, Kazu, you can't put toothpaste back in the tube," said the general. "But it's alright; I probably should've told Kenji anyway."

"Told me what?"

"These damn notes. This isn't the first one. I've been getting them for a while now. Same kind of notes – all words cut out of newspapers or magazines, glued to a blank sheet of paper or, like this one, typed up. I couldn't make any sense of them. They were always, how should I say, unflattering, or maybe even threatening, but they were just notes in the mail or left in places for me to find them. They had never been accompanied by the sender."

"Until today," said Kenji.

"Yes. Until today," repeated the general.

Kenji thought he detected just the slightest bit of concern in his father's voice. Whoever was behind this orchestrated plot had succeeded in planting seeds of genuine uneasiness in the old man's head, try as he might to deny it.

"What did the other letters say?"

The general shook his head and waved the question off with a firm hand through thick smoke. "Nonsense. Cock-and-bull nonsense is what they said."

"You're going to have to be more specific than that."

The old man shook his head again, clearly annoyed at being interrogated on the subject. "They were so ridiculous I can't remember a damn thing – I swear."

"Let me see if I can help you there, General," said Kazu without being asked. "Didn't the last one say something about you being a gutless coward, a bully using your power to hurt people, but that soon you'd be getting yours?" A smile came to his face, proud of his adroit memory until a sidelong glance from the general informed him that his memory needed to be boxed.

"Dammit, Kazu, haven't you fucked up enough for one day?" said the general. "Just drive the damn car and keep your mouth shut."

"Alright, let's have the truth," Kenji said. "When did you start getting these things?"

"I don't know. Six months ago, maybe a year."

"How many have there been?"

"Maybe five, six."

"What did the others say?"

"I can't remember," said the old man with undisguised agitation at the grilling. "I haven't given it that much thought, and I'm not planning on thinking about it now. I'm officially on vacation, and I'm going to sleep." He tossed his cigar out the window and reclined in his seat.

Kenji knew better than to ask Kazu any questions at the moment. The subject would have to wait until they were alone. He sat and watched Kazu drive his way out of the crowded city and onto the rural roads that would lead them to their destination. Kenji spotted the moon over the mountains making an early entry into the evening sky. He had enjoyed his first moments of freedom from the bonds of the city since childhood. There was an exhilarating joy in abandoning his suit at the house in favor of jeans and a T-shirt, and now he was feeling the ropes of urban life releasing as the balmy evening air swept through the sedan carrying the countryside scents of honeysuckle and pine. The croaking of frogs from the rice fields and the chirping of the crickets floated and mingled with the air so perfectly that the senses of smell and sound became indistinguishable. The general was snoring in the front seat, and Kazu had traditional Japanese folk songs playing on the radio. Kenji decided not to interfere with the trance of stimulation he was experiencing by starting up an unnecessary and unappealing conversation with Kazu about the previous notes received by his father, so he laid his head back, closed his eyes, and within a matter of seconds was drifting away.

CHAPTER 8

Monday, August 14th: Morning
Karuizawa, Nagano

When Kenji awoke the following morning, he marveled at the rare, deep, and peaceful night's sleep he had enjoyed. Everything was different in the country. The unmistakable pungent smell of the cedar logs, the warm yellow sunlight flooding the room, the aroma of a country breakfast, all brought a feeling of peace not possible in the city. He imagined for just an instant that he was eight years old again, ready to bolt out of his futon, put on his favorite old clothes, grab a banana and his favorite fishing rod, and head out to the lake. The past was palpable here, but it only lasted for a fleeting moment before the reality of his true age and circumstances trumped the fantasy. He lay in bed for several minutes trying to remember life as a boy in this room, trying to recapture the innocence of that age – a time in life when he had not been jaded or cynical. After a few moments reminiscing, he dressed and went downstairs for breakfast.

The stairway led directly into the living room, which adjoined the dining room and kitchen, the latter of which was visible through a serving hatch. Kenji's mother, Ami, the general, and Yoshi were having breakfast at a table outside.

"Good morning," said Kenji in an unusually pleasant voice as he walked out onto the front deck.

"It looks like you still love that old room of yours," said his mother. "I thought about waking you, but from the sound of your snoring I thought you must be in need of some extra sleep."

"I just can't tell you how much I love this place," said Kenji. "This is the year I'm going to do it. I'm selling the house in the city and moving out here for good."

"That makes about twenty years in a row now that you've been saying that," said his mother. "And who knows how many years you begged me to do it before that."

"You mark my words; this is the year. Where's Masa?"

Ami said, "He left early this morning to have breakfast at the French Bakery, and then he said there was a new history museum he wanted to visit."

"And why didn't you go with him?" Kenji asked Yoshi.

"He wanted to go the museum, and I wanted to go to the temple."

Kenji smiled and shook his head. "I don't know if these boys are really mine. It's summer. I'm letting you ditch schoolwork for a few days. What about playing some tennis? What about going fishing? What about *girls?* What kind of kids go to museums and temples during summer vacation?"

"Let's be thankful they're nothing like you, dear," said Ami as she stroked the hair of her youngest son.

"Any problems on the drive last night?" Kenji asked Yoshi.

"None at all. That car can fly."

Kenji gave him a stern look, and Yoshi said he was only kidding. Kenji doubted it was a joke, but let it go.

They all finished breakfast and spent the day taking hikes in the woods, watching high school baseball on television, reading books, cooking, and taking naps. Yoshi visited the temple. Everyone spent the day in some form of leisure, purposely refusing to call, or accept calls, from the outside world. Masa returned home in the early afternoon and joined Kenji watching baseball in the living room. The general was also present but was napping in an armchair. Yoshi was still away, and the women were in the kitchen preparing dinner.

"How was the museum?" asked Kenji.

"Fun. Quite interesting."

"Wouldn't it be more fun to spend time with your friends or family instead of being alone all day in some sterile museum?"

"Who said I was alone?" said Masa vaguely, keeping his eyes on the game and pretending not to notice the intrigue he had aroused.

"Oh yeah. Who went with you?

"No one."

"I thought you said you weren't alone."

"I wasn't."

"Would you quit pulling my leg – who was with you?"

"I met someone at the museum."

"Oh, I see." Kenji alternated between watching the game and watching his son for a few minutes as he waited for some further explanation, but it never came. "So, who did you meet – do I know him?" he said nonchalantly.

"No, you don't, and it's not a him."

"Ohhhh. Now I get it," Kenji said as he sat up in his seat, smiling with fatherly pride. "That's great, Masa. You had me going there. Now I see what you've been up to, you sly little devil. That's more like it. I was getting a little worried about you guys, but I should've known. Heck, Yoshi's probably doing the same thing right now. Tell me all about this mystery girl."

"I don't know too much about her yet, Dad. I just met her."

"Well, you must know something."

"She's nice, okay? And I'm going to see her again tonight."

"That's my boy," Kenji said. "Where are you taking her?"

"Dad, let it go, will you? I don't know – maybe just for a walk or something. Can't I meet a girl without getting the third degree?"

"Let me give you some money just in case you want to take her to a nice restaurant or out for a game of tennis," he said as he pulled a couple of large bills from his wallet and held them out for Masa.

"Thanks, but I've got money," said Masa, frowning at the cash.

"What did you say?" said Kenji with a perplexed expression as if Masa had said he enjoyed seeing the dentist. "You're turning down money? What the heck is up with you? Here," he said shoving it against his arm, "a little more can't hurt. I don't want you to get embarrassed getting caught short of cash."

Masa looked at his father and shook his head, the expressions of distaste becoming more and more frequent. When Kenji saw the look, he remembered telling Mrs. Ishii how much he hated the way his parents had flashed money, and here he was doing the same thing.

"I promise I will not be embarrassed," he said without taking the money. "Besides, if she's the kind of girl who's interested in money, I doubt I'll be interested in her."

Kenji laughed at the comment as he put the money back in his wallet. "Masa, I can assure you they're all interested in money, but I do admire your morals." They watched the game without talking for a few minutes as Kenji listened to the serene sounds of the relaxing afternoon: the old man's snoring, soft voices in the kitchen over the sounds of their cooking, a television with the volume turned low, and insects humming outside in the forest.

"Come on, Masa, I'm your dad. Tell me about her. Is she pretty?"

Masa sighed and decided to give in. "I guess. She's really nice, though. I care about that more than I do about being pretty. But, yeah, I guess she's pretty."

"You are wise beyond your years my boy," said Kenji in disbelief. "Some men go their whole lives without learning that crucial fact. Everybody says 'beauty's only skin deep,' but hardly anyone really understands how true that is. What's her name?"

"Kayo."

The name caught Kenji by surprise. Surely it couldn't be *that* Kayo. However, it was possible that she could be in town, he thought, and she was about the same age as Masa. And she would definitely be the type of girl to visit a history museum in her free time.

"Uh, what does Kayo's father do?" asked Kenji.

"Believe it or not, Dad, that subject didn't pop up today," Masa said. "I'll make sure to address that tonight along with checking on his annual salary and portfolio investment strategy."

"Smart ass," Kenji mumbled under his breath. "What about brothers or sisters – is that too invasive for a first meeting?"

"Actually, that did come up. She doesn't have any."

"Hope you boys are hungry," said Ami as she came into the room with a tray of appetizers. The general awoke with the announcement, and they all chatted about baseball and other light topics as they ate the snacks and drank coffee. Kenji was unable to find the right time to get back to the subject of Kayo, and before he knew it evening was at hand.

There was a knock at the front door, and Kenji went to answer. Three smiling young children, two little girls and a younger boy, stood proudly looking up at him, each with a gift in hand. Kenji couldn't remember their first names, but he knew they were the children of the caretaker that watched over all the houses in the neighborhood while the owners were away. The children were well behaved, but lacking in education and not at all well to do.

"Good afternoon," they said in unison.

"And good afternoon to you," said Kenji as he walked out onto the deck. He observed that their clothes were clean, though a bit threadbare – threadbare being normal, clean being anomalous. The wealthier children from Tokyo usually wore pressed and cleaned western-style clothing as though they were on their way to the country club. The local kids, especially the Fujiyama children, wore more traditional Japanese clothing covered in dirt. Today, however, they looked freshly bathed, their gift-bearing hands and fingernails scrubbed, and Mrs. Fujiyama had gone to the additional trouble of braiding the girls' hair and adorning their heads with ribbons.

"It's nice to see you again, Mr. Watanabe," said the eldest girl, using her best, and obviously rehearsed, formal Japanese language. The people of the town had a strong country accent, but she was doing her best to use the more formal Tokyo dialect.

"And how is it that you know my name when I don't recall ever having had the pleasure of meeting such a lovely princess?" said Kenji. The younger two giggled and the *princess* turned away to hide her blushing face.

"We're the Fujiyamas," said the younger girl with the normal country accent. "Our Daddy takes care of this here place whilst you and your family is off in Tokyo making the big bucks." Kenji smiled as he imagined Mrs. Fujiyama trying to prep the children on what to say and how to say it. He could picture old Mr. Fujiyama complaining after a hard day's work: *Here I am busting my ass all day to make a measly dollar for all these rich folks while they're off in Tokyo making the big bucks.*

"Don't you remember us?" said the little girl.

The elder sister cleared her throat and glared at the younger sibling for failing to follow the prescribed protocol. The younger girl lowered her head.

"But the Fujiyama children are just little kids who only come up to about here," said Kenji with feigned disbelief, holding his hand down low. "You couldn't be *those* children."

"Yep, them's us," said the little boy, who Kenji guessed was not supposed to be part of the speaking cast.

"Shhhh Kaito," said the older sister, fearing that the youngster's speech was nullifying her glorious performance.

"Well look at you," said Kenji. "Yeah, I suppose you are the Fujiyama children alright, but what have you been eating to get so big?"

"Who is it?" interrupted Kenji's mother as she came out of the house behind him.

"Why it's the Fujiyama children," he said. "Can you believe how they've grown?"

"I don't care how they've grown. What do you kids want?" Kenji pretended he hadn't heard his mother. He smiled at the children and tried to avoid the question and the embarrassment he felt because of it. The children stared up at Mrs. Watanabe the same way they would regard a menacing bear, then the younger two looked to the older sister for direction. She swallowed noticeably, her eyes darting away from the old woman to collect her thoughts, and then began again with her practiced script.

"Please pardon the interruption, Mrs. Watanabe. Our parents asked us to bring these small gifts to you. They aren't much, just a token of our appreciation for you allowing us to take care of your property." She looked at her younger siblings and nodded her head, one, two, and then they all looked up and said, "Thank you," together as they held out their gifts.

Kenji hoped that his mother would respond favorably to such a charitable gesture, but he knew she would find a way to stomp out their attempt at magnanimity. In the mind of Mrs. Kimiko Watanabe, it was an inexcusable act of insolence for the lower classes to address her or her family unless the superiors initiated the encounter. Today, she would remain true to form.

"Tell your father that if he values his job, he'll pick up the trash twice a day while we're here this year. Last year he was so late picking it up that the flies and crows held their own family reunions in our front yard." Without accepting or even acknowledging the gifts, she turned and walked back into the house.

Kenji did his best to mitigate the insult by changing the subject. "Is that *sake*?" he said to the little boy. Luckily, the boy was far too young to understand the slight he had just received.

"Yep. My daddy says it's the good stuff, not the rotgut he drinks." Kenji couldn't resist a smile.

"I can see that," he said as he took the bottle and held it out admiringly. "And what do we have here?" he said to the younger sister.

"Mushrooms. I picked 'em myself, but Momma fixed 'em."

"They look absolutely delicious," he said with an affectionate smile as he accepted the plate.

"And this is fried rice with chicken," said the oldest girl as she placed it on a deck table. "I made it myself, so it's probably not as good as what you usually eat," she said timidly with her head bowed.

"She made it," said the boy, "but I caught the chicken and helped Daddy kill it. That there was our best bird."

"Kaito," said the elder sister, "do you remember our conversation on the way up here? Would you please let me do the talking?"

"I can smell it from here," Kenji said in a most convincing tone, "and I believe it smells better than any chicken and fried rice I've ever had in my life. Thank you all so much. Make sure to tell your parents how much we appreciate this. Now, wait just a minute while I take all this inside," he said as he picked up the chicken and rice and disappeared into the house with the gifts. When he returned, he began leading the children off the deck and down the steps.

"Don't worry, Mrs. Watanabe," called the eldest girl into the house before leaving. "I'll see to the trash myself." There was no response from within.

Kenji walked with them down to the road in front of the house, continuing to marvel at their growth. He reached into his pocket and pulled out three shiny 100-yen coins and gave one to each of the children. Their faces lit up in ecstasy, and they looked at one another as if they had just discovered a treasure chest.

"Wow. I've never had one of these before," said the little boy.

"If your mom says it's okay," said Kenji, "maybe you can go down into town and buy an ice cream cone. Also, tell your dad that I'll be stopping by your place later and that he might get a little bonus, too."

The children's faces became even brighter as they exchanged looks of disbelief. "Thanks, Mr. Watanabe. I'll tell him," said the oldest girl as she took to her heels after the others down the dirt road. The sisters outraced the little boy and disappeared through distant trees, leaving a trail of dust that rose into the branches above. Kenji stood and stared for several minutes, contemplating what a different life they led, and envied the simplicity. A magpie screeching snapped him out of his trance, and he went back into the house thinking about the gifts they had brought.

All eyes were focused on the last inning of the baseball game when Kenji entered and went unnoticed to the kitchen to sample some of the goodies the Fujiyama children had brought. He searched the counters and refrigerator but couldn't find the dishes. Ami came in with her arms full of dirty plates and glasses and began unloading them into the sink.

"Where's the food the children brought? I left it right here."

"Your mom threw it in the trash," she said matter-of-factly.

"In the what?" he asked. "Why? What happened to it?"

"Kenji, you weren't seriously considering eating that garbage, were you?" said Ami with her hands on her hips. "Do you want worms? Your mother and I spent all morning at the supermarket and butcher buying good quality meats and fish. That slop they brought belongs in the trash. Those mushrooms could be poisonous for all you know. Do you want to spend your vacation in the hospital?"

Mrs. Watanabe entered the kitchen with more dishes as they were talking. Kenji stared at the two of them. They were the two women in his life that were supposed to mean the most to him, the two women he should love more than all others. But at the moment he couldn't think of anyone he despised more.

"What's wrong with you?" his mother said when she noticed him glaring. He went on staring in silence.

"I think Kenji's upset with you," said Ami. "It appears he was planning to eat that junk those filthy kids brought." His mother burst into a revolting, high-pitched laugh, and Ami joined in with her own wicked giggle. The thought of telling them both how he felt about them crossed his mind, but he only stared, loathing their pompous arrogance and superior airs.

"It's in the backyard, dearest, if you really want it," said his mother with insincere empathy. "If you want to eat like a peasant, please don't let me stop you." After seeing the hatred in Kenji's eyes, Ami and Mrs. Watanabe attempted to act remorseful, but when their glances met, they were unable to refrain from bursting into another fit of laughter.

Kenji walked out the back door and onto the rear deck to get away, but the sounds of mocking derision poured out of the open windows and echoed in the forest. The duet continued to berate and insult the Fujiyama children and family. Looking down he noticed a brown paper bag on top of the trash in the gray metal trashcans at the bottom of the porch steps, wet and leaking. Even from a distance, it was clear that the mess was a broken bottle of *sake* covered with the food the children had brought. Chicken and rice were strewn about the cans that the Fujiyama family would soon be coming to empty. There was no doubt in his mind that his mother intended that the gifts be discovered by them like this, but he couldn't understand why she gained such satisfaction from crushing the kindness of others. Could this shameful treatment of people, especially children, somehow elevate her status in her own mind?

Crows began to gather on the branches of the trees around the yard, so Kenji returned to the house in the hopes that they would remove the evidence of his family's snobbery before the children arrived to carry it all away.

CHAPTER 9

Monday, August 14th: Evening
Karuizawa, Nagano

Shortly after sunset, Masa stopped watching TV and went into the bathroom. Kenji noticed him combing his hair and brushing his teeth as he passed by the open door. After a few minutes of grooming, Masa came out and put on a light windbreaker as he headed toward the door.

"I'm going out for a while," he said. "Don't worry about my dinner – I'll pick something up in town."

"You don't want to take the convertible?" asked Kenji.

"Thanks, but it's a little much. I don't want to give the wrong impression."

"Wait a minute. I need to go to town myself," Kenji lied. "I can give you a ride." Kenji was still looking for a way to learn more about the girl Masa had met. Masa was not thrilled with the offer but couldn't come up with a valid reason to decline. Kenji snagged the keys off the coffee table and hustled out to catch him before he could get away. Once they were in the car, Kenji began to fire away again.

"Is Kayo from Karuizawa?" he asked.

"She lives around here somewhere; not sure exactly where, but she said she hopes to move to Tokyo soon." Kenji remembered Ai saying that her Kayo was thinking about moving to Tokyo.

"Why does she want to go to Tokyo?"

"I don't know," Masa said, not attempting to mask his annoyance at the second round of questioning. "Maybe because it's boring as heck around here." Kenji drove in silence for a minute, taking streets that would make the trip longer than it needed to be so he could think.

"What does Kayo want to do in the future?"

"You mean as in a career?"

"Yeah, what does she want to be?"

"Dad, I just met this girl. Who the heck talks about careers the first day they meet? We talked a little bit about art and what bands we like and stuff like that. Only a serious loser would go into all the details you're asking me about when you first meet someone. What is with you and all these questions about careers and her father's occupation? We're not getting married."

"Okay, calm down. I'm sorry. Just thinking like an old man I guess. Where are you supposed to meet her?"

"Tell you what, Dad, this is good enough right here. I don't want you meeting her and freaking her out, asking her bra size and how many children she plans on having."

"Let me at least get you to the edge of town," Kenji said to buy a little more time and a few more questions. He knew that Masa didn't want him to see this new girl, and if this Kayo was Ai's Kayo, he didn't want to see her either.

"I realize you don't know much about her yet, but did she happen to mention if she's from Nagano?"

"Interesting you should ask. She was born in China. Her mother is Chinese."

Damn, thought Kenji. It *was* Ai's Kayo.

Kenji made a wrong turn so that he would have time to think. He needed to come up with a solution pronto. It was imperative that this friendship be nipped in the bud, but he knew he needed to proceed with caution.

"Where are you going, Dad? Town is..."

"Look, I just don't know about this. I don't know this girl."

"Don't know this girl? Since when did I start needing your permission before making friends?"

"Yeah, but this is a young lady," said Kenji running his hand through his hair, a nervous habit that didn't escape Masa's notice.

"Yeah, and you were pretty excited about that a little while ago. What happened to 'That's my boy,' and 'You sly little devil?'"

Kenji continued driving parallel to the destination as he tried to think.

"Oh, okay. Now I see," said Masa. "I would have expected this from Grandfather, but it's a little surprising coming from you."

"What do you see – what's surprising?" said Kenji.

"I see your problem now."

"What are you talking about, Masa?"

"Well, you were all excited about me going out to meet a girl until you found out her mother is Chinese. It doesn't take a brain surgeon to figure out your problem with her."

Kenji opened his mouth to defend himself from the accusation but stopped before saying anything. Being viewed as a bigot was undoubtedly something he would prefer to avoid, especially knowing how he felt about Ai and Kayo, but if the false knowledge got him out of this predicament, it might be the lesser of two evils.

"Maybe you're right, Masa," he said as if he were giving it consideration. While he thought through what needed to be done, he drove closer to the rendezvous location but pulled over at a point where there would be no risk of seeing Kayo. "Perhaps I did let that affect my judgment. Go on, have fun, have a good time, but I do want you home by ten-thirty. Most places close by ten, and you can't get into anything after that except trouble. Agreed?"

Masa stared at his father dumbfounded. "Ten-thirty? I'm not a child. You have noticed, haven't you?"

"Good, then you can tell time. I'll see you at ten-thirty."

Masa got out without losing the dumbstruck gaze at his father and without saying another word. Kenji felt it best for his credibility to stare straight ahead and not look into the eyes of his son.

"Ten-thirty sharp or I'll have the police looking for you," he said as he pulled away and darted down the empty roadway.

Kenji's relationship with Kayo had been a close, but unique, friendship since she was a child. Ai had brought her to Japan after the war, and he had helped them financially and otherwise as best he could but was forced to keep the relationship with her, and of course the relationship with Ai, a secret. She called him Kenji or Papa, and thought of him as her father, but she knew nothing about his real life away from her and her mother. Through the years, many of her questions, such as was he her father, did they have the same last name, why didn't he live with them all the time, and many others that were too difficult for Kenji or Ai to explain had gone unanswered. She knew nothing about the Watanabe name or family. But now the lines had crossed, and there was no way to get across to either Kayo or Masa that they should not see each other in this way. There was nothing wrong with them being friends, but *what if...* He couldn't take a chance; this relationship needed to end before it turned into something immoral or illegal. He stopped at a phone booth and called Ai.

"Hello."

"Ai, it's Kenji."

"Hi there, I wasn't expecting to hear from you while your family's in town."

"That's what I'm calling about. Listen, this is important. Where is Kayo?"

"She said she was going down to the Karuizawa Ginza to meet a new friend. Why?"

"Because that new friend is Masa."

"What? Are you sure? She's never mentioned him."

"Did she go to a museum this morning?"

"As a matter of fact, I think she did."

"They must have met each other there and struck up a conversation. When Masa began telling me about this new girl he met named Kayo, of course, my radar went on high alert. Now I'm sure it's her. Anyway, I'm going to get him out of town first thing tomorrow. In the meantime, we need to make sure they don't exchange any contact information. If they get each other's numbers, we'll have to get them changed. I'll just have to stay on top of this and adjust the plan depending on how things go tonight. I'll call you again tomorrow when I know more."

After hanging up, he drove back to his house trying to think of a good excuse as to why Masa would need to get out of Karuizawa pronto. Everyone was out on the front deck eating strawberries and ice cream when he arrived. Based on the redness of his father's face, Kenji knew that he was well along in drink.

"Dad, can I see you inside for a minute?" he said as he reached the top of the steps. The old man laughed heartily, a sure sign of his intoxication, as he went into the house with a glass of *sake* in one hand and a stogie in the other.

"What is it, Son?" he said in a jovial tone as they sat down facing each other in the living room.

"I've been thinking," said Kenji, "about what you said regarding the boys, and I think you're right. Can you set up an interview for them with your friend at the university tomorrow?"

"Tomorrow? What's the hurry?"

"I think the sooner, the better. If we prolong it, it'll just give them more time to try to talk me out of it."

"That's pretty short notice," said the old man, "but he owes me a favor.

I'm sure he'll do it if he can – if I can reach him of course."

"It doesn't need to be anything formal or official – just a chance for them to meet without any strings attached."

The old man agreed and called his secretary to get the number. The dean was delighted to be able to be of assistance to the notorious General Watanabe, and the meeting was set at 11:00 a.m. the following morning.

Only Kenji was still awake when Masa made it home promptly at 10:30. He waited for him on the front deck, smoking one of his father's cigars and sipping Jack Daniels on the rocks. Masa got out of the taxi, paid, and ran up the steps to be sure he made the curfew.

"Have a good time?" said Kenji.

"Oh, hey Dad. I didn't see you. I thought everyone was asleep," Masa said. "Yeah, we had a great time. She's *unbelievably* interesting. We have so much in common."

The beaming smile on his son's face told Kenji everything he needed to know. Not surprisingly, they had hit it off, making what he was about to do all the more difficult.

"Sit down here with me. I saved you some strawberries," Kenji said as he slid the bowl in front of him. "They're really sweet."

"Thanks," said Masa, sitting down.

"Where did you go?"

"We did a little window shopping on the strip, but mostly we just sat and talked. She said her favorite food was *tonkatsu*, just like me. Can you believe that? So I told her about my favorite restaurant. You know the one on the second floor beside the place where we used to buy fireworks? Anyway, I wish I didn't have to be home so early because we were having a great time. We're going to meet again tomorrow night."

"Did you get her number?"

"No, thanks to this ridiculous curfew. She was going to give it to me, but then I just happened to glance at the clock on the wall and saw that it was already almost ten. I had to walk her back to the station and get a cab, so I told her I can get it tomorrow night. You're right, these strawberries are good."

"What's Kayo's last name?" Kenji was digging for all the information he needed before dropping the bomb.

"Wang. It's Chinese of course. Oh, and I couldn't believe it. Guess what her dad's name is?"

Kenji stared out into the night, unable to look his son in the eye, sipped his whiskey and said, "No clue."

"Kenji. Isn't that funny? We were laughing so hard in the restaurant I spit rice all over the floor. So many things we had in common. Isn't that incredible?"

"What a coincidence," Kenji replied, barely audible. "What does he do?"

"I got the feeling it was a bit of a delicate subject, so I didn't ask too many questions about him."

Kenji now knew all he needed to know and decided to get it over with. "Oh, by the way, I almost forgot to tell you," he said, still staring straight into the darkness. "Your grandfather was lucky enough to get you and Yoshi an interview with the Dean of Admissions at the University of Tokyo tomorrow. The appointment's at 11:00 a.m. You'll need to get an early start so you might want to head off to bed."

"Tomorrow?" said Masa. "But we're on vacation. And I'm supposed to meet Kayo tomorrow night."

"It's one day, Masa. I'm sure Kaz can get you back in time for your date tomorrow night. If you're running a little late, I'll go tell Kayo myself."

"Why does it have to be tomorrow? I don't meet many people that I like, Dad. I like this girl. And I think she likes me too. Can't I go when we get back next week?"

Kenji's conscience was wreaking havoc, but there was no looking back. "Look, your grandfather went to a lot of trouble to set this up for you and tomorrow was the only time the man had an opening. I think he's leaving the country on business the following day. Surely you know a man like that has a busy schedule. We can't call him back and tell him we're sorry for all his trouble, but we'd like to come some other time when it's more convenient for us. Believe me, Kayo will understand. Now go on and get to bed."

At last, Kenji was compelled to look at his son and saw the disappointment on his face as the boy stood up and moved listlessly into the house. *What kind of father takes his son's delirious joy and chokes the life out of it?* Although he was confident that his course of action was justified, there was little consolation in the thought. He was doing precisely what he planned, what needed to be done, but he felt terrible about it nonetheless. Allowing their friendship to flourish without the full truth of Kayo's birth, which he could not reveal under any circumstances, was out of the question. It seemed to Kenji that, just as with most relationships, absolute and total candor was not a feasible option. Only Ai and Kenji knew the truth, and Kenji believed that it should remain a secret forever.

He took a long draw from the cigar, drained his glass of whiskey, and poured another shot.

CHAPTER 10

Tuesday, August 15th: Morning
Karuizawa, Nagano

Kenji stayed in bed late so that he wouldn't have to face Masa before they left for Tokyo. He told Ami to confirm the time and location of the planned meeting with Kayo, and also to tell Masa that he would go meet Kayo himself and let her know about Masa's appointment should they run late getting back that evening. Kenji failed to mention, however, that he had made arrangements for the meeting at the university to be postponed until after lunch and for Kazu to return with Masa no earlier than 6:00 p.m. Ami also told Masa that if they did not make it back in time, Kenji would be sure to get Kayo's telephone number so that he could contact her later to set up another date which, of course, was nothing but a lie.

In addition to the distaste created by the deception he was practicing on his beloved firstborn son, his anxiety level increased with the knowledge that his entire family would soon descend upon the house for the dreaded annual family reunion. There would be several hell-filled, bitchy-attitude, snide, sniping, drunken, miserable days. Insults would be hurled and denied, feelings would get hurt, old grudges would be rekindled, and presiding over all the chaos would be the instigating family Svengali – his very own father. They all made plans and reservations for this hell every year. He lay in bed planning numerous escape routes from the nightmare that was sure to ensue at any moment. What he wanted was a vacation from his vacation.

The unmistakable voices he heard downstairs confirmed the sobering fact that his little sister and her family had arrived. As much as he wanted to roll back over and sleep for a few more hours, he managed to force himself up and into the shower. As he toweled off and dressed, he dreaded having to meet and go through the motions of pretending to be excited to see everyone again. He tossed his mind a little candy by promising to break away for a few hours in the afternoon to spend some time with Ai. That thought gave him the strength to put on a smile as he walked down the stairs to greet round one of the relatives. Most of them were gathered around the breakfast table. The first wave looked simple enough to handle. In addition to his mother, father, and Ami, his sister Yumi, her husband Naoto, and her two brats, an eight-year-old daughter and six-year-old son, were present.

The relationship between Kenji and his sister had always been complicated, even since his first memory of her. There was familial love and that quintessential role of protector that older brothers feel for their little sisters, but apart from that, he found her to be wanting in so many ways. When she was a child, born when Kenji was just three, he viewed her as the most selfish creature on the planet. Of course, he didn't know at the time that all babies were selfish, but, then again, most children grew out of it, which was where Yumi parted ways with the rest of humanity. Kenji was often beyond confounded at the degrees of self-centeredness his sister could attain. She was the least productive individual that he had ever met, or could even imagine (although his little brother could give her a run for her money), and yet, there was no limit to her sense of entitlement. Of all her shortcomings, however, there was one that chafed Kenji far more than all others: the total lack of supervision and discipline of her children.

Mei, the daughter, and Koutaro, the son, were vile, devilish, obnoxious, and just as selfish as their mother. Whenever they were present, it took all of Kenji's powers of self-control not to slap them. They constantly fought and tried to irritate each other and everyone around them, whined incessantly, threw temper tantrums, and used language usually reserved for drunken sailors, and all the while, his sister sat oblivious to her iniquitous offspring.

Naoto, who Kenji viewed as a perfect match for his sister for all the wrong reasons, rarely said a word to anyone, content to either read comics, newspapers or magazines, or just sleep all day. The children were already in full form, trying to kill the goldfish he had just put into the fish tank by dumping in a year's worth of food. Kenji patiently forewent the initial urge to slap and simply nudged the mischievous delinquents out of the way and scooped out the excess food. Yumi was too busy with her makeup to notice what her children had done, or what Kenji was doing, and Naoto had his face buried in a local newspaper.

"Hello, Yumi," he said. "It's great to see you as always."

"Kenji! It's so good to see you. When did you come down?"

"It appears just in time to keep your kids from killing these poor goldfish," he said as he worked the strainer.

"Did they feed your fish for you? Aren't they the sweetest things you've ever seen?"

Kenji opted to forego the futile explanation.

"I trust business is well," Kenji said to Naoto, forcing him to lower his paper just enough to make eye contact.

"A little slow at the moment," Naoto replied.

"There just aren't any good jobs these days for a man of his qualifications," said Yumi. "We're making plans to start up a new business very soon though if you want in on it."

"What exactly," said Kenji, trying to decide to whom he should address the question, "are his qualifications?"

"Oh Kenji, you are so hilarious sometimes," said Yumi. "His qualifications? How long do you have? You know his father's automotive supply company was the largest in Japan, and Naoto was the driving force behind its success."

Kenji sat down on the couch beside Naoto, encroaching slightly on his space, and considered whether he should waste his time on this or let it go. As usual, the allure of the scrimmage was too much of an invitation for Kenji to refuse.

"But Naoto, didn't that company go out of business a few years ago?" he said.

"Sold the business, Kenji," interrupted Yumi. "Sold at the perfect time. Naoto and his father knew the time was right to move on. That's why we're planning to start the new business next year."

"Oh yeah?" he said to Naoto with a shove.

Naoto put the paper away and confirmed his wife's assertion with a cautious nod.

"No kidding," said Kenji. "What's the new business?" He just couldn't wait to hear what ridiculous scheme was next for them.

"Go ahead and tell him, sweetheart," urged Yumi. "No one here is going to steal your idea."

Naoto sat up from his slumping position and sat on the edge of the seat, looking uncomfortable at being thrust into the spotlight. The general and Mrs. Watanabe had heard the conversation and turned to listen.

Naoto had also been a wealthy child growing up. He and Yumi had attended the same private school, and she had been smitten with the dashing, young captain of the swim team who exuded wealth and prosperity with his fashionable attire and expensive cars. Naoto had been the leader of the It-group, and Yumi had fallen for him, totally ignorant of the high-wire act his father performed with his highly leveraged company.

"It's just in the early stages at the moment – nothing solid yet," said Naoto. "We're still in the exploration phase at this juncture."

The general already had a give-me-a-break expression on his face. Kenji loved Naoto's spiels and was happy with his decision to force the discussion.

"Go ahead, Naoto," demanded Yumi with a laugh, putting down her compact mirror and staring at him. "Don't be so close-lipped all the time. This is my family. They may want to invest."

Kenji looked at his father who flashed a smile in his direction. Yumi and Naoto were becoming famous for their get-rich-quick investment opportunities.

"Well," he began, wringing his hands, "you see, I have a connection in Europe. Of course, it's huge in Paris."

"Lingerie," blurted out Yumi.

All eyes shifted to Naoto, and not a few eyebrows were raised. Kenji had to fight hard not to break down laughing and was doing well until he looked at Ami and saw her *Oh-for-the-love-of* rolling eyes. Once he saw her reaction, he needed the assistance of a couch cushion to suppress his amusement.

"Yes, that's right," said Naoto, attempting to affect a dignified air. "European lingerie." After a pause, he added, "Women's."

Kenji knew his family well, and he desperately wanted to indulge in the pleasure of the hilarity burning in his belly. One word from any of them would be too much.

When the general stood up and quipped, "Well, we can all thank our lucky stars they're not opening a shop to sell French panties for men," Kenji had to let it out.

The eruption sent Naoto back behind his newspaper. Kenji gave him a few slaps on the shoulder as he was releasing the pent-up laughter.

"You guys stop it now," said Yumi good-naturedly. "You just wait, Dad – you guys won't be laughing when you see how much money we're making a year from now."

Loud greetings and acclamations were heard coming from the front yard, and everyone got up to go greet the new guests – except for Naoto whose face had not yet returned to its natural color. Taro, Kenji's little brother, was outside introducing his girlfriend. She was a new one, as usual, and also, as usual, she was a knockout. It occurred to Kenji that he hardly ever saw his brother with the same girl twice. In fact, he had only seen him with the girl Taro married at the wedding. They were divorced in less than six months. The little playboy liked to shower young girls with lavish gifts and exotic vacations but had never held a job in his life.

Cut from the same cloth as his sister Yumi, Taro had no concept of what was required to make the money deposited into the accounts that he depleted with reckless abandon. There had been numerous invitations and suggestions, both lighthearted and earnest, that he pursue some vocation, or avocation, instead of constantly traveling with his latest fling. The general had even been so benevolent as to offer to allow him to seek his own path outside of the Watanabe empire. The little glamour boy had ignored all these offers, as well as those of the nepotistic variety, and everyone, except Ami, had looked the other way. The one saving grace that set him apart from Yumi, in Kenji's opinion, was that he had had the common decency not to procreate.

When he walked out onto the front deck, it wasn't Taro or his trophy that caught Kenji's eye. There was another family further down the slope.

"Kenji," his father called to him, "come see if you can guess who this is. You haven't seen her in years."

Kenji greeted Taro and his girlfriend and continued down the steps. It was hard to believe that the woman standing before him with her husband and two daughters was the same person with whom he had spent so much of his childhood, yet there was no doubt. She stared at him with the same shy, girlish smile she had years ago, but the reality of time hit Kenji like a punch in the gut.

"It's your cousin Naomi," exclaimed his father, as if Kenji couldn't tell.

"Yes, of course," Kenji tried to recover. "This must be your husband." His body was on autopilot, exchanging greetings, pleasantries, and hearing names and ages but remembering virtually nothing. All he could think was how cruel time had been to his once-perfect cousin. Years ago, she had been the envy of every girl and the heart's desire of every boy she met. There was an awkward embarrassment as though their minds were still fourteen while their bodies had been transformed to mid-forties. He wondered if she was casing his looks in her mind the same as he was doing in his. There were still the remnants of the beauty she once had, but the years and childbearing had obviously taken a heavy toll on her figure. The roomy white chiffon dress she wore was probably meant to conceal as much as possible, but Kenji could see enough to shatter his previous image.

"So you had two boys, and I had two girls," he heard as he became aware of the conversation again. "Nice symmetry, don't you think? But I always imagined just the opposite – you with girls, and me with boys." Kenji nodded and laughed, trying to participate in the uneasy small talk, but his mind kept drifting back to how different she looked. She was still charming, her voice vaguely familiar, but the changes were almost inconceivable to him. The last time he saw her, which had been around thirty years ago before he left for the war when they were still teenagers, he was sure that she didn't have a single ounce of unplaced flesh.

"Speaking of your boys, where are the young gentlemen? I've heard so much about them. I can't wait to meet them." Kenji explained that they were in Tokyo but would be back this evening.

The entire herd eventually moved indoors where the men congregated in the living room around the television set to watch baseball and the women sat at the dining room table drinking coffee and talking about the children.

"Dad, let's take a little walk," Kenji said when everyone seemed occupied elsewhere. "It's time we figure out who's sending these letters."

●   ●   ●

Once they were well out of range of the house, Kenji said, "Tell me about the others."

"Not much more to add to what Kazu already blabbed. Just some jackass who obviously doesn't like me and is trying to scare me."

"When did you get the first one?"

"I guess it was about a year ago, more or less."

"What did the first note say?"

"Some proverb. They all sound like bullshit proverbs. 'A single slip causes lasting sorrow,' or some such nonsense. Hell, ask Kazu. Seems like he remembers all this better than I do."

"Did that coincide with any disagreements you were having at the time

– family, business associates?"

"I don't know. I didn't even take it seriously at first. After I got a couple more and started trying to figure it out, I guess I've suspected just about every person I know, including you."

"Me? Why me?"

"Why the hell *not* you? Why the hell anybody? I don't know. Don't get me wrong, I'm not accusing you, but the truth is that I've made mistakes in my life as a father, a husband, a businessman and a friend, as a human being, and let's not forget as a grandfather. The point is that a lot of people don't like me. Hell, more than a few actually hate me. So in trying to figure this thing out, I've discovered that I've given cause to just about every person I know to want to do me harm."

The midday sun was blazing in the cloudless sky, but it was comfortable under the overhang of elm trees lining the road. The cicadas sang their lulling summer song, and a steady breeze carried their music throughout the serried forest.

"What do you intend to do?" asked Kenji.

"I'm not letting this idiot ruin my vacation – I can promise you that," said the general. "I'll think about it again after we get back to Tokyo."

"That's fine, except for the fact that the last note seemed to indicate they were threatening imminent action."

The old man bristled at the comment. "Kenji, I've been through two world wars and hundreds of battles, and you see me standing before you at the ripe old age of seventy-two. Let the son-of-a-bitch take his best shot. I'm done talking about this character. We can talk about it at the office when we get back."

The two of them walked on and changed the subject to business before looping around and heading back for lunch. When they returned, several plates of sandwiches, pickled vegetables, fruit, and desserts had been spread on the dining room table for a self-service lunch. The old man told Kenji, Yumi, and Taro to load up a plate and meet him upstairs on the rear deck.

Before going up the steps, the general told his wife and Ami to make sure they were not disturbed unless his lawyer called. The three children did as instructed and followed their father upstairs, through his room, and onto the deck overlooking the backyard. After they were all seated around the table, Yumi poured from a bottle of chardonnay for everyone, and the old man began speaking in his most authoritative somber voice.

"When a man of my stature reaches a certain age, difficult decisions must be made regarding the division of assets after death." If he hadn't had their undivided attention before, he had it now. This was not going to be a fatherly lecture about the virtue of tenacity. "I don't want to alarm anyone, but I've become increasingly concerned about my health and feel that it's time to make the tough decisions. Until recently, I was of the somewhat reluctant opinion that the three of you, after seeing to it that your mother is set up for the remainder of her life, of course, should share my fortune equally at the time of my death." The *until recently* screeched in the ears of Yumi and Taro like a train attempting an emergency stop.

The old man was in a chair closest to the outer railing, facing the house, so that he was silhouetted in the pale blue sky. After he gave the preceding ominous introduction, he leaned back in his chair and helped himself to a bite of his sandwich. He washed it down by finishing his glass of wine, which all three children reached to refill with Taro edging out his elder siblings.

The spellbound trio was oblivious to everything except their father's voice. Two wagtails flew their peculiar swooping pattern through the yard and alighted on the railing completely unnoticed by the group. They did not sense the heat of the sun; the shrilling of the cicadas was at its apex for the year but was not heard. Such was the interest in the present topic, the subject that all three had pondered at great length through the years. And now, the old man was about to reveal his decision at this unannounced and unexpected moment.

"Yumi, Taro," there was a pause as he considered his words. "I care for both of you and want the best for you in the future, but..." He paused again and looked at Kenji. Yumi, knowing that the *but* within that particular sentence structure was not likely to be followed with desirable information, cocked her head in a threatening angle. Both sets of eyes narrowed. Kenji knew his siblings well enough to know what was going on in their minds. *But? Did he just say 'but?' But fucking what?* The tension was palpable for several seconds before the old man continued.

"But, you have not lived your lives in a prudent and productive manner worthy of a legacy of one-third of my estate. I realize that I am to blame for spoiling you, and I share in the blame for what you have become. However, I do not believe that the proper remedy is to leave money to you to be squandered away on whatever it is that you two blow all of my money on. I do intend on seeing to it that you are financially sound for the remainder of your lives, but it will not be in the way you had in mind. I know damn well that the two of you would run through any cash I left you within a year or two, and that's probably being optimistic. Therefore, I intend to leave you very little; cash, that is. You both already have houses, purchased by me, and I will leave you a second house as well."

The old man watched for their reactions. "Everything else will be left to Kenji, who has already agreed to look after you and provide for you as needed. You and/or your spouses are free to take positions within the company at any time you should decide to avail yourselves of that opportunity. And, of course, this is all open to revision if either of you should ever show any signs of initiative. I wanted to tell you this before I'm gone so that you understand my reasoning."

Kenji watched for reactions as the gears clicked in their heads. *Would defiance be prudent at this point? What about playing on the old man's emotions?* Their eyes moved like cornered animals searching for the next move, both hoping that the other would say something first.

Meanwhile, the old man helped himself to more fruit, but when he downed his glass of wine this time, only Kenji was mindful to reach over and refill. As the eldest son, Kenji had enjoyed a certain hierarchical privilege bestowed by Japanese culture. Taro, the youngest of the three, had accepted his lesser status without protest, especially since the youngest child had the least responsibility in terms of family maintenance and support. He spoke first.

"Father, I can obviously understand your reluctance to leave Yumi and I a fortune in cash." His gaze left his father's eyes and fixed directly on Kenji. "And I, too, trust that my brother would see to it that our needs were met in accordance with your wishes. However," his eyes returned to meet his curious father, "let's say, heaven forbid, something should happen to our dear brother, and he should also pass away. Do you have the same confidence that Ami, who is not our blood relative, would have the same benevolence toward Yumi and I as Kenji? Your entire empire, everything you've worked for your whole life, it would all be hers. You, Father, would be gone, and we," he pointed to Yumi and himself, "we would be at her mercy." Kenji had to give his little brother credit. That was a pretty compelling argument on short notice.

The general, who was chewing in his typical, arrogant, self-assured manner, put down his chopsticks and reclined in his chair as if the argument had struck a discordant note in his flawless plan. The truth was that he had always considered Ami to be materialistic and greedy, which was fine with him as long as she knew the score and he controlled the purse strings. The thought of her inheriting all he had acquired in life and telling his own children to fend for themselves was one of first impression. The old man turned to Kenji for a response.

"I'm thankful that you have that much trust in my judgment," Kenji began, "and this is undoubtedly a momentous decision for you."

"While I'm sure it's disappointing that Father has decided not to leave you the full share you were expecting," Kenji continued, looking back and forth between his sister and brother, "I don't think either of you can fault his logic and reasoning in reaching this decision. Father has worked his whole life to amass this fortune, and I've worked my entire adult life trying to contribute what I could, while the two of you have done nothing but help spend it as fast as humanly possible. Neither of you has worked a day in the company offices. You take money like it's water flowing in a river with no appreciation at all for the hard work needed to earn it. I agree with Father that, no matter what he leaves you, it would just be a matter of time before you squandered it. Other than just being born into the family, what have either of you done to deserve a large inheritance? As far as the question raised by Taro, I think that can be handled best by me preparing a will naming you as beneficiaries in whatever amount Father thinks appropriate."

"That's my Kenji," said the old man with a relieved smile. "That's the kind of thinking that gives me confidence in my decision. Can't you two see that what I'm doing is best for your futures? If I leave you a fortune and you throw it all away on lingerie or some other such nonsense, when you come back to the money tree like you've done all your lives, it'll be gone."

Taro couldn't believe what he was hearing. In his entire life, he had never once considered what it might be like not to have everything he wanted. The thought of not having money, or actually having to work for it, terrified him. But if something didn't change fast, he faced the likelihood of actually being broke – like the people he scorned and mocked. And what would happen to his women?

"So, you made this decision without any regard to what we might have to say or how we feel about it?" Yumi said, bringing on the tears for the sympathetic approach.

"Now, now, there's no need for that," said the old man. "You've been free to express your opinions all your lives, and we're having this discussion now so that you can speak your mind."

"Does that mean that you have not yet made these changes that you're talking about?" she asked.

"My lawyer and I are still discussing all the options. He is on standby awaiting my instructions. I will probably have him bring a new document here for my signature within the next day or two. As for the changes, I would be interested in what the two of you have to say as to why I shouldn't do as I've proposed. After all, as I say, it's not meant to be a punishment or a snub. It's just that Kenji has always been more frugal and able to manage money better than the two of you. Do you disagree?"

"I don't disagree," said Yumi, "that he's *frugal*," speaking the last word as if it were an expletive, "but I don't see why I need to come begging to him or Ami every time I need something. Couldn't you leave our money in one of those trust fund things to be administered by your lawyer if you don't trust us?"

"Your money can't work for you the same way Kenji can work it if you have it tied up in a trust fund. I'm confident that Kenji can turn a fine profit on the money if I leave it with him. As I've told you, it takes money to make money."

"Are we to receive some agreed upon yearly payment?" asked Taro. "How much are we talking about here? And are we just at the mercy of their good graces to collect this money, or can your lawyer write this in such a way that we have a legally enforceable right to it?"

"You sound as if you don't trust your big brother, Taro," said the old man. "But I can understand your desire to protect yourself, and I believe we can word it in such a way that you will have a legal right to the money. I was thinking that ten million yen per year each should be enough to keep you out of the poor house."

Taro knew he could go through that easily in a month in Vegas. When traveling abroad, that would get him maybe 30,000 U.S. dollars – for a year. Yumi's tears were no longer an affectation.

"While that is kind of you, Father, perhaps not necessarily generous," she whispered, "it will never reach one-third of everything you own. While Kenji may deserve slightly more than us, don't you think that's a bit unfair? Kenji will probably get a hundred times more than we get."

"And Kenji is worth a hundred times more than the two of you," said the old man bluntly, holding his glass in front of Kenji for a refill. Taro and Yumi stared at their food.

Mrs. Watanabe came onto the deck from the bedroom and announced that the lawyer was on the phone with some questions. The general said he would take the call alone downstairs in his study and got up to leave. Kenji excused himself as well under the pretext of needing to run an errand and caught his father on the way down the stairs.

"I think things went as well as we could have expected," he said. "Just let them cool off for a while. I'm getting the heck out of here." The old man told him he wanted to discuss matters further when he was finished with the lawyer and walked toward his study. As Kenji made his way past the guests in the living room, he announced that he was going into town to meet an old friend. The general yelled from his study that he wanted Kenji back pronto.

Kenji decided that it would be a good time to spend an hour or two with Ai before he went to meet Kayo. *It was only fair*, he thought, *they were getting what they deserved*. Yumi and Taro had never done a damn thing for the family; things were as they should be. On the deck outside the general's room, however, his younger sister and brother were discussing the matter with very different sentiments.

CHAPTER 11

Tuesday, August 15th: Afternoon
Karuizawa, Nagano

Kenji waited alone in a quaint coffee shop across the street from the spot where Masa told Ami he was to rendezvous with Kayo at 5:00 p.m. He was a little put off that he had tried to visit Ai and found no one at home. The restaurant served an excellent cheesecake with blueberry sauce and the best Dutch-brewed black coffee he had ever tasted. The smoke from his Lucky added just the right mix to the aroma, perfecting the ambiance of the coffee shop, he thought. The only other patrons in the restaurant were an older couple from Australia who were trying to get directions back to the train station from the owner who understood absolutely nothing they said. The futile gesticulations of the Aussies were quite comical and about as useful as if they had been trying to explain quantum physics to a poodle. Kenji considered assisting in the situation but thought it better to stay focused on the task at hand. He had arrived at 4:30 to be sure he had the right spot and a good parking arrangement, and it was already a quarter before the hour. He sipped his coffee and enjoyed the entertainment provided by the old couple.

"The big train, don't you see, with the wheels that go round," said the man as he and his wife made what they hoped were useful gestures. "Toot, toot, it goes as the smoke comes out. I don't believe he's catching a bloody word of it."

"Oh, move over Henry," said the wife. "Men are of no use in these circumstances. Now here, we need to find the T-R-A-I-N."

"Oh good god, Alice, why the bloody hell didn't I think of that?" The shopkeeper shook his head.

As he sat chuckling, Kenji noticed Kayo on the other side of the road, coming from the direction of the station. She was wearing a white summer dress, far shorter than Kenji would have preferred, with a light blue shoulder bag that hung to her waist as she sauntered up the sidewalk, looking in shop windows along the way. There was a bench near the entrance of the Karuizawa Ginza Strip – a cobblestone thoroughfare closed to motor traffic during the crowded summer months – which was where she was supposed to meet Masa.

She strolled over and sat on the bench, crossed her legs rather too seductively for his liking, and looked around for the young man with the audacity to keep her waiting. Kenji couldn't help noticing how much she looked and acted just like her mother. He half expected her to pull out a cigarette and light up but was pleased that she did not. To the neglect of his coffee and dessert, he watched her attentively as she read a magazine, uncrossed and crossed her legs repeatedly in evident agitation, and stood up to leave at 5:30. She took one final look around with her hands on her hips before marching briskly back toward the station.

Kenji paid up and walked to his car. He drove down a parallel street so that he could pass her before doubling back in her direction. The traffic was barely moving, and he had no difficulty spotting her. She turned in surprise when he beeped the horn and called her name, then crossed the street and jumped into the front seat.

"I'm so happy to see you," she said. "You won't believe what just happened to me. This guy asked me to come all the way here to meet him, and he didn't even show up. Can you believe that? A boy standing *me* up? I'm so angry I can't think."

"Oh my," said Kenji. "But you can never trust boys. Haven't I always told you that?"

She leaned over and kissed him on the cheek. "But I can always trust you, Papa. Right?"

"Let's take that up some other time, shall we?" he said as he cut off the main road. "And who is this boy with the nerve to stand up a girl as beautiful as you?"

"Masa Watanabe," she said with dramatic flair.

"Would you like me to stop at a phone booth so you can call and give him a piece of your mind?"

"That would be fantastic. The problem is, I don't have his number, but if I did..." Kenji was pleased to hear that. Now he had confirmation that neither had the other's number, and neither had their names listed in any city directories. If he could make sure they didn't bump into each other for the rest of the short vacation, they would be off to Tokyo where they would almost certainly forget about each other and never meet again.

"I tried to call your mother today, even stopped by, but no one was home – where is she?"

"I think she went out somewhere with Uncle Shou and Aunt Fan this morning."

"Shou and Fan are in town?" Kenji said.

"Yeah, they've been here a week now."

"She didn't tell me anything about it."

"Hope it's not a secret."

Ai was the firstborn of five children, coming into a world of chaos and uncertainty in China in 1926. A younger sister, Lin was born the following year, and the twins, Shou and Fan, were born in 1935. Another little girl, Jiao, the youngest child in the family was born in '38. Kenji had met Shou and Fan in Manchuria during the war, and they had visited Ai in Japan several times in the years since. Their family history was fascinating, and Kenji loved to meet with them whenever they were in town, so he found it odd that no one had told him of their visit.

It was a little after 6:00 p.m. when they reached Kayo's house. There was still no one home, so Kenji dropped her off and was back at his father's place by 6:30.

Everyone was on their way out to the street when he arrived, and Kazu was packing picnic blankets and coolers into the back of the general's car.

"Good timing," his father said. "I thought you were going to miss it."

"Where are we going?" said Kenji.

"Down to the lake to watch the fireworks, of course. Don't tell me you've forgotten." But in all the events of the day, he *had* forgotten. Tonight the general was to be honored by the mayor and town council at their yearly festival.

"You guys go ahead without me. I have to get something from the house. I'll just be a minute."

As he ran up the steps, he met Ami on her way down. "Where's Masa?" he said.

"That child of yours," said Ami. "He ran down the mountain to find that girl. We couldn't stop him. Kazu said he hounded him all day to hurry and get back, and Masa was furious with him for not taking him directly to the Ginza once they returned."

"It'll be okay. You guys go ahead without me. I'll find him and meet you at the lake."

Kenji drove down the mountain and found Masa on the same bench where Kayo had been waiting earlier, sitting alone and dejected. He felt guilty, but gathered his thoughts for the final stage of the fraudulent scheme. He pulled up in front of the bench, turned off the engine, and went to sit beside his son.

"Hi, Dad. Did you get her number? It's not too late for me to give her a call and have her come back for the fireworks."

"Sorry. I waited for over an hour, but Kayo didn't show. I'm sure it must have been something important that kept her away." Kenji could see the heartbreak he was causing as Masa lowered his head with the false knowledge that he had been stood up. Kenji watched and imagined the thoughts that must be going through his son's head: maybe his dad had missed her, perhaps he had been late, maybe if he hadn't gone to Tokyo, or perhaps she had an emergency and was still on her way. Kenji reached over and put his hand on his shoulder, deciding to pass on the *there are lots of other fish in the sea* routine that he knew would only succeed in making things worse.

"I suppose we could sit here all night," said Kenji, "feeling terrible about a girl that isn't going to show, or we can go watch the fireworks. Let's go have a beer."

Whether it was the thought of the fireworks or the beer, he couldn't say, but Kenji thought he definitely saw an encouraging look on Masa's face as he stood up and walked to the car. The ruse now complete, Kenji spun the Corvette around and sped off to join the rest of the family.

●　　　●　　　●

Each year, the mayor chose a member of the town's exclusive summerhouse citizenry to be feted at their annual summer festival at Black Bear Lake. This year's honoree, who had coincidentally made a munificent cash donation to the town for a new eponymous park, was none other than General Tatsurou Watanabe. The event was copiously advertised in newspapers, handbills, the radio, and television, and was also the most talked about shindig among the small town's inhabitants.

The lake was a donut-shaped body of water with an island in the center about fifty meters in diameter. A single bridge, on the southern side near the lone entrance to the lake, spanned the roughly thirty meters from shore to island, which was the approximate breadth of the water all around. As there was usually an admission price to the lake and the surrounding park, there was a tall, wrought iron fence around the perimeter of the ten-acre grounds.

The outer edge of the lake was packed with townspeople on blankets feasting on junk food, juices, and alcohol of all varieties in anticipation of the fireworks. Afterward, the general was to give a speech and then they would have traditional dancing, singing, and other entertainment. Vendors had set up stalls all over the outer banks selling everything from fried chicken to pet goldfish.

A raised stage three-meters high had been erected in the center of the island, which could be viewed from all directions. A small hospitality tent for the guest of honor had been put up on the northern side of the island, opposite the bridge. Picnic blankets were only permitted on the southern side of the stage, and authorized-guests-only signs had been posted on the eastern and western sides so that the general would have privacy in his tent.

The town band played festive music as the special guest arrived to grand pomp and circumstance. The entire police force, fire department and volunteer fire department, former military brass, the mayor, and town council were all on hand for the town's most anticipated annual event. The captain of the police department and eight officers rigorously monitored access to the island at the bridge entrance, and only those possessing the proper credentials were allowed to pass. The officials whisked the Watanabe family through the crowd, across the bridge, and onto the island in front of the stage where a prime section of ground had been reserved for their picnic blankets. The general was led around the outer banks to greet the many guests who were present to salute his achievements. Kenji and Masa arrived just before 7:30 p.m. and sat down on a blanket with Ami, Yoshi, Kazu, and Mrs. Watanabe.

"I hope we haven't missed anything," said Kenji.

Masa sat without saying a word, resentment still showing on his face. Kazu, who was having fits with his guilty conscience for his role in the masquerade, handed Masa a beer but received nothing but an icy stare.

"Come on now, Masa," said Kenji, "I've told you Kaz was following orders. And besides, even if you had been there on time, the girl didn't show." Masa stood up, walked away, and sat alone on the grass under a chestnut tree near the water's edge. A few seconds later, Yoshi got up and joined him.

The ladies had spread four picnic blankets in a square pattern on the thick grass; one for Taro and his girlfriend, one for Yumi's family, one for Naomi's family, and one for Kenji's family. They began passing out plates with fruits and cheese and filling cups of juice for the children. The men commenced in serious summer-night beer consumption. The children, gorged on sugar and giddy with the thought of the upcoming fireworks, ran and played with beetles and other insects near the water.

The general was escorted across the bridge by the mayor just before the fireworks were to begin. The mayor stopped by to wish the family a good evening and told the general that a tent had been set up behind the stage where he could wait in private. He informed everyone that he would come back when the fireworks ended to introduce the general for his speech and then returned across the bridge to hobnob with other dignitaries.

"Are you just going to shoot from the hip, or do you actually have a speech prepared?" Kenji asked his father.

"Absolutely no idea," the general said. "Kimiko," he looked to his wife, "write something down for me – what an honor this is, and how we need to prepare our children to face the challenges of a changing world – manly stuff, none of that mushy crap. Bring it to me backstage when you get it ready, I'm going for a smoke and a belt of whiskey."

With that, the general left his family and walked around behind the stage. The canvas tent, which was stocked with beer on ice, *sake*, whiskey, and the general's favorite cigars, had an open entrance facing the back of the stage which was not visible to those on the banks of the lake.

As soon as the fireworks began at precisely 8:00 p.m., Taro and his girlfriend took their drinks and strolled around the edge of the water hand-in-hand. Mei was doing her best to shove Koutaro into the lake and, as usual, the parents were clueless to their little darlings' movements. A few minutes later, Yumi, still seething over the discussion of the will, left the group saying that she needed to speak with her father; however, she returned in a short time and said that he wasn't in the tent.

"Probably just went to the bathroom," said Kenji.

At that point, the general's wife decided to take her handwritten notes backstage. She also returned declaring that he was nowhere to be found. Kenji, too absorbed in beer and fireworks to be bothered, told Ami to go look for him. The general's speech was to begin right after the 8:30 finale, so when

Ami returned at 8:25 shaking her head, Kenji had no choice but to take on the task himself.

The fireworks exploding in the clear night sky were cresting toward the crescendo as Kenji made his way around the stage to find his father. The white canvas of the tent lit up to all the colors bursting overhead. A quick panoramic scan revealed no one except the revelers on the shore across the lake staring up at the pyrotechnics. He entered the tent, which was dimly lit by a single electric lamp, and saw a glass of whiskey on a table but no sign of the general. Kenji walked around the inside of the tent, looking behind and under tables, and it was clear that his father was not there. He had no idea where he could have gone or why. As he turned to leave, the sky was filled with fireworks that threw a bright light over the green grass, where Kenji noticed a curious red streak on the lawn in front of the tent.

The light faded and the streak vanished. It appeared to have led from the tent toward the lake, so Kenji began moving that way until the next set of fireworks lit the sky and revealed the streak's end at the border of the water. There was a shiny metal object protruding straight up at the point where the red streak ended. As he approached it, a momentary quiet darkness prevailed over the lake, but when Kenji neared the water's edge he could clearly see that the object was a sword – his father's sword.

As he tried to imagine what it was doing there, the night exploded under the fierce brightness of the finale, and the light revealed his father's face staring up through the shallow water with the weapon planted in his stomach. Kenji seized the sword and pulled hard, as if the action could somehow undo the harm that had been done. Yumi, who was approaching to see if he had located their father, screamed when she saw the general's body in the water. Everyone on the shore looked just in time to see Kenji holding the sword over his head, though they couldn't see the general's body under the surface of the water. Kenji threw down the sword and began pulling his father out onto the grass. Taro and his girlfriend came running, followed by the police and the mayor. The spectators on the shore had given up all interest in the fireworks and were standing and pointing at the spectacle. Once the police chief, Captain Miyabe, realized what was happening, he took charge and ordered everyone to stand back. He went down on one knee beside the body, took the general's wrist, and felt for a pulse.

"He's dead," he said as he looked up at Kenji.

Yumi shrieked again and put her arms around her big brother. Kenji stared in shock at the body of the man who had raised him, not able to accept that this was real.

Captain Miyabe ordered his officers to seal off the exit and perimeter of the park. "No one leaves this island or the park until we have names and any information they have regarding the general's murder," Miyabe said to a subordinate. "Make a list of everyone on the island and then move them across the bridge and into the restaurant. I want to speak with everyone who has been on this island tonight. And make sure everyone on that shore," he said as he pointed to the onlookers staring at them from the bank, "is questioned to see if anyone saw anything suspicious over here."

Officers guided the wailing Watanabe family members across the bridge while others strung police tape around the tent and the area where the body had been found. Captain Miyabe left orders that nothing was to be touched until crime scene experts arrived from Nagano City, the capital, to photograph the scene and body. After the criminalistics team was finished, the body was to be taken to a hospital and stored for an autopsy which the captain himself would schedule and observe. Miyabe left the island and pushed his way through the murmuring crowd to the restaurant where the family members were gathered in various states of shock and disbelief.

"Mr. Watanabe," Miyabe said to Kenji, "I will need to ask you a few questions. It would be best if we speak in private." One of the officers motioned them toward the kitchen where a table and chairs had been arranged for an impromptu interrogation. The captain motioned for Kenji to have a seat across the table and had an assistant come in with a pencil and notebook to record the interview.

"I know this is difficult for you, Mr. Watanabe, but I need you to tell me everything you know about this and spare no details, no matter how minor."

Kenji's head moved as though he had awakened from a deep sleep and was trying to determine where he was. The captain's words bounced around and echoed before he could grasp what he was saying.

"I don't know," he said. "I, I can't...he was fine. I don't know."

"Mr. Watanabe, let me see if I can bring some clarity to this situation. Someone has just murdered your father, and we've received information that you were seen holding the apparent murder weapon over his body. Let me be blunt, sir. Did you just kill your father?"

"What?" said Kenji. The question had had the effect of a bucket of cold water to the face. "What the hell? No! What the hell kind of question is that?"

"Given the circumstances, sir, I think it's a very logical question. As I say, someone has just killed General Watanabe, and I need to know who did it. I must ask that you begin telling me what happened tonight without any further delay."

Kenji began relaying the events of the evening from the time he and Masa had arrived, as best he could remember. Several people had tried to find the general unsuccessfully, so he had gone on the errand and discovered the body after following a bloody trail to the water's edge. He had grabbed hold of the sword and pulled without thinking, entirely a reflex action. That's why he had the sword in his hands.

"Do you have any idea who may have done this?" the captain asked. Kenji shook his head without any thought of the threatening letters.

"Did you see anyone else behind the stage?"

"No," Kenji replied. "No one."

"I'll need to speak with the rest of the family now. I'll have one of my men take you down to the station for additional questioning later."

Kenji shook his head, incredulous. "Wait a minute. Are you arresting me?" he asked.

"No sir. Not at this time. We're conducting a murder investigation, and I assume you'd like to help. You would like to help us solve your father's murder wouldn't you, Mr. Watanabe?" The threat and suspicion were crystal clear in the captain's tone.

"I will not be interrogated like some common criminal," said Kenji. "I'll be at my father's house if you have any questions. I assume you know where that is."

"I'm sorry, Mr. Watanabe. I truly am, but that will not be possible. If you prefer, you can wait outside while I finish questioning the others, and I'll make a decision on how to proceed after I have additional information." Kenji stood, still confused, and walked out of the kitchen.

"Bring me the general's wife," ordered Captain Miyabe.

CHAPTER 12

Friday, November 24th: Morning
Karuizawa, Nagano

In the days and months after the death of General Tatsurou Watanabe, age 72, on the evening of August 15th, 1967, Captain Miyabe spent every waking hour investigating the murder. The autopsy findings confirmed the obvious – that the general had been run through once with his own sword. The assailant had been facing the general, and the stab wound originated just above and to the left of the deceased's navel, continuing on a slightly ascending path through his bowels before exiting to the left of his spine.

The medical examiner's opinion was that the thrust could have been delivered by someone of average strength, but most likely by someone who had training. Given the ascending path of the wound, it was plausible to believe that the perpetrator was shorter than the deceased, but there were numerous scenarios in which the same injury could have been inflicted by a person of equal or greater height; Kenji Watanabe was two centimeters taller than his father.

There were no signs of a struggle, nor were there any defensive wounds, which led to the opinion that the general was probably caught off guard by the attack. Although the injury was not immediately fatal, it would have left the general debilitated entirely. The general ultimately died of asphyxia brought on by aspiration of water into the lungs in the lake.

The blood trail evidence and disturbance of the lawn indicated that the general had been stabbed near the entrance of his tent and dragged into the water. Considering the weight of the general at the time of his death, and the slight downward slope from the tent to the water, moving the body would not have required extraordinary strength. Given the short distance from the point where the general was stabbed to where the body was found in the lake, the killer could have moved the general in less than a minute.

The general went behind stage just before 8:00 p.m. and was discovered at approximately 8:28 p.m., and the pathologist who performed the autopsy could not narrow the time of death with any greater precision. Kenji Watanabe's khaki trousers were wet up to the knees, but there were no traces of blood on him or anyone else at the scene. The wet trousers were not necessarily inculpatory, however, as the son had pulled his father out of the lake. No one else's clothes showed signs of being in the water.

All witnesses identified the weapon through firsthand knowledge as General Watanabe's sword, which he had owned and used in his service to the Imperial Japanese Army during World Wars I and II. Due to the fabric used to wrap the handle of the *katana*, they had been unable to lift any fingerprints from the weapon. Kenji stated that the sword had been stolen, according to his father, from the general's home in Tokyo the previous Sunday, August 13th, which was verified by the Tokyo Metropolitan Police Department and Mr. Kazu Ishii.

His investigation into that burglary led Miyabe to believe that the burglar must have had keys to both the front gate and to the residence because there were no signs of forced entry, and the general and his wife had strict rules about keeping the street entrance doors and house doors locked whether they were at home or away. Furthermore, Miyabe believed that the intruder had specific knowledge of the residence and had entered to steal the general's sword and leave a threatening note.

Kenji had informed Captain Miyabe what little he knew about the mysterious letters, however, after searching the general's Tokyo home, the house in Karuizawa, and the offices on the Ginza, only the final note had been recovered. Kenji and Mr. Ishii were the only people the general had ever confided in regarding the existence and content of the earlier letters. All the captain could rely upon and presume, if he was to believe the veracity and accuracy of their accounts, was that someone may have been stalking and threatening the general through anonymous letters for the past year. The fact that Miyabe found just one of the mysterious notes troubled him, but the captain did believe that Kenji and Mr. Ishii were telling the truth on the subject. Their accounts, which the captain had discussed with them separately and on numerous occasions, were consistent, and he couldn't perceive the slightest sign of dishonesty by either of the gentlemen.

Therefore, he leaned toward the theory that someone had sent the general threatening messages, but he had no evidence or supposition yet as to who it might have been. The contents of the one letter they found indicated that the general would die by the sword and mentioned his will, but Miyabe had still not constructed a theory that pointed to a particular suspect.

Apart from these findings, if the killer were someone other than Kenji, the captain was left with very little evidence to catch his man – or woman. There was nothing left behind by the killer of any use: no clothing or fibers, and no fingerprints. Whatever footprints had been left by the killer were destroyed in the chaos after the general's body had been discovered, and although he had hundreds of people within sight of the area, no one could testify that they had seen someone run the general through with his own sword or drag him into the lake. By 8:00 p.m., the sun had been down for over an hour, and the spectators, over thirty meters away, were packed tightly and watching the fireworks, which had been exploding in the sky west of the island.

The most prevalent theory among his officers and the public was that Kenji had killed his father out of greed because he thought the old man was going to change his will and reduce his inheritance. Rumors spread rampantly in the small town, and there was no shortage of experts with their own theories on why the wealthy businessman had killed his famous father in such dramatic fashion. Miyabe had listened to them all.

It was the talk of Nagano. Kenji was the Lizzie Borden they had never had.

But Captain Miyabe felt he didn't have enough evidence. He could have Kenji arrested, but he knew that he would need much more if he was ever going to get a conviction against a man as wealthy and powerful, with all the clout and connections both politically and within the legal system, as Kenji Watanabe. And more than that, Miyabe was a conscientious man who had never wished to get convictions just to put an end to his cases, and he still had his own doubts about Kenji. Even if it were possible to get a conviction, he felt he needed more before he was satisfied that Kenji was his man.

The most significant source of confusion in the case, and the piece of evidence Miyabe thought held the key to solving the murder, was the general's will. But the truth of what the general actually intended to do, and what everyone perceived he planned to do, was one of the most convoluted matters he had ever investigated.

At first, Kenji, Yumi, and Taro had informed Miyabe about the events of the afternoon of August 15th, when the general told them that his original will would provide a substantial sum for his wife, with the rest of his estate to be left to the three children in equal shares, but that he was thinking of changing it to give almost everything to Kenji. It stood to reason that if that were the case, Yumi and Taro would have been the ones with a motive to kill the general before he changed it. Kenji would have had an interest in making sure the general was safe until the changes had been made.

But later, when the will was administered, and Kenji received the majority of the estate, the only thing clear to Miyabe was that nothing was clear. The general, it seemed, was playing mind games with everyone concerning what was in his will, and, ironically, the document that he used to control his children's lives may have gotten him killed. The tricky part for Miyabe was to try to put the truth of what was in the will out of his head and focus on what each individual *thought* was in the document, true or not. That had proven easier said than done.

Miyabe had taken a long look at the pros and cons of the case against Kenji. Although Kenji was found with his hands on the murder weapon standing over his dead father, many facts did not add up in the case against him. First of all, Miyabe could not fathom why Kenji would have killed him in such a brazen and reckless manner when so many other simpler methods existed. He could not devise a plausible theory as to why a rational and intelligent man, as he had found Kenji to be, would kill his father in such a risky, theatrical manner. Neither a spur-of-the-moment, heat-of-passion killing nor a planned, premeditated killing in that fashion made any sense. The fact that the general died by drowning created problems in the case against Kenji as well because of the short time he had been behind the stage. Further, Kenji's actions that day and evening did not appear consistent with a man preparing to commit murder. Although this was Miyabe's first time leading a homicide investigation, his gut feeling was that Kenji was not the killer.

On the other side of the coin, when Kenji received the lion's share of his father's estate, to everyone's apparent surprise, Miyabe had decided he could not give up on the possibility of his guilt. The loss Kenji would have suffered had the general changed the will closer to the one-third-per-child scenario would have been astronomical. It seemed that the general had told so many stories about his will that no one, except his lawyer, knew what the situation was at the time of his death. And even his lawyer never knew from one day to the next what the general's true intentions were. The attorney did tell him that the general's will at the time of his death left the largest share to Kenji, but he had spoken to the general on the afternoon of August 15th, the day of his death. General Watanabe had expressed concern over the possibility that Kenji's wife would be in control of everything if something ever happened to Kenji and had asked his lawyer to come up with some possible solutions to prevent that eventuality.

As Miyabe was driving through the tree-lined, twisting, uphill course that led to the Watanabe home in Karuizawa, he combed through every fact of the case hoping for an epiphany, like the ones that always came to the great detectives in movies. Dead leaves in the road rose and fell back, spinning to the ground in the car's wake as he reviewed every suspect's file in his mind.

Kenji Watanabe. He was found standing over his deceased father holding the murder weapon. He received a fortune, far more than he would have inherited if the will had been changed to three equal shares. Did someone in the house overhear the general's call to his lawyer? But, and this applied to all suspects, how could he have gotten the murder weapon onto the island and behind the stage?

Mrs. Kimiko Watanabe. The general's wife did go behind the stage to look for her husband to give him his notes, but otherwise, there was little reason to believe her to be a serious suspect in the case. She was seventy years old. The general's philandering was a poorly kept secret, but the wife appeared to have accepted her husband's ways long ago. The threatening notes made no sense coming from her.

Ami Watanabe. She profited just as much as Kenji. She had been to see the general behind the stage within the accepted timeframe of his death. Could she have overheard the call to the lawyer? There was another phone in the kitchen. Could she have listened in on the conversation without the general's knowledge? But again, with so many other less complicated and secretive ways to kill a man, why would she do it this way? She could have been the burglar at the general's house perhaps, but the notes didn't make any sense coming from her either.

Masa and Yoshi Watanabe. They were not happy about being forced to change schools, but murder? They gave each other an alibi on the night he was killed. They were seen by several people sitting together, and there was no evidence that they went back to see the general. Very unlikely suspects.

Yumi Watanabe. She could have believed, as her father had told her, that he was changing the will to drastically cut her inheritance. But all the stalking and threatening notes would have been a wholly unnecessary, elaborate hoax. She had just learned of her father's intention to change the will that afternoon. So, while she may have had a motive and opportunity, as she had been behind the stage within the appropriate window of time, it seemed highly unlikely that she had anything to do with the threatening notes.

Taro Watanabe. Just as Yumi, he probably believed that his father was about to substantially reduce his inheritance. He said that he had never left his girlfriend's side that evening, something she had corroborated, but two witnesses had seen her standing alone at about 8:15, which meant that he was alone on the island for a short period of time. However, as with Yumi, while he may have had motive and opportunity, none of the other pieces of the puzzle made any sense regarding him. He would have had no previous knowledge of the general's plan to reduce his inheritance, and, thus, no reason to write the notes or steal the murder weapon. And again, how could he have possibly gotten the sword behind the stage?

Kazu Ishii. The general's driver was on the island on August 15th and moved about freely with, perhaps, an opportunity to go behind the stage, but he had denied doing so. And no evidence had been found to the contrary. No disputes or acrimony of any kind between the general and Mr. Ishii had been discovered.

Others. There had been one potential lead provided by the company hired to cater the event on the island on August 15th. The owner of the company, a Mr. Sakamoto, had brought and put up the general's tent and stocked it with food, alcohol, and cigars. He had hired a man and woman who had helped set it all up. Sakamoto had thought little about them at first but found it strange that they had left early and never came back to receive their pay. The pair had been on the island working to set things up throughout the day but had disappeared at some point; he could not remember when, possibly after guests had begun to arrive around 6:00 p.m.

Sakamoto stated that the two had answered a help-wanted advertisement and had been introduced by an Asian woman with a foreign accent. She had given their names as Masahiro and Yuki Takahashi, a brother and sister with special needs who spoke very little but could follow instructions. Mr. Sakamoto was proud to have used special needs part-time workers in the past and was happy to hire them for this event as it was simple manual labor. They had worked hard but had not spoken throughout the day. He estimated their ages to be between 30 and 35. They were of average height and weight and had both worn head coverings as they worked – the man a towel and the woman a scarf. He wasn't sure if he could recognize them if he saw them again.

The man and woman had worked all day helping to set up the tent and stock it for the general and were supposed to work at one of his stands selling hot dogs that evening beginning at 7:00 p.m. but never showed. They had not filled out any paperwork as they were temporary workers and he was going to pay them in cash. Miyabe and his men had searched high and low for Masahiro and Yuki Takahashi but had come up empty. They had checked with all special needs facilities in the area, but no one had ever heard of such a brother and sister.

Other than that, there were other family and friends on the island that night; however, none were seen going behind the stage, and no motives were uncovered as to individuals who wanted to harm the general. He had interviewed all of his men who had been on the bridge checking IDs that night, and they were confident that no one other than the authorized family members and guests had been allowed to pass. One of the men did, however, bring up a valid point which gave him cause to reflect. Their main concern had been stopping people on their way onto the island; they had paid no attention whatsoever to who was leaving.

After conducting hundreds, perhaps a thousand interviews, he had not uncovered a single witness who saw anything that happened behind the stage where the general was killed. He had no theory or useful evidence to show who had broken into the general's house, stole his sword, and left the mysterious note on his bathroom door.

No epiphany.

•   •   •

Having hit dead ends again and again, Miyabe decided to try to go back to the beginning. He thought he had successfully convinced Kenji that he now believed everything about his story. The detective told Kenji he was trying to develop other possible leads and wanted to speak with him again to see if there was something they had missed about anyone who had enough of a grudge in the past to want to kill his father. Kenji and his wife had agreed to visit their home in Karuizawa, the general's former house, to facilitate the interview and save the captain a trip to Tokyo. Miyabe arrived at the house at eight o'clock as agreed and found Kenji and Ami on the front deck having breakfast.

"Good morning," he called out from the bottom of the hill as he made his way up the steps. The sun was bright, but the dazzling fall colors had turned to brown, and an overnight frost covered the lawn. The squirrels went about their fall activities, oblivious to the more enlightened and evolved species around them. The wind was helping relieve the forest's deciduous members of their dead leaves, revealing empty and forsaken nests that had been so active and full of life through the spring and summer.

Miyabe took a seat and the three engaged in meaningless small talk, with Kenji and Ami attempting to mask their disdain for the situation and the captain's presence. The truth was that Miyabe still had to consider Kenji to be a suspect in the murder of General Watanabe even though he pretended otherwise. Kenji knew this and resented Miyabe for suspecting him when he had tried to be as honest as he could. Ami, who was angry with both men for bringing trouble into her fairytale existence, got up and walked into the house.

"What a day for breakfast on the veranda," Miyabe said. "How I envy this type of life."

"We call it a deck," said Kenji, already tired of the man.

"Here's your coffee, Captain," said Ami, returning. "I don't recall if you take cream or sugar."

"Black, please," Miyabe said with a friendly smile. "This is very hospitable of you." Ami did not reply before walking away again.

Miyabe looked up at the clear sky through the many trees that towered overhead. "What I wouldn't give to have a place like this. But on a policeman's salary I guess I can only dream," he said with a laugh. There was an awkward moment of silence as Kenji was unable to find a sincere reply. He didn't feel like placating the captain anyway. After all, this man was here to build a case for murder against him.

"As nice as it is though, I guess it must be bittersweet for you to visit here now," said Miyabe.

"How's that?" replied Kenji.

"Well, it's just that this is where you spent your last day with your father, or do you try not to think about that?"

"My father had a brilliant career," Kenji said with a somber expression, "a family who loved him, and he was regarded as honorable by most, I believe. Like everyone, he made some mistakes along the way, but we have many great memories of my father here. It would be foolish to dwell on his death."

"Words to live by," said Miyabe. "I'm glad you find comfort in that." He paused, looking down from the sky, and looked at Kenji. "But today we are going to have to do just that – dwell on his death – and, as I see it, there must be at least one person who did not view your father as an honorable man. This was not a crime of passion. This was cool, calculated, premeditated murder designed to inflict maximum exposure, and yet, I don't know why. If someone had been writing letters over a period of time, and if they had gone to the trouble of burglarizing his home to steal the very sword they would use to murder the general, *and* if they committed the murder in front of hundreds of spectators who had gathered to honor the man, it stands to reason that they had a vendetta against your father. People do not have vendettas against those they venerate."

"I had no vendetta," said Kenji calmly, assuredly.

Miyabe ignored the self-serving declaration and pressed on. "By the way Kenji, I had a thought the other day. When you were telling me what happened the day your father died, you said something about Masa being rather down earlier in the day – that you were trying to cheer him up. What was that all about?"

Kenji knew well that this wasn't something that had just popped into the captain's head as he was pretending. "I can't recall. There were so many other important things going on at the time I suppose I've forgotten."

"Think back," said the captain. "I'm sure it'll come to you."

There was no doubt that it had come to him. The question was, where was the captain going with it? Kenji recalled all too well why Masa had been upset that evening, and he was fully aware that Masa's agony had been the result of the devious plot he had concocted to keep him away from Kayo. As he looked up into the trees as if to search his memory, he was actually contemplating what effect a true answer to this question might have on the potential case against him, or perhaps even Masa. He decided to tell the truth, sans, of course, the chicanery on his part.

"Ah yes, now I remember. Some girl had stood him up that evening. If I remember correctly, he met her the previous day and was supposed to meet her again that night, but she didn't show. Actually, I was the one who went to meet her because Masa and Yoshi had gone to Tokyo and didn't get back in time."

"What were they doing in Tokyo?" the captain asked.

Kenji again weighed his response carefully, trying to anticipate the captain's goal here. "They had an interview at the University of Tokyo. Their grandfather wanted them to enroll there and had set up the meeting." As the words 'Their grandfather wanted' rolled off his tongue, Kenji sensed the pricks of a snare.

"Wow - the University of Tokyo. Have they been accepted?"

Kenji nodded as an ambiguous smile creased his face.

"Were they happy about that change?" asked Miyabe, pulling a pencil and tiny notebook from his jacket, leafing through pages and scribbling.

"They were not at first, but they've come to understand and respect the decision we made."

"Have they now?" asked the captain rhetorically.

Miyabe did not regard Masa or Yoshi as likely suspects, but he wanted to press in that direction so that Kenji would be one hundred percent forthright, give up any secrets he might have about the general or the murder. Ami came back and placed Miyabe's breakfast on the table and returned to the house. The conversation then shifted to a review of the detective's findings. The captain touched on alibis, the physical evidence at the murder scene and the house in Tokyo, and other benign matters without a flicker of interest, but his eyes and manner became noticeably more animated when he turned to the subject of the will.

"Now, as to your father's will, it appears that the lion's share was left to you. That's the easy part. However, it seems that your father attempted to use his money and the threat of disinheritance, or virtual disinheritance, to keep all of you, his children, your spouses, and his grandchildren, living in accordance with his wishes. The actual will itself, unless I find proof that someone knew the precise contents, is irrelevant. What matters is what everyone *thought* was in the will, and that's where things begin to get interesting."

"The truth," the captain continued, "as you are aware since you've received most of his fortune, was that he had one will. And in that one will, he leaves a substantial sum to your mother, some property and nominal cash to Yumi and Taro, and the remainder, including the family business, to you.

However, all three of you have told me about the meeting on the rear deck the day of his death at which he said that his original will was one third to all, but that he was going to change it in your favor because, basically, Yumi and Taro refused to take positions within the family business and act as he wanted them to. So, at that moment, Yumi and Taro had every reason to believe that your father was about to substantially reduce their inheritance, ergo, they had a motive to kill him before these supposed changes could take place."

"However, now I've learned that the truth was just the opposite: the real will left the majority of assets to you and your father was discussing options with his attorney because he was worried that everything might end up under the control of your wife. Yumi and Taro had gone to him that afternoon to tell him that they would be taking positions in the company within the next month. This, some people might say, would have given *you* the motive to kill your father."

"But as you have just said," Kenji remarked, "what matters is what people believe to be the truth, and I had no knowledge of this plan you say he had of changing the will to three equal shares. I believed what he said that day to be the truth. And let me add this absolute fact for your edification, Captain Miyabe – I would never kill anyone, let alone my father, for any amount of money."

"And I must say that I would be inclined to believe you. It's just…" he paused as if troubled.

"It's just what?" said Kenji with a hint of irritation.

"I have the statement from your father's attorney that the general was asking about the possibility of changing the will, leaving things in equal shares to the three of you. I have no doubt about the veracity of that statement, but I ask myself, how could you have known about this? And then I hear, I apologize that I cannot reveal my sources on these things because of the ongoing investigation, but I hear that you and your father were quarreling that very afternoon about the point Taro had raised at lunch – that your father was truly fearful of the idea that his fortune might someday be controlled by your wife to the neglect of his own flesh and blood."

"Your sources are mistaken on this point, Captain. My father and I had many discussions about family matters that afternoon, but there was no quarrel."

"Let me see – I have it here somewhere," said Miyabe, flipping through the pages of his notebook. "Ah yes, your father yelled at you in a loud voice from his study as you were leaving him the afternoon of the 15th after your meeting on the deck to 'Get back here pronto,' or something to that effect, but you left the house anyway. Does that ring a bell?"

"No. Well yes, but it isn't as it seems."

"There's a lot of that in this case," said Miyabe.

Kenji put his cup down and looked at Ami who was coming out onto the deck to refill their coffee.

"Well, it wasn't a quarrel. Anyway," continued Kenji, "I thought you were of the opinion that the author of these mysterious, threatening messages and the murderer were one and the same. Are you now of the opinion that the answer lies in who felt they were being cheated out of their rightful inheritance?"

"I'm a firm believer in turning up all the stones, Mr. Watanabe. It could all be connected to the notes, all connected to the will, there could be a connection between the two, or it could be something else entirely. I guess I'm like one of the wild boars you have around here – just plodding and rooting until I find the morsel I'm looking for."

"I'm sure my words will not dissuade you in this search," said Kenji, "but I didn't kill my father. I can promise you that. I didn't see anyone kill him, so it appears I have no morsel to give."

"Ah," said Miyabe, raising his index finger in the air, "but Mr. Watanabe, that is where I believe you're wrong. Does the oyster know the value of the pearl within its own shell?"

Ami came back and sat down with them, still wearing the frosty look that made it clear she wished to be anywhere other than with the captain and discussing this topic.

"I must be honest with you both," said Miyabe. "Most of the evidence I have in this case points toward you, Mr. Watanabe. I have enough evidence to charge you and have you arrested for the murder of your father, and that is exactly what some people want me to do."

Kenji and Ami glanced at each other when Miyabe made this declaration. It might just be a bluff, and, then again, it might not. Regardless of the outcome of a trial, however, the Watanabe name would be ruined by the scandal with rumors of disputes over inheritance, infighting, and other unseemly behavior. The empire that had taken generations to build would be lost, and the riches consumed in an unquenchable lust for the family secrets. Their honor would be irrevocably annihilated.

"I'm running out of reasons *not* to charge you, Mr. Watanabe," said Miyabe. "But…"

That one word, such a small word, and nothing yet giving it credence, dangled like a rope for a man about to fall into an eternal pit of damnation. It lifted their spirits like the commutation of a sentence of death at the last moment. It was hope.

"I have to say that I have this lingering suspicion that there is something I'm missing, something I can't put my hands on, something I don't know about this case just yet. Call it a hunch, or intuition, or a sixth sense, whatever you like, but this is how I see it. Number one, it's just like it looks, and you killed your father over money and hatred over how he's treated you and your family. Or number two, there's a secret about your father's past that was dark and serious enough to make someone hate him enough to patiently plan and carry out his execution; a real life, modern *Count of Monte Cristo*. And since I believe you knew your father better than anyone, if someone had a reason to kill him I believe you would know it. In short, under either scenario, you're the key. Since you deny killing your father, that leaves me with but one final question for you."

The captain's question was obvious to Kenji, and he was surprised that it had taken him this long to get around to it. To someone like Kenji, who valued his family name and honor above all else, however, the true answer to the question could never be revealed no matter what the circumstances.

Miyabe leaned forward, placing his clasped hands and forearms on the table, his eyes fixed on target to detect any signs of deception. It was as if the captain and Kenji were alone in an interrogation room at a police station. Ami, all but forgotten, held her breath in anticipation of the question.

"If you didn't kill your father Kenji, then I want you to tell me – who did?"

BOOK 2

WORLD WAR II

CHAPTER 1

Saturday, August 29th, 1942: Early Morning
Port of Nagasaki, Japan

"The forces of Our Empire," said the young private as he proudly recited the military code of conduct, "are in all ages under the command of the Emperor. It is more than twenty-five centuries since the Emperor Jinmu..." he continued, reciting the document decreed by the Emperor Meiji in 1882.

The boy had committed the document to memory, as all soldiers were encouraged to do. The mania surrounding the text was such that one fledgling officer, having made a mistake in his recitation before his men, committed *seppuku* to atone for the disgrace. Every serviceman was required to study and meditate on the document each morning. "Soldiers and Sailors, We are your supreme Commander-in-Chief. Our relations with you will be most intimate when We rely upon you as Our limbs, and you look up to Us as your head."

Twenty-year-old Second Lieutenant Kenji Watanabe, dressed smartly in his new uniform, stood at attention and watched as the 17-year-old private he had handpicked for the occasion spoke to his fellow soldiers and guests before they sailed for China. Kenji had graduated from the Imperial Japanese Army Academy in Sagamihara, near Tokyo, the previous year where he was first in his class, excelling in martial arts and horsemanship. He had completed a four-month apprenticeship, had been formally commissioned as an officer, and was now ready to lead his men into whatever role his superiors commanded in furtherance of the Rome-Berlin-Tokyo Axis powers in World War II.

"Whether We are able to guard the Empire," continued the youth, "and so prove Ourselves worthy of Heaven's blessings and repay the benevolence of Our Ancestors, depends upon the faithful discharge of your duties as soldiers and sailors. If the majesty and power of Our Empire be impaired, do you share with Us the sorrow; if the glory of Our arms shine resplendent, We will share with you the honor."

Kenji moved his eyes without moving his head to watch the effect on the callow soldiers, most of whom had only a grade-school education. Their mouths moved silently, imagining themselves to be the one honored to speak the words of their god, a few of them shedding tears. Dignitaries stood at attention and the crowd of guests, including many young men who had been rejected as candidates, pushed their way closer to see the selected group who had made the grade to fight for their great country. The few parents and relatives fortunate enough to make the trip to see the new soldiers off glowed with pride watching their sons – the chosen, the elite – who had been given the honor of fighting and dying for the Emperor.

"If you all do your duty and, being one with Us in spirit, do your utmost for the protection of the state, Our people will long enjoy the blessings of peace, and the might and dignity of Our empire will shine in the world. As We, thus, expect much of you, Soldiers and Sailors, We give you the following precepts."

There were five.

Soldiers and sailors should consider loyalty their essential duty. They should respect their superior officers and seniors, and the superiors and seniors should treat their inferiors and juniors with consideration and kindness so they could work together in the service of the Emperor. They should esteem valor, never despising inferior foes nor fearing superior enemies. Soldiers and sailors must value faithfulness, keeping one's word, and righteousness, the fulfillment of their duty. And, finally, they should make simplicity their goal.

Kenji strove hard to believe that The Imperial Precepts to the Soldiers and Sailors embodied the spirit of his army. These were the divine words of the Emperor – surely, they were to be followed to the letter.

It was all true. It had to be.

Yet, like a neophyte disciple of religion, he had pangs of discomfort trying to reconcile certain passages with his own experiences thus far in the army, and with accounts of the war he had read. He felt the onset of reservation and skepticism taking root.

He was a Watanabe he often reminded himself. His ancestors were samurai. The blood of great warriors flowed in his veins. There could be no doubt about the honor of the mission he was about to undertake for his country.

Yet...

The most invigorating sentence, the truly poetic verse, was coming. While Kenji found it inspirational, there was still something about it that troubled him. With a voice that faltered with the enormity of his task, the private approached the sacred text with all the solemnity and poise he could gather. Every mouth in the platoon and audience moved now, and there was nary a dry eye amongst the throng. The words took on an ethereal aspect and seemed to come in slow motion.

The private, unlike Kenji, had no uncertainty about what he was saying. He continued, "Therefore, neither be led astray by current opinions nor meddle in politics, but with single heart fulfill your essential duty of loyalty, and bear in mind..." He paused as he had been instructed to do and proudly scanned the eyes of his fellow soldiers about to speak words like those proclaimed by samurai reciting the *Bushido Creed* before leading warriors into battle.

"Duty is heavier than a mountain; death is lighter than a feather."

•   •   •

The transport vessel headed west with the tide, and the cavalier lieutenant stood alone on the bow contemplating the events of the morning. Like all soldiers and citizens, he had been indoctrinated to believe that Japan was invincible – that their march to victory would be swift and dominant. To almost all Japanese, it was clear their Emperor was a god, and the successful outcome of the war was simply a matter of time; but the Japanese had been suffering setbacks recently which brought into question their invincibility in Kenji's mind.

His father, General Tatsurou Watanabe, was one of the most respected and decorated officers in Japan. General Watanabe had been instrumental in forming alliances with Axis powers Germany and Italy before the war. It was well known also that he had been hawkish on the attack of the United States at Pearl Harbor. Kenji had always considered his father to be a great military man, and he thought soldiers like his father always seemed to need battles to quench their thirsts and showcase their talents.

"A soldier without a war is like a king without a kingdom," he often told young Kenji. Even as a boy, Kenji had been mystified by the desire of men like his father to be in a perpetual state of conflict. The fear that he was not made of the same grit as his illustrious ancestry had plagued Kenji all his life.

Kenji returned to his cabin and retrieved a pen and paper. Every soldier was advised to write home on the voyage because of the uncertainty of their orders in the near future, and Kenji decided he would write the two women who were most important in his life: his bride and his mother. The letter to his mother was the easier of the two, which he filled with patriotic tenets that she would be proud to show others in the event her son was killed in battle. The letter to his new bride, Ami, contained many of the same sentiments, but there was also a personal message he wished to express. He wrote:

> *Dear Ami,*
>
> *We are on our way to do our service for the country at last. You needn't worry yourself as the mission we are to accomplish is righteous and our commanders honorable.*
>
> *Your words of support and encouragement at my departure have inspired in me a will to survive so that I might be of the utmost service to the Emperor and our nation. Once we are victorious, it will be my greatest desire to return to you and begin our domestic life, building the large family which we both so passionately desire. Your tears, like rivers of devotion, have spawned in me an insatiable, undeniable thirst to vanquish all obstacles in my path and all enemies of our great Empire.*
>
> *But please, dear Ami, let those tears be the last. Be strong as an example to others around you. Be positive and support Mother, Yumi, and Taro until Father and I return victorious to march in parades of glory through the streets of our motherland. If I have the luxury of even a moment of free thought, I will think of you.*
>
> *With devotion,*
>
> *Kenji*

He read through the note several times, recognizing little of his true self in the words. It was not his style – nor was it the impression he wished to convey – it was what the army would have him say. It was the mantra his instructors had instilled in his mind. He feared that he really was becoming a limb without a head with which to think independently. He was being brainwashed to join in lockstep the thinking of the army.

The only truths he could find were that he did wish to return to Ami and have a large family. She had been such a sincere and charming girl when he was introduced to her at their first formal meeting, and the seeds of love had sprouted and grown with each successive encounter. When she had agreed to marry him, he felt as if he could know no greater joy in life. He would think of her, and he would be faithful to her. That was true.

But the doubts, his personal demons, gnawed at his vitals as if they were living creatures. They were visceral, and they were strong.

As the ship rolled over the waves, Kenji lay down on his bunk and recited passages of the Imperial Precepts again. He told himself that his doubts were wrong; that what he had been taught about the invincibility of the Imperial Japanese Army was right.

It was all true. It had to be.

CHAPTER 2

Monday, July 12th, 1943: Early Afternoon
Hsinking, Manchukuo (Changchun, China)

It took less than two months after sailing from Nagasaki for Kenji to abandon hope that his fellow soldiers had any regard for anything so noble as imperial precepts. The excitement he once had in donning his new uniform with its shiny insignia was long gone by winter. By the end of '42, he had not only lost respect for his superiors, but had also begun to loathe them. Now a first lieutenant in the Kwantung Army, the esteemed division of the IJA in Manchukuo, Kenji's doubts about his suitability as a soldier, and the morality of conduct he regularly witnessed by his fellow servicemen, had only increased.

After an excellent meal of roasted chicken and wonton soup, he sat outside on the porch of his favorite dining establishment, which had no sign to advertise for business but was known by most as Lu's Place. In the street, he saw two Japanese privates begin to harass a Chinese girl who had dared to walk down the road of the town in which she had been born.

Kenji hadn't seen the infraction committed by the poor girl, if she had indeed done anything wrong. He had learned by now, however, that doing something inappropriate was not necessary to incur the wrath of his fellow servicemen. The locals were often harassed for merely encountering a soldier who happened to be having a bad day. The girl was no more than ten years old and was on her knees bowing and doing her best to apologize in Chinese while the privates cursed at her and ridiculed her threadbare clothing. The eggs she had been carrying were broken and strewn about her, congealing in the dirt under the hot sun. Kenji noticed a man, probably the girl's father, peeking around the corner of a building across the street but lacking the fortitude to come to her rescue. He thought about the third precept: *Esteem valor...Those who appreciate bravery should daily set gentleness first and aim to win the love and esteem of others.* What a crock of shit that turned out to be. He sipped his beer and considered how much he had changed, because the urge to stand up and do something every time he witnessed such behavior had calloused over the last year.

"*Yamero*," he barked at the soldiers, using a vulgar language he would never have used before the military changed him. They turned with sneers but bowed and backed away when they realized who had spoken to them. The girl stood and ran to the man at the corner who managed a quick bow in Kenji's direction before hustling down the street with the child under his arm. Kenji wondered if he was going to be able to turn this coarse language off after the war. Ami would be mortified if he slipped and spoke this way in public once he was back in Japan.

Kenji had been coming to Lu's almost every day since the beginning of the year, usually alone. The food was good, and the owners kept to themselves.

He had developed very few friendships in the army and spent much of his time reflecting on what he was doing with his life and what he would do when he got back to Japan after the war. And today, July 12th, 1943, happened to be his twenty-first birthday, which gave cause for more soul-searching than the average afternoon.

In addition to the food and privacy, there was an even better reason for Kenji's attraction to Lu's Place. While he had not been the most earnest student of science and math in school, he had found the study of history fascinating from an early age. The battles of the samurai and palace intrigue had leapt off the pages and come to life in his mind, and he had sought knowledge of the past wherever he could find a willing lecturer. And that was precisely what he had discovered at Lu's.

His train of thought was interrupted when a handsome, middle-aged Chinese man with a long, black queue came outside with a beer and placed it on the table before him. The man's head was modestly ornamented with a round, black felt hat, which was in turn adorned by red tassels, a common headdress among the Manchurians. He wore a plain, long-sleeved gown that reached his ankles, and a black vest.

"On the house," he said in excellent Japanese.

"You read my mind, Wei," said Kenji. "My compliments to the chef. Where were we when I had to leave yesterday?"

"We have to take care of our best customer," replied the Manchurian with a smile and overdone bow. "However, perhaps we should not talk so freely out here," he said as he ran a wet cloth over the table. "Eyes are upon us as we speak. It would not be prudent for me to be seen chatting with Lieutenant Watanabe."

Kenji had met Wei soon after arriving in the country and had found him to be a walking encyclopedia – and therefore a man to be treasured – of everything about China that Kenji wanted to learn. Communication was not a problem because Wei had studied Japanese and had worked as an interpreter for many years.

During their last conversation, Wei had taught Kenji that the Opium Wars in the mid 19th century had exposed China's vulnerabilities – backward ways and a failure to move with the times – to Western powers. Kenji had been surprised to learn Wei knew that Japan, during the Meiji Restoration, had decided to modernize their military so as not to meet a similar fate. The two had discussed how Japan began to establish a strong presence in China, starting with the First Sino-Japanese War in 1894, and again in the Boxer Rebellion in 1899. Kenji knew many facts about all the wars and battles that Wei discussed from a Japanese point of view, but Wei gave him knowledge from a wholly new perspective. Wei did not, however, go into *how* or *why* he had come into such a profuse understanding of Asian history. Lieutenant Watanabe would not learn the details behind those omissions for a few days to come.

Kenji had learned much of the history of Japan and Asia in school and from his father. The general had taught young Kenji about the hostilities between Japan and China dating back to the battles between the Tang Dynasty and the Japanese Yamato clan in the 7th century. During his meals over the last few months, he and Wei had spent countless hours discussing Asian and world history from the Middle Ages up through the present day.

Wei had been equally enthused when Kenji taught him about the Japanese battles against the great Kublai Khan and the Mongolian invaders that had been repulsed by the first *kamikaze* – divine winds – which had sunk thousands of invading Mongol ships in the 13th century. Kenji explained that the Japanese saw the powerful typhoons as signs of divine protection for their outnumbered soldiers from the invaders and their superior weapons. The sense of invincibility and divine selection which was common among the citizens and soldiers of his country dated back to those victories.

In another session, Wei taught Kenji about the vast Ming Dynasty, uniting much of China which had ruled over the land in which they now lived from the latter part of the 14th century to the mid-17th century. Kenji added in what he remembered about the Japanese Daimyo Toyotomi Hideyoshi who had invaded Korea late in the 16th century with the intention of conquering both Korea and China, successfully capturing Pyongyang. The Japanese were eventually defeated and forced to retreat home, but Korea had suffered significant casualties during the war. Wei had explained that as a result of the damage done by the Japanese, the Ming Dynasty was so weakened that they had soon fallen to the Manchu – a people of which he was a member, as were Mr. and Mrs. Lu. The Manchurians, an ethnic minority in China, established the Qing (pronounced Ching) Dynasty in 1644 and had ruled from that time until 1911. It would be the last dynasty to reign in China, a country which had been governed by the dynastic cycle for the last four thousand years.

Kenji enjoyed the discussions of the Middle Ages and of things long ago, but his greatest excitement came when Wei began to talk about the tangible story of his life. History from a book was one thing, but hearing it from a man who lived and breathed it, a man who walked before him and spoke as Kenji ate his meals, gave the stories a special, irresistible allure.

Typically, there was a distinction, a condescension, by Japanese over their Chinese hosts. But with his immense knowledge, Wei had been able to maneuver himself onto an equal plane with Kenji. They talked as friends.

The Manchurian had regaled with stories about the waning days of the Qing, limping to its demise when he was just a boy. Wei gave fascinating accounts of the chaos and how it left the country divided between an array of vicious warlords. He taught Kenji that, due to all the infighting and interference by foreign powers, by the end of World War 1 China was in shambles and almost entirely at the mercy of Japan and others; China's inability to coalesce and unify allowed foreign powers to creep in and claim large parcels of his country.

There was, though, unbeknownst to Kenji, a great deal more to this Chinese waiter than met the eye. Although Wei had occasionally hinted at his fealty to the Qing, there were several secrets about his life that he had, thus far, chosen to withhold. He had not been 100 percent forthright with Kenji about his personal connection and participation with the former dynasty, or his genuine desire to see it return to power to unify the country again someday.

The two had discussed the notion, held by many Japanese, and some

Chinese at the time, that Japan was needed to assist China in repulsing Western powers: they had common cultures and were Asian brothers in battle against foreigners that would devour China first and then move on to Japan and the rest of Asia like the Europeans had done in the Americas. It was well known Japan lacked the necessary resources needed to wage war, and the Chinese had all the land and materials they needed right next door. And, since the Chinese were unable to unite and expel the enemy alone, Japanese assistance was necessary – or so some argued.

While Wei was generous in his dissemination of knowledge to Kenji, and rarely refused to lay out facts contradictory to Kenji's education (which he did with the utmost politeness), he was hesitant to speak to Kenji outside the walls of the restaurant. China and Japan were at war in various parts of the country, and although the Manchurians and Japanese were supposed to be allies in Manchukuo, many Chinese in the area, both Han and Manchu, were radically suspicious. Wei feared that the eyes of rebels and spies lurked at every corner.

"I think it's time for dessert," said Kenji in response to Wei's admonition. "I think I've had enough of the view from here for one day anyway," he said as he rose and returned inside to his regular table.

Mrs. Lu, a slight woman in her seventies, brought out a plate of red bean buns and placed it before Kenji, babbling away in Chinese, not one word of which he understood. Neither Mr. nor Mrs. Lu spoke a single phrase of Japanese and had no intention of attempting to learn it. They endeavored to hide their abhorrence for the Japanese through purely survival instincts, but they had grown fond of Kenji over the last few months.

"What's the topic today, Professor?" Kenji asked.

"I am afraid I know very little, but will be glad to add whatever I can to any subject you like," said Wei with insincere humility.

Their discussions the previous week had reached a contentious level when they had discussed the fact that since the end of the Russo-Japanese War in 1905, the Japanese had lawful rights to operate the South Manchuria Railway, which helped deliver many of the resources Japan needed for its ambitious war agenda. They agreed to disagree about the rumors that in 1931, Japanese soldiers had dynamited their own railway line, causing minimal damage and used the affair, known as the Manchurian Incident, as a ruse to invade and occupy Manchuria. Regardless of who actually damaged the railway line, the situation had devolved into full-blown war in 1937, with

Japan dominating a China divided by Chiang Kai-shek's Nationalists, Mao Tse-Tung's communists, and a seemingly endless plenitude of warlords and foreign powers. Kenji decided it would be a good idea to steer clear of confrontation today.

"What can you tell me about Emperor Pu Yi?"

The country where they now lived was formally called the Great Empire of Manchukuo, but was known by many as Manchuria, in northeastern China. The inhabitants were a mixture of Chinese, Japanese, Koreans, Russians, and Mongolians. The Japanese puppet state's puppet emperor was a man named Pu Yi, who had been the last emperor of the Qing Dynasty as a child. Japan used him to give the Manchukuo regime credibility and authenticity on the world stage, but truthfully, he was an impotent figurehead held captive by the Japanese with no authority at all.

"The Son of Heaven – excellent choice," said Wei with relish. "His Majesty is a truly great leader and the only one, in my opinion, who can unify our people. Power hungry liars," he said changing expression, wiping a table with more force than necessary, "who had no divine calling to lead China unjustly dethroned him. They have done nothing but lead us on a path to destruction ever since."

Kenji referred to Wei as a professor in jest. However, Wei did indeed have an air of absolute authority when he spoke, and Kenji had complete confidence in the accuracy of his information. Wei constantly moved, wiping tables, polishing dishes, moving furniture around the establishment, but never sat with his guest for fear of rumors of collusion with the enemy. The Japanese were permitted, even encouraged, to interact with the Chinese in Manchuria, who they claimed were their allies, but most Chinese had a more pragmatic view of the arrangement.

This was because, as much as the Japanese harped on Asian unity, there was ample and growing proof that Japan had little regard for the best interests of China. As Kenji had begun to see the reality of life in Manchuria, he had become increasingly uncomfortable. He had never been to Nanking but remembered seeing articles in Japanese newspapers when he was a teenager in Tokyo about a killing contest – a competition to see which Japanese officer could kill the most Chinese with his sword – with a running tally like a home run contest. The words "Rape of Nanking" were not used in the Japanese newspapers or in social studies books, of course, but rumors spread quickly in armies. And Kenji had heard enough stories of rape, looting, and murder of innocent civilians, both by Japanese and Chinese soldiers, to instill in him a fervent desire to be back in the peaceful mountains of Nagano with his new wife. His father's beloved army had not lived up to its billing.

"The rumor is," said Kenji lightheartedly, "that Emperor Pu Yi is – how shall I say – more of a queen than a king."

The comment froze Wei, the astonishment on his face unequivocal. "Now, why would you go and say such a thing?" he said through a pained expression. "Were we not having a friendly, stimulating conversation? I would never disrespect your emperor in such a way. There have been many strange occurrences in the royal house of your nation, but I would never speak of the Emperor of Japan with such jocularity."

"Sorry if that offends you, Wei," said Kenji, surprised at the seriousness with which Wei had taken his remark, "but I think you and I both have an interest in Emperor Pu Yi's offspring, which he has yet to produce. And there are rumors about his lack of...effort, shall we say. I'm not saying that he is, of course, but if the rumors that he is homosexual prove to be true, it would not be the most conducive way to fill a palace with little heirs to be."

"That is a certainty, but as you well know, the Son of Heaven has a wife and has had various consorts. These rumors you speak of are just fabrications created by his innumerable enemies, who themselves are nothing more than gutless swine."

"Okay. It was only a joke," said Kenji. He stored the topic away in the *What-Gets-Under-Wei's-Skin* file, should he ever wish to use it in the future.

As Wei's face softened to an imperious grin, Kenji noticed for the first time that Wei had absolutely no facial hair on his chubby, cherub cheeks. There was something effeminate in his manner, and Kenji recalled that he had neither wife nor children. He wondered if he had struck a personal nerve. "So, please continue. Tell me all about the Son of Heaven."

As they were talking, a messenger arrived, coming through the back door in the kitchen to summon Wei to follow him for an undisclosed task. Kenji had begun to suspect that Wei held a position of authority among his people although Wei denied any such honor.

"I'm sorry," Wei said, "but we'll have to continue this conversation tomorrow."

"I can't come tomorrow," said Kenji. "I'm taking a few days off to hunt renegades. I'll see you when I get back."

"Renegades? Where are you going?"

"I haven't decided yet. Any recommendation for the best scenery in Manchuria?"

"Ah, I see. The Changbai mountains to the east have some magnificent views. Take care, and I'll see you when you return," Wei said as he slipped out the back door.

Kenji had decided he needed to find a way to disengage and extricate himself from the army, if only for a short time. There had been reports of insurgent activity in the countryside, and he had received orders from his commander to seek out and annihilate the culprits in such a way that would convincingly discourage others who might contemplate similar conduct contrary to the dignity of the Emperor. Kenji decided to masquerade his desire to get some fresh air away from the army as a scouting expedition.

After he left Lu's, he went back to his barracks and ordered the men in his company to be ready to move at 5:00 a.m. the following morning. He then spent the evening mapping out a route which would lead his excursion toward the Changbai Mountains in easternmost China near northern Korea. The roads were impassable at points by automobiles, making travel on horseback the only feasible option, which was precisely how Kenji wanted to make the journey. Thanks to Wei's advice, coupled with his own knowledge of reconnaissance in the area, he was able to choose secluded areas where there had been no reports of insurgent attacks as his destination. If all went according to plan, his company would meet with nothing but farmers, wild animals, and mountain scenery for the next few days.

At the same time Kenji was meeting with his men to plan their mission, another group of men were meeting outside of town at a location known only to the Chinese elders and their invitees. At that assembly, the hot debate was between those elders that wanted to try to approach the relatively new young officer, and those opposed. Acquiescing to the impassioned entreaties and a recommendation from their most trusted spy (a handsome middle-aged man named Wei), they voted, over heated opposition, to allow a messenger to contact the Japanese officer.

And that vote would change the course of Lieutenant Kenji Watanabe's life.

CHAPTER 3

Tuesday, July 13ᵗʰ, 1943: Early Morning
Hsinking, Manchukuo (Changchun, China)

At daybreak, the company mounted their horses and set off on their journey with a few days' rations. Kenji felt a burden lifting as he led the expedition eastward out of town toward the rising sun. The sounds of the horses' nickering in the morning air and the songs of the birds already at work gave him a sense of peace that he had not felt since arriving in China. He kept away from the others to avoid conversation and let his mind drift to thoughts of his bride back home.

His parents had chosen Ami through the common Japanese practice of *omiai* – or arranged marriage. Extremely well bred, educated adequately for a young lady, and submissive, Kenji had no doubt that she would make an excellent wife and mother. Yet, all the traits which made her a good choice in the eyes of his parents had caused some apprehension in the beginning in his own estimation of what he wanted in a partner for life. Ami was prudent and thoughtful, whereas he might have chosen someone carefree and spontaneous if he had made the decision on his own. She had deep-rooted beliefs and training in traditional Japanese culture and mannerisms – subservience of women, humbleness, unquestioning adherence to the demands of one's elders and superiors – whereas Kenji wondered if it might not have been more exciting to have chosen someone more modern and independent. But his parents had not consulted him on the character traits he was seeking in a wife, and, even if they had, they would have dismissed them as the ingenuous notions of a young man who didn't know what he needed in a spouse.

Ami had grown on him, however, and he had gradually been charmed by her refinement. Within the first few meetings, she had successfully dispelled all his reservations and methodically bound the young officer's affections.

After leaving the city, roads that could be traveled by car were few and far between. Kenji guided his men to a trail which ran alongside a broad river. Ahead in the distance, the majestic Changbai mountain range came into view, and Kenji estimated it would take them another two hours to reach the foothills. The constant clip-clop of the horse's hooves had a hypnotic effect that allowed him the escape he needed, and his mind continued to roam over pleasant thoughts of the past and his dreams for the future.

When he returned to Japan, he would settle down in Nagano with Ami, and they would have a large family – many sons and daughters, living in the country. They would live on a farm and raise horses, and there would be no other women in his life. Most wealthy and prominent men, including his father, kept at least one mistress; the practice was well known, sometimes even to the wives. It was a status symbol, another method of distinguishing the wealthy from the lower classes, but Kenji wanted to have a monogamous relationship with Ami. The thought of marrying with the pre-conceived intention of carrying on an affair seemed immoral and dark, something to bring about perpetual schemes of subterfuge and disharmony. And he didn't want to continue the practice just for the sake of honoring tradition. It was yet another aspect of life where he would break from his father's mold and teach his children a better way of conducting themselves.

Only an occasional farmer was seen working in the fields, but they tried to have as little contact with the Japanese soldiers as possible, keeping their heads down under conical farming hats. After reaching the foothills, they found a rugged path and began their ascent to the summit. Kenji separated himself some fifty yards in front of his soldiers, ostensibly as the lookout, but in truth trying to eliminate any useless small talk that might interfere with his mental excursions. After several hours of uninterrupted, exhilarating climbing, on horseback when possible and occasionally leading on foot, they reached a highland plateau with a spectacular view abloom with summer flowers. As his men prepared camp and began a fire for supper, Kenji strolled off and looked out over the valley from where they had come and considered what a magnificent sight this must have been years ago without the Japanese military compound and other manmade structures to spoil the scenery.

The view of the valley was expansive, and he allowed his imagination freedom to block out the reality of war and to pretend to be back home alone, taking in the sights after a day's climb. After a few minutes lost in thought, he walked to the opposite side of the plateau to look out over the land to the east where they would explore tomorrow, and the prospect was splendid with nothing but woodlands and mountains ensconcing a comely lake.

At sunset, he returned to camp and over supper explained to his sergeants that they would divide into two groups in the morning. Half would scout along the plateau to the north until midday, then move down the mountain on the opposite side to the east, and then ride south until they reached a lake which Kenji pointed out for them on the map. The other half would move in the opposite direction and mirror the movements of the first group, first south until noon, down the mountain to the east, and then north to the lake, with the two groups essentially creating a large rectangle. They would then meet at the westernmost tip of the lake. He instructed them to report any suspicious groups or gatherings to him when he met them at the rendezvous but was confident that their journeys would be uneventful. Kenji told them that he would move alone to the east, exploring the land between the two groups, and would meet them at the lake either on the following evening or the day after at the latest.

They ate their dinner, laughed and talked about life in China, and what they missed about Japan. None of them had the slightest idea that they were under surveillance.

CHAPTER 4

Wednesday, July 14th, 1943: Early Morning
Changbai Mountains in China, Near Northern Korea

There was a downpour just before dawn when Kenji sent the platoons off in opposite directions, but the weather had cleared considerably by the time he mounted up and began his journey at sunrise. The freedom – the absence of the army and all the rogues that seemed to go hand-in-hand with armies, conflicts, and battles – along with the beautiful mountain scenery, allowed for a peaceful descent toward the lake. It dawned on him that he hadn't enjoyed this type of peace very often since he was a child. From the time he had reached adolescence he had felt an unrelenting, intangible force compelling him forward to be the kind of man everyone expected from the first-born son of General Tatsurou Watanabe. There were high expectations everywhere he went: when he was introduced, when in school, when in the officer training academy, and now as a lieutenant in Manchuria. It was always so serious, but here he was in the mountains – free – without a soul in sight. It was as if he was a youth again, with that exhilarating suspense brought on by a game of hide-and-seek in the forest.

There was a good trail that allowed him to make it down to the lake much faster than he had anticipated. There were occasional reports of gunfire as he walked his horse along the shore of the lake, but it sounded so far away that he felt there was no need for alarm. Probably just hunters. After stopping for a late breakfast of rice balls and water, he sat on the bank and watched as a skein of ducks flew over the mountains and landed in the lake.

As he watched them at play, he heard a horse neigh in the forest behind him. He turned to look but all he saw was woodland. As he was standing to get a better look, he heard the horse break into a gallop and caught a glimpse of a rider through the trees at the base of a mountain to the east. He saw very little of the horseman because of the foliage but could hear the horse climbing energetically. The mountaintop was bare, and he saw the horse and rider reappear, still charging at full speed, and then disappear over the hills. The curious incident supplied all the intrigue he needed to make his plans for the rest of the morning. He retrieved his grazing horse, mounted up, and took off in the same direction.

When he reached the summit, he looked back over the valley he had traveled and found the lake where his men would be meeting soon. As for the mystery rider, all he could discover was a trail leading further east. He followed the tracks, which took him to the opposite side of the mountaintop where the hoofprints abruptly ceased. Although he was puzzled at losing the trail, he realized the spot where it ended had one of the most charming views of nature he had ever witnessed. The shades of green rolling over the vast landscape and the shades of blue where it met the mighty heavens were overshadowed by a goshawk gliding through the sky, shrieking out its call of domination. An old wish, the one he had had as long as he could remember – that he could soar just like that goshawk, free through the open sky, wherever and as far as he wanted to go – came roaring back.

As he watched, mesmerized by the graceful creature banking away, his trance was disrupted by the sound of laughter – children's laughter. For a moment, he thought he was hallucinating. It seemed quite unlikely that children could be here, but there was no doubting that he heard the voices. The view downward was partially impeded by a narrow shelf, some one hundred meters below. When he looked back up the goshawk was gone. He dismounted, tethered his horse to a tree, and began down a trail to seek out the source of the mysterious sounds. By the time he reached the plateau, the voices had begun to fade and drift out of range, as if being carried off on waves of a receding tide. Walking out into tall grass, he picked up the sounds again, ever so faintly.

He ran across the field to where it entered a woodland and, as he had guessed, the voices could be heard not far away. There was a descending path which he took at a pace he thought might mirror the movement of such a party so that he could follow them without being detected. While he couldn't pick up any of the conversation, from the cadence and intonation, he thought it sounded like young Chinese girls. But the playful and innocent banter was unlike anything he had heard from the Chinese he had encountered thus far in Manchuria.

They sounded happy.

When he began to close the gap, and the voices grew louder, he spotted a ledge off the path, dropped to the ground, and crawled over for a look.

There were three girls, one of which was carrying a child in a sling on her back, and a boy, making their way around the edge of a pond twenty meters below. The smallest girl removed her clothes and waded into the water laughing and was soon followed by the boy. The two older girls, who he could now see were actually young women, stopped and sat down in a clearing a few feet from the water's edge. The one carrying the child was dressed in typical peasant clothing, the other in a stylish red dress that seemed out of place. The girl with the sling made a bed in the grass and lay the youngster on a blanket. This was clearly not a matter of military significance, but he found it reassuring, even entertaining, to see Chinese children enjoying themselves as if there weren't a war being fought not so very far away. As he watched the younger children splash and frolic their way around the edge of the pond away from him, he thought of Ami again, and imagined the day when he would be a father.

What happened next was something that Kenji would remember for the rest of his life. So much of life is occupied by the routine, the mundane, the unmemorable – only a few images become indelible in our minds, and we often have no warning that they are about to happen. This moment was just such an incident in the life of Kenji Watanabe. The scent of pine bark, the muffled drilling of a woodpecker in the forest, or the sensation of lying face down on the bare earth would forever bring his mind back to this moment when he saw her for the first time. His body pulsed with excitement as the girl in peasant clothing stood on the bank and began letting her hair down. Never in his life had he seen such pure beauty. Although she wore the clothes of an ordinary farmer, he could see immediately that her skin and features were delicate and soft. When she bent down and removed her sandals, Kenji anticipated with excitement what might follow, and his body coursed with energy. And when she crossed her arms over her stomach and lifted the gown over her head, allowing tresses of long hair to fall over her bare chest, he experienced an astonishing euphoria that overrode his sense of decency. Even though the earth below him was cool, he began to sweat. The girl tossed the garment on top of a rock, crossed her arms modestly over her ample breasts, and waded into the pond.

Kenji was in a state of ecstasy.

The intoxication of the moment was short-lived, however, as he heard the sound of a man gently clearing his throat behind him to announce his presence.

CHAPTER 5

Wednesday, July 14*th*, 1943: Early Morning
Village in Changbai Mountains – Ai

In the summer of 1943, Ai Wang was only seventeen years old – but what a seventeen years they had been.

It would be difficult to find a more eventful, up and down, topsy-turvy, unpredictable equivalent among other girls her age anywhere the world over. The eldest of five children, she had been forced to mature beyond her years when most girls were still playing with dollhouses and make-believe princes. Secrecy and chaos pervaded the world into which she had been born, and the concept of home now was as elusive to her as to a teenage pirate.

Ai and her siblings had rarely been able to stay in the same house for more than a month since leaving the only home they had ever known in Changchun the previous year. Their current living conditions – a life on the run, constant changes in accommodations far below those to which they were accustomed – constantly taxed the minds of the children. Ai had recently begun to suspect that certain private matters of her family's history, things of which she expected she knew little about, were likely the cause of both the reason they had been forced to flee their home, and also the reason why so many kind people went to great lengths to keep them safe.

As she sat in yet another new and strange house in the mountains, she wondered about the father she had never known. She had found it odd that she had never seen a picture of the man, and also that her mother and her caretakers attempted to avoid any discussion of the subject. He existed – that much she had been promised. Her father was a great man, so she had been told. He would be coming for them soon, but here she was at seventeen, without ever once having met the man.

"What's for breakfast?" asked Lin, the second eldest, as she came out of a bedroom. Lin, beautiful jade in Chinese, was fifteen, two years younger than Ai by the calendar, but many years distant in terms of maturity. While Ai accepted the current circumstances with stoic patience, Lin was apt to pout and rail against their plight with childlike impudence. Both girls were beautiful, and looked almost exactly as their mother had looked at that age. They both had long hair, Ai preferring to keep hers in a compact, matronly bun, while Lin let hers fall freely. Ai had cautioned Lin on several occasions that her hair did not resemble the peasants they were trying to emulate, but to no avail. Lin was obstinate and, as usual, did as she pleased regardless of the merits of well-intentioned advice.

Both girls had light complexions but had recently begun to tan to look more like farmhands. Again, as with all such efforts, Ai had taken to the project much more seriously than her younger sister.

"The grandmother cooked some meat and rice this morning before she left for the fields," Ai said.

"How do you know she's a grandmother?" asked Lin.

"We had a nice little talk this morning while you were sleeping. She has three sons, four daughters, and thirty-two grandchildren."

"And precisely two teeth," quipped Lin. "I'm amazed you were able to understand a single word the woman said. Her dialect must have survived from the Stone Age. And look at this shack she calls home. Mama would die if she saw us in this squalor."

The house was indeed quite small. The main room, which had both a front and rear door, was just a few paces wide and served as a combined kitchen, living room, and dining room. On one side of the home were two meager bedrooms, which would have barely qualified as closet space in their Changchun home. The dirt floors in the bedrooms were covered with straw for comfort and insulation from the cold. A few old, musty blankets had also been provided for their accommodation. On the opposite side of the house was a wood stove used for heat and cooking. The only other furniture in the main room were two decrepit chairs and an ancient dining table with benches on either side.

"What would kill Mother is your lack of appreciation," said Ai. "She's really a pleasant woman considering such harsh conditions. Can you believe she's seventy-four years old and lost her husband of fifty-seven years just last winter?"

"Those blankets she gave us must have been wedding presents," continued Lin. "Honestly, Ai, I don't know how you expect me to continue to live in these squalid conditions. I think I would be treated better if I took my chances with the Japanese."

Ai didn't respond to the ludicrous comment and moved about the room tidying what she could. Lin followed her with her eyes awaiting a response.

"How is Jiao this morning?" said Ai changing the subject, referring to their youngest sister.

"Obviously not well. I couldn't sleep at all last night with her constant moaning and coughing. And something needs to be done about her stomach problems soon. The few times I was able to fall asleep, you both woke me up when you went outside to go to the bathroom."

Jiao, which meant dainty and lovely, was their five-year-old sister, so named because of how small and fragile she had been at birth. The fact she had survived at all had been considered a miracle.

"I'm sorry, but it couldn't be helped. When the grandmother comes back, I'll ask about a doctor."

"I can just imagine the kind of witch doctor one might find in these hills."

"By the way," said Ai, "Chang said we should be prepared to leave at any moment. The Japanese are sending out patrols, and he's worried they might be coming this way."

"I'm tired of living like a rabbit," said Lin. "All we ever do is run and hide. Tell Chang I'm sick of it. I want my old life back, and I want to be left alone."

"Please don't be angry with Chang. He's doing everything he can. Things will be better soon."

A boy and girl, twins, walked out of one of the bedrooms yawning and stretching.

"I need to pee," said the little boy.

"Go outside and find someplace private," Ai said. "Fan," she said to the little sister, "go with Shou and I'll get your breakfast ready."

Shou, born first of the twins, was the lone boy in the family, and because of that distinction, had been spoiled rotten by his mother. Fan, his *little sister,* was a sensible child cut from a very different cloth. It was evident from their names – Shou, meaning defender, and Fan, meaning lethal – that the father who had named them was obsessed with protection. When considering that the older girls' names meant love and beautiful jade, it seemed clear that there must have been something different about them.

Shou and Fan were eight years old and, though twins, complete opposites in character. They were the best of friends in times of peace and very protective of each other, but were rivals more often than not.

The two darted out the door, playfully pushing each other to be first, laughing, and understanding little of the dangers lurking about. Ai retrieved the food that had been left in a covered bowl on the stove and placed it on the table along with three metal plates which looked as if they had been used as drums at some point, then took a pitcher of water from the countertop and put it beside the breakfast with three gourd cups. The twins came back the same way they had left, laughing about the way Fan had tinkled in such an unladylike fashion.

"Wash your hands in the basin outside by the front door before you eat your breakfast," said Ai, sounding like their mother. The pair dashed back out the door and transformed washing their hands into a game of splash. The tranquil, family-in-the-country scene was interrupted by a gunshot in the distance, a warning that Japanese soldiers were coming.

"Everyone, back inside, we have to get ready to go. Hurry."

"But you said we could have breakfast," whined Shou. "I'm hungry."

"Everyone gather your things quickly. We have to go. We'll eat on the way," Ai said as she ran to the bedroom and picked up Jiao. The little girl started to cry as soon as she awoke. Lin began her own preparations but did nothing to help Ai or her younger siblings. Ai grabbed all the food she could find, stuffed it into her bag, had everyone fill up on water, put Jiao in a sling and spun it onto her back, and was out the door in a matter of minutes.

The house sat near a bluff that overlooked a lake. Ai walked over to have a look and saw a lone Japanese soldier on horseback walking beside the water's edge. She turned and had the others follow her along a road that she hoped would take them out of danger. They were all dressed as peasants, except for Lin, who insisted on wearing her favorite bright red dress. They had never been to this village before and had no idea where they were going, but Ai felt better in motion away from the soldier. She urged them all to move as swiftly as they could on the old dirt road and to keep an eye out for people in both directions.

They ran for several minutes until they couldn't take it any longer. Ai told them they could walk but to keep a sharp lookout for soldiers. She readjusted the sling on her back where it had rubbed her skin red. Shou was the first to spot a horse and rider coming from behind, and they all ran for cover in the weeds and trees off the roadway. Ai whispered for everyone to stay still and keep silent. Jiao did her best not to cry. They were terrified when the rider stopped on the road in front of them, but relieved when they heard his familiar voice.

"We really need to work on your camouflage and survival skills children."

They sheepishly came out from their hiding places.

"How could you tell, Chang?" asked Shou.

Chang dismounted and bowed reverently.

"Well, if you will look down the road, Shou," he said, pointing in the direction from which they had come, "you will see, in addition to my horse's prints, four sets of fresh tracks where children have been dragging their feet on this dirt road. And here," he said pointing straight down, "the tracks stop and disappear into the underbrush. And one more thing – Lin my dear, you shouldn't wear red when trying to hide in a green forest."

"I knew it was you all along," snapped Lin. "I don't need you to lecture me on peasantry. I'll wear whatever I please. You should be beaten for your disrespect."

Chang was on his knees in an instant. "Yes, of course. How foolish of me to speak so rudely."

"Chang, please get up," said Ai. "We're so happy to see you."

"Lin is right. I should be punished. I have forgotten proper manners in the long days since the revolution."

"Nonsense," said Ai. "You're the kindest man I know, and we owe you more than we can ever repay. Now please, escort us somewhere we can have a nice bath and wash these clothes."

Chang stood but continued with his apologies to Lin until Ai convinced him to stop. When he saw Jiao's face, he inquired as to her health.

"She's not feeling well," said Ai. "She needs to see a doctor soon. She's been having diarrhea for two days now."

"Ai*iiii*," protested the little girl feebly, "that's embarrassing."

"Sorry dear," said Ai, smiling to Chang at her little sister's modesty.

"Very well," said Chang. "I will get to work on that right away."

"Oh, I almost forgot," said Ai. "The reason we left the house is that we heard a shot, and I saw a soldier near the lake."

"Yes, we are aware of him. He is actually the one we wish to speak with," said Chang.

"Are we in danger, Chang?" asked Shou.

"I don't think so; not from this man. But others are coming over the mountains, so it would be best for you all to stay out of sight for a while. If you stay on this road, it will lead you to a field where you will find a path between two large cedars. Follow that down to a pond, and either Gang or I will come to see you this afternoon and let you know where to go next."

"Thank you, Chang," said Shou. "Don't worry, I'll take care of everything. These girls are safe with me." Chang smiled at the boy's bravado.

"Meanwhile, I'd better get back to that soldier you saw," said Chang. He bowed deeply and waited for them to begin walking away before mounting his horse and galloping away.

The children walked along the road for half an hour and came out into a field where Shou and Fan raced to see who could find the path between the cedars. They both claimed victory, and everyone walked down to the pond. Fan was out of her clothes and into the water in seconds.

"Maybe I'd better patrol the area while you girls take a bath," said Shou, the sentry.

"That's very brave of you Shou, but I think we're safe for now. Why don't you join Fan and make sure you get all that dirt and sweat off," said the substitute mother. Shou didn't need to be told twice. Ai found a spot of soft grass in the shade and lay Jiao down on a blanket.

"Are you getting in?" she asked Lin.

"I'm not going to bathe like a duck. I'll wait until we have proper indoor facilities."

"That's your choice, but I don't know how long that might be," said Ai, letting her hair down. It felt good when she was finally able to get her dirty sandals off. She felt liberated when she pulled her gown over her head and shook out her hair, totally oblivious to the fact that the Japanese soldier she had seen by the lake that morning was watching her undress from above.

CHAPTER 6

Wednesday, July 14ᵗʰ, 1943: Late Morning
Changbai Mountains – Kenji

As Kenji began to push back from the ledge overlooking the pond, he heard a man telling him to stop in Japanese. He turned his head slowly and, beside him on the forest floor, was a bare brown foot, and although he couldn't see the rest of the being to which it was attached, he knew that anyone who had gained this position on him without being heard was capable enough to make any wrong move his last. He held up his hands to show they held no weapon and waited for whoever it was to make the next move.

The man spoke in Japanese, albeit broken and with a Chinese accent, and told him to put his hands behind his back. Kenji did as he was told. His hands were bound with a thin rope, and the man rolled him over with his foot. The man appeared to be a simple peasant, but this simple peasant had nimbly gained the upper hand on him without a sound. The man turned his head to one side as if he could somehow read Kenji's character better from a different angle.

"Why you here?"

Kenji thought for a moment and decided on, "I'm lost. I got separated from my patrol and lost my way." Kenji thought that sounded believable under the circumstances.

The man, who Kenji assumed to be a Manchurian, had a slender build, but Kenji sensed a martial superiority in his manner. He had a long queue of white hair braided in a ponytail and a matching white Fu-Manchu mustache and goatee. He wore a loose-fitting tunic with sleeves falling just below his elbows and baggy trousers. His face was stern and rugged but not without compassion.

"Why you spy on children?"

"I wasn't spying," said Kenji with a nervous laugh. "I heard voices and just came to see if they were rebels."

Even as it was leaving his mouth, Kenji knew that it sounded preposterous. He had spoken without thinking – never good. The Manchurian smiled and reached down, undoing the buckle on Kenji's holster belt and rolling him back over, taking the holster with his pistol and knife. It was clear that the hands of this man did not lack strength or dexterity. The Manchurian pulled him to his feet and blindfolded him from behind before leading him back up the trail toward the spot where he had left his horse.

"So you like young girls, do you?"

"I told you I didn't know who they were."

"Oh yes. Sometime I have same problem. I think Japanese army coming, only find out it's little girls bathing in pond," said the Manchurian. "My daddy teach me, very hard to tell difference in fierce warrior and naked girls taking bath. I make same mistake all the time."

Realizing the uselessness of continuing with the flimsy argument, Kenji decided to change the subject. "Where are you taking me?"

"You not dead yet. Less you know, better for you." Although Kenji didn't like the sound of *yet*, he found the overall tone of the complete sentence promising. "What's your name?" said the Manchurian.

"Watanabe."

"No, I mean what name parents give you?

"Kenji."

"You keep your mouth shut, Kenji, and you be okay." Kenji wasn't sure how he knew, but he felt he could trust the Manchurian's word on this.

"Your Japanese isn't bad," said Kenji.

"I work for Japanese family long time," said the man.

Kenji walked along with the Manchurian, hoping that he was merely taking him back to his horse and wondering why it was necessary to be blindfolded since he had already been through here without one. He tried to imagine what the Manchurian could be protecting. They had moved along for several minutes in silence, but Kenji was curious to find out more about these people.

"So who are they?"

"I told you, Kenji, less you know is better." But then after a few steps, the Manchurian spoke as though he was merely thinking out loud. "Let's just say their safety is important to me."

"Do you honestly think this is a good idea – arresting an officer of the

Imperial Japanese Army?"

"Maybe it look like arrest, but believe it or not, I'm helping you."

"Helping me? What are you talking about?"

"Best to just be quiet for now."

Although it looked as though the man leading him along the mountain trail was his enemy, Kenji had no fear that he was to be killed or even harmed. In fact, he felt a remarkable sense of curiosity. Strangely enough, he was actually enjoying the experience. If the Manchurian had wanted to kill him, he would have already done so. If he had cut Kenji's throat under the pine tree and buried him in a shallow grave, which would not have been a complicated matter, no one in the army would have ever known what happened. So, if he wasn't going to be killed, he was curious to learn what this was all about. Then the disagreeable thought that he might be taken for interrogation occurred to him, and he knew that certain Chinese methods were notoriously cruel. But the voice and actions of this odd man seemed uncharacteristically friendly.

When they reached the summit, Kenji heard the whinny of his horse and what he thought to be two horses trotting from a distance until they were beside them. His captor said something in Chinese that Kenji could not understand and heard only a grunt in response from the newcomer. He felt the restraint from behind his back being loosened and then refastened in front of his body. There was only a brief consideration of resistance – there were at least two of them, they had his pistol, there was no imminent danger, and one of them had already established himself as a formidable character. Definitely not worth the risk at this point, he thought.

"Put hands on saddle," said the Manchurian. Kenji blindly held out his bound hands and found the front arch.

"Now put your foot in stirrup," said the Manchurian. Kenji lifted his leg and was soon hurled upwards and into his saddle. He heard the Manchurian mounting another horse, and the third took off with its unknown rider. The Manchurian spoke to the horses, and they began to move.

They rode without speaking, Kenji deep in thought as he heard the leather of the saddles twisting, the rhythmic clip-clop of the hooves, then the sounds of horseshoes on rocks, splashing water, then more rocks, and earth again. Kenji lost all sense of direction and location. There were the calls of hawks circling overhead in search of prey, the smell of damp forest at times and summer flowers at others, all other faculties heightened and magnified by the nullification of his most trusted sense. His mind ventured back to the girls by the pond, then to the sarcasm of the Manchurian. Good thing the Manchurian didn't know about Naomi, he thought, about his first time and how young she was. Kenji's thoughts drifted back to that field when he and his cousin were still teenagers. Summer heat, summer sounds, and summer grass, far enough away from the summerhouse and summer guests that they wouldn't be seen, he and Naomi had roamed without any thought of erotic fantasies. Innocent thoughts of child's play filled their heads as they ran through fields and forests, splashing in streams, sometimes laughing, sometimes fighting, but mostly running. Without consciously doing so, they had wandered far away from the house for hours.

And all of those senses came rushing back to Kenji now – the fresh, soft bed of grass in which his knees had landed while they playfully wrestled in a green meadow, the smell of her scented hair, her laughter as he had flipped her through the air over his body with his foot between her legs, and the sound of her soft impact as she rolled onto the lush green grass. There had been the same rush of manhood he had just experienced at the pond, but back then he hadn't been as familiar with the sensation, as he rolled up onto his knees over her, pinned her wrists to the ground, and realized that her kimono belt had come undone and her chest was bare. Naomi's face came back to him now; her mouth open and the disingenuous *I-can't-believe-you-did-that* look on her face as if Kenji had done it on purpose. But she hadn't moved. Kenji could remember the sensation of falling, as a man might fall from a cliff, only without fear, and there was no way to stop the fall. He hadn't consciously moved, merely lowered slowly on top of her as she closed her eyes and received him. As with most youthful escapades, the fact that their behavior was absolutely prohibited was drowned out in the heat of the moment. Or perhaps, as he would consider years later, the fact that it was forbidden made it all the more enjoyable. It's a damn good thing this man didn't know about that, he thought.

"Have some water," said the Manchurian, touching Kenji's arm with a cup.

"You still haven't told me who the children are," Kenji said before taking a sip.

"Why you ask so many questions about children? I think I don't believe you. I think you spy on girls taking bath. It's my job to take care of kids, protect them from Japanese soldiers like you."

"I wasn't going to do anything to them, I told you. I'm just curious to know what all of you are doing here."

"What *we* are doing here? That's a good one Kenji-san. My damn country and you want to know what *we're* doing here. You a funny man."

They rode on quietly for a while until the Manchurian, apparently the talkative sort, began again. "Pretty dangerous for you to come here alone, no?"

"My men and I are just on patrol. Not looking for trouble."

"Hope that is true. Too many Japanese soldier do just that. Look for trouble."

"So is that the reason you fight against us?" asked Kenji.

"Maybe you not understand me, Kenji, but I not for this army or against that army. Don't care about armies. Care about people, and I don't want to see bad things happen to nice little boys and girls."

"And you think taking me prisoner was necessary?"

"How many time I tell you, Kenji? You no prisoner. It's a little more dangerous out here than you think. You should thank me."

"Oh, so you're helping me. Now I get it," said Kenji sarcastically.

"Maybe I tell you a little something, Kenji-san. I will be honest with you – a little anyway."

"That would be nice."

"I already know some things about Watanabe Kenji-san. It is not complete accident that we have met today."

CHAPTER 7

Wednesday, July 14th, 1943: Early Afternoon
Changbai Mountains – Ai

The twins had eaten well after their swim and lay near Jiao, sleeping in the shade of a Korean pine. Ai had washed everyone's clothes, save Lin's, and hung them on branches to dry. Lin had also found a soft spot in the grass to nap.

Ai sat, wrapped in a towel, watching Shou and Fan sleep, protector Shou with his arm wrapped around his sister's neck. It had been such a happy time when they were born. Ai was eight at the time, almost nine, and had only a vague concept of where babies came from, but she had still wondered how her mother could continue to have children without a father in the house.

There had been discreet guests, including Chang, who visited, bringing gifts and congratulating them on the births. They had been especially congratulatory for the success their mother had finally achieved in giving birth to a male child. Mother had even told her that her father might be coming soon to celebrate. But he never came.

Never.

Everyone continued to talk about what a great man their father was, how important he was. They had all said that it was just business that kept him away, that he truly loved his family and would return soon.

There had been untold promises that he would be coming on such and such a date or for this or that event, but they were always left disappointed in the end. Through the years, they had all been affected by his absence, but little Shou had suffered the most. The pampered man of the house had demanded that his father attend their sixth birthday party, and Mother had promised that he would be there. But, of course, as usual, he didn't come.

Shou had spent the entire day brooding, wearing his finest Manchurian gown yet refusing to talk to anyone or participate in the celebration. He stared out the front window of their house all day, waiting.

Meanwhile, there was Fan, who never understood her brother. Of course, she would have welcomed a visit from their father, but was it really worth ruining their birthday party just because one guest hadn't shown, she had asked. Weren't the cakes still as sweet? Weren't the presents still wonderful? Why, she had asked him, did he *choose* to feel bad when it just wasn't to be? Some things simply were, and no amount of sulking or pouting would change it, she had reasoned with him.

They were so different.

Ai heard the hoot of an owl, the signal that a friend was approaching. She stood, slid on her gown, and watched as her grandfather came into view through the forest. Her mother's father, a man named Gang, was a rugged warrior who could stand up to the strongest of enemies but found it difficult to engage in the shortest of conversations. He was intelligent, but he had very few people he cared for. And even those he liked had a hard time getting him to speak more than the bare essentials.

Their grandfather walked up quietly, careful not to wake the sleeping children, and told Ai that Chang was busy at the moment with an urgent matter. He and Chang had decided it would be best for the children to remain out of sight for a few days. He gave her directions to an abandoned barn far off the beaten path and told her that no one would find them there as long as they stayed out of sight and were not followed. There was a cellar under the structure, accessible through a door in the barn floor which she would find under some bales of hay. There was a well behind the barn, and the cellar had been stocked with enough bread and cheese to last a few days. He offered to escort them there if she felt any concern about being able to find it, but Ai had promised they would be able to make it on their own.

The grandfather apologized for the inconvenience and told her he needed to get back soon because there was to be an emergency meeting of the village council that afternoon. He bowed to her and left.

After a few minutes more she woke the children, put Jiao on her back, and led them through the forest to the road her grandfather had told her she would find. Within a few minutes they saw the large stone with the snakeskin beside it, the landmark they needed to find the barn. They took the overgrown path, and Ai could see why her grandfather told her that no one would ever come this way. After a ten-minute journey, they came to a clearing with a dilapidated barn standing in the center surrounded by waist-high weeds and brambles. Shou and Fan were excited and ran in to see what types of adventures might be discovered.

Ai and Lin stopped and stared.

"You have *got* to be *kidding* me," said Lin.

Ai took a deep breath and told herself it was temporary, things would be different soon. She walked into the barn knowing Lin would be watching her and that the others would look to her for guidance. The building was ancient, smelling of moldy hay. The boards making up the walls had cracks which allowed in parallel streams of bright yellow sunlight. In other less precarious circumstances, the light would have been a welcome sight but, at the moment, Ai felt vulnerable. Old yokes, hoes, tillers, and the like sat in corners or hung on the walls as if someone had planned to come back and use them the next day but changed their mind and deserted the place. Old feed sacks and tiny mice carcasses lay strewn about twisting in the wind. The A-framed thatch roof added to the odor of must and mold but held out the light from above and gave a sense of protection to the room. It had a dirt floor where she stood by the door, but there was a section of wood flooring on the other side with the bales of hay that Grandfather had told her she would find.

She immediately lay Jiao down, opened her bag, and pulled out some food. The twins dug in, looking rather more like savages than the wealthy children they had been. Lin sauntered in with what was becoming a permanent look of disgust as she looked around at their new accommodations.

"Another Chang special I see," she said.

"We don't have time for your self-pity right now," said Ai as she moved to the other side and got down on her hands and knees and began to search. She pushed aside bale after bale and felt beneath them as the others watched. At last, she found a latch and pulled open a hidden door in the floor. Shou and Fan looked at each other, amazed at their sister's resourcefulness.

"Have you been here before, Ai?" said Shou.

"Grandfather visited us at the pond this afternoon and told me about this room while you were asleep. I'm glad we found it. He said we can hide here until Chang finds a new place for us to stay."

"No doubt the Forbidden City would have to be the next logical *new place* in Chang's parade of stunning architecture," scoffed Lin.

"I think we should appreciate all the trouble he goes to for us," said Ai.

"So the transformation appears complete," said Lin, ignoring her sister's advice. "We are now officially rats living under the barn floor."

"I told you we don't have time for that today, Lin," Ai said without looking up as she continued her preparations to ready the chamber below. "All of you need to eat something, and that includes you, Jiao. Lin, there's a water well behind the barn. Go draw some for us." With that, she flung her legs into the cellar and started down the ladder.

"I don't know how to do that," shouted Lin after her.

"I'm sure you'll figure it out," was the reply from the cellar.

There were six steps to the bottom. Other than the light from the door directly above and a few small cracks between the boards, only a faint light penetrated the room from an iron grating located along the rear wall of the barn. The room was square, about four paces wide with two support beams in the middle and some wooden benches around the edges. The walls and floor were mostly covered with boards, but there were many openings that gave the room the smell of damp earth. Ai walked over to the lone wall letting in light through the grating, stood on a bench and tried to look out. The view was mostly obstructed due to the angle because the bars were parallel to the ground, but she was able to get a glimpse of Lin walking by. She stepped down and continued her search of the room and found that some blankets had been folded and placed in a corner under a bench along with two clay water jars. Beside these, she saw a bag filled with bread and cheese. While she felt comforted by the thought that someone had gone to all this trouble for them, she hoped they would never be forced to live in such a dark and gloomy hole. When she climbed back out into the barn with the jars, she found the twins continuing to eat the provisions she had brought but saw that Jiao was lying on the floor staring up at the ceiling.

"Jiao dear, you have to eat something. You're skin and bones. You haven't eaten anything in two days; this has to stop. Now have some rice and water."

"I can't. My tummy hurts," said Jiao in a frail voice, her normal ruddy complexion pale and white.

"Shou, Fan," Ai said, "make sure she has something to eat and drink."

She went out through the open barn doors, taking the jars, and walked around to the back where she found Lin leaning against the wall peering down into the well.

"You can daydream later, Lin; I need you to fill these quickly and get inside in case we need to hide."

Lin scowled and shook her head as she moved from the well and picked up a pail and rope. Ai went to the side of the barn, found the iron grating, and pulled a piece of plywood away to let more sun and air into the room. As she finished and turned to go back indoors, she heard the distinct sound of horses in the forest. She told Lin to hurry back inside and dashed into the barn and had everyone descend quickly into the cellar while she checked the room for any signs that could give them away. Lin came in reluctantly with the jars of water and passed them down to Fan before climbing in. Ai shut the large outer doors, grabbed a couple of bags that had been left behind, and tossed them down into the secret chamber. After a final look around, she pulled two bales of hay and some loose straw near the cellar door, slipped into the hole, and pulled the door shut over her head. Still standing on one of the ladder rungs, she reached up, found two loose boards beside the door, dislodged them, and stuck her head up through the opening. She grabbed the bales, which she pulled into place camouflaging the cellar door, and scattered the straw. Once that was accomplished, she ducked back into the cellar and replaced the boards to their original positions, just as Grandfather had instructed her to do.

"What is it, Ai?" said Fan. "Did you see someone?"

"We need to keep perfectly quiet," Ai replied. "I didn't see anyone, but I heard horses. I can't say who it might be, but we can't take any chances. Let's just practice being quiet for a while. Sleep if you like, but no talking."

Ai sat down beside Jiao and put her little sister's head on her lap. She ran a finger along her face and stroked her hair to put her at ease. They sat for several minutes, listening for any sounds of soldiers but hearing nothing other than the wind, a creak here or there in the barn, birds chirping outside, and occasional fidgeting from a restless child. After Ai felt certain that whoever she had heard was gone, she whispered to Lin to take her place caring for Jiao and told them she was going up to take a look. She felt her way to the ladder and up to the boards, pushing one and then the other out of place, then rose slowly up until she could see into the barn. She continued to proceed cautiously in moving the bales of hay and opening the door. Once out of the cellar, she crept to the door, opened it, and confirmed that no one was there. She took a quick walk around the barn and then returned and reported the good news.

"Whoever it was is gone," she said, looking down into the cellar. "You can come up, but leave the door open, and leave your bags down there in case we need to hide in a hurry."

"What am I supposed to do with Jiao?" called Lin. "I'm not holding this sick child all day and night."

Ai looked down and saw Jiao on the floor and knew that she was not well. She looked ghostly white and had begun to cry again. She was afraid that even if Chang returned with a doctor that it might already be too late to do anything for her baby sister.

"Use some blankets to make a bed for her and use one for a pillow. Make sure she stays warm. Do your best to have her eat something, and she absolutely must drink some water. I'm going to go see if I can find Chang or a doctor myself."

"Oh, no, no, no you're not," cried Lin bounding up the steps. "You're not leaving me here alone to take care of these brats by myself. *I'll* go find Chang or a doctor."

Ai had already thought of that possibility, and it would definitely make more sense to let Lin go, assuming she could be trusted to give her best effort. There was no question the children would be much better off under Ai's care, and Lin was much faster if she would just give one hundred percent to the effort. The main drawbacks to the plan were Lin's lack of discretion and selfishness.

"Do you think you can find your way to town safely and back?" asked Ai.

"I'm not a child."

"Alright. If you'll promise to stay off the roads when possible and keep a sharp eye out for anyone you don't recognize. You need to eat and drink before you go since you might be gone all afternoon. And make sure you pay attention as you leave so you can find your way back. Make sure you're back before dark. And make sure to describe her symptoms precisely so that a doctor can send what she needs. And, if you see anyone you can trust, don't tell them where we are because we can't trust anyone that much, but tell them to try to get word to Chang that we're waiting for him at the spot he told us about. Don't say any more than that. And..."

"I'm not an imbecile if you hadn't noticed," yelled Lin. "Do you honestly think I'm going to go marching down the middle of the streets in town, talking to soldiers and strangers, calling out for a doctor, and then not tell him what's wrong? You act as though you're the only one around here capable of rational thought. I think I can manage just fine. While I'm gone, don't stab everyone in the eye with your fingers, and don't go outside yelling

'Defenseless young children in need of a hero,' and don't set fire…"

"That's enough, Lin. We don't have time for this."

Ignoring the advice on nourishment, Lin pushed past Ai and headed out the door. Ai knew she treated Lin like a child but couldn't stop herself from giving some last-minute instructions. She ran out into the field and pulled her by the arm.

"I didn't want to say anything in front of them, but I think this is serious. Her sickness has lasted too long, and I can't get her to eat or drink. What little I've been able to force her to drink, she's thrown up. Do you understand that she needs a doctor? Now?"

Lin sighed loudly, a sign that indicated she might be listening at last.

"Yes. I'm sorry for being difficult. This absolute nightmare we're living is too much for me at times, but yes, she's my sister too. I understand. I'll run as fast as I can."

Ai gave her a hug, and Lin took off running down the overgrown path. Ai wiped away tears watching her go.

"Make sure you're back before dark," she called out as Lin disappeared from sight. She shook her head and worried that she was making a mistake by entrusting this job to anyone else as she walked back into the barn. The twins were beginning to go stir crazy, and Ai knew she needed to find a way to keep them occupied. She went and got Jiao and brought her up into the barn and had the twins bring blankets. She made a comfortable bed and urged Jiao to drink some water. After she had Jiao settled, she told the twins to sit together with her on the barn floor.

"Okay, let's practice our multiplication tables. Shou, you go first and start with your 2's."

"Two times one is two. Two times two is four…" he began.

In all her life, there had never been a time when she wanted to cry so badly, but she couldn't. She was the leader. There had to be a good example for the rest to follow.

If only her mother were here, this would not be her problem. If things were as they had been in her childhood, she would be teaching Shou and Fan their math lessons in a beautiful library with books from around the world while sitting on courtly, comfortable chairs instead of hiding in an old barn with a sick little sister who had no doctor to care for her. This was not how life was supposed to turn out for them.

Shou, the boy who considered himself the man of the house, should be clothed in Manchurian robes and treated like a king. It was almost unbearable to see him forced to adapt to this new life of poverty and desolation. She remembered how their mother doted on him: the fierce, yet sensitive, boy who had tried to intervene when he heard the cry of a mother pheasant as a fox chased down one of her chicks; how he had been so happy and pleased with himself when he found the wounded bird, the defender defending. Ai recalled his devastation when he learned that the fox had probably gotten away with another baby pheasant and the mother had abandoned her chick because of its injuries. The memory of the six-year-old boy crying when the little pheasant died the next day brought back fresh grief as she listened to his voice.

And there, sitting beside him, was the intellectually superior Fan, watching and waiting for the first mistake – ready to pounce like the cool-hearted fox she was. She wasn't evil. She was simply different – made of different stuff. She had been perplexed as to why her twin brother cared, actually went so far as to shed tears, over some wild bird that meant nothing to them whatsoever. The remembrance of little Fan questioning whether the pheasant could be eaten brought a much-needed moment of levity into Ai's troubled mind.

"Where do people go when they die?" asked Jiao out of the blue.

"Of course, they go to heaven dear," replied Ai, obviously taken by surprise. "But why do you ask such a thing?"

"What do you think heaven is like, Ai?"

The question halted the mathematics recitation, and the twins were riveted on this new and intriguing subject. Ai tried to remain thoughtful yet cautious, treading in such delicate territory. It couldn't be ignored, but she didn't want to lend credence to any school of thought that one of their members might be in imminent need of this information.

"Well, Mama always said, *says*, that heaven is a beautiful and peaceful place with green pastures, rolling hills full of tame animals, and all the people are kind. There's no hunger, no sickness, no pain, no war, no sadness."

"That sounds like a lovely place to live," said Jiao with fondness. The innocence with which she spoke caused the older sister's eyes to moisten, and she felt a tightness in her throat.

"Do you miss the people you loved on earth?"

Ai couldn't bring herself to answer. Silence could be explained later whereas the broken speech and tears that would surely come if she spoke at this moment would betray her fears. After a forced swallow and time to compose, she proceeded guardedly.

"Of course, my dear, you wouldn't," she paused, "that is to say, *one* wouldn't miss their loved ones, because that would be a form of sadness, and, as I've already said, there is no sadness there. Perhaps, they know that they will be seeing their friends and family again soon, so there's no need to feel bad. They will all be together in heaven someday. The concept of time probably doesn't occur to them, so if they have to wait fifty years of our time on earth, it may seem like a long afternoon to them. So, no, I don't think you...*they* miss the people they love.

"I'm not afraid anymore," said Jiao softly. "I just hope the people here aren't too sad."

"Jiao, please, you must stop talking this way," said Ai, breaking into tears. "You aren't going to heaven – at least not anytime soon. Shou, please continue."

"Eleven times twelve is one hundred thirty-four," he began, staring at Jiao as if she were already a ghost.

"You made a mistake," said Fan. "It's one hundred thirty-two."

"I know that. You're all breaking my concentration."

"No fighting. It's our fault, Shou. Fan, why don't you try now."

Ai tucked and pampered Jiao as her little sister stared straight up as though she could already see all the way to paradise and all its beauty. Ai stood up and walked outside, fell on her knees, and wept.

A hawk soared overhead searching for prey, oblivious to the misery of the destitute figure kneeling on the grass below.

CHAPTER 8

Wednesday, July 14ᵗʰ, 1943: Afternoon
Changbai Mountains – Lin

Lin ran through paths in the forest, and on the roads when necessary, down to the valley below, occasionally stopping at houses to inquire about anyone practiced in medicine. One elderly farmer informed her that he had never seen a doctor in these parts, even before the war, and that it was a good two days journey on foot to a large town which might have one. There were some people though, in the small town just a bit further down the road who could help with herbs and medicine.

When she reached the town she was disappointed to see the streets empty. There wasn't a car or person in sight, not a single sign of life. She glanced up at the mountains to the west and saw that she was running out of daylight. As she stood, looking around and contemplating her next move, she noticed a curious establishment on the street corner, the business of which she couldn't say. The door was ajar so she decided to see if anyone inside might be able to help or point her in the right direction.

Like many places in the area, the room fronting the street was open to the public for business, and the remainder of the structure was the owner's home. When Lin entered, she was alone, but a bell attached to the front door rang. Even after entering the room, she was still not sure what type of concern it was. She took a seat on a creaky bench beside a decrepit table and wondered whether it was sturdy enough to support her weight. Layers of dust covered everything in the room. After a brief time peering about the place, she heard a tapping noise and slow, shuffling feet. When the door on the opposite side of the room slid open, Lin's hand went to her mouth to cover her gasp.

A woman, who looked to be in her nineties, wearing a ragged white shawl, which matched her tousled white hair, stood before her with her mouth drawn into an eerie smile. With wrinkled skin covering a cadaverous face and recessed, pale gray eyes, the old woman had the appearance of one already deceased.

"Don't be frightened my dear; I assure you I am harmless," said the old woman, which only succeeded in producing additional terror in the mind of the stricken teen. Lin desperately wanted to turn and run, but her limbs were not under her control. The old lady tapped the cane on the floor as she made her way behind a counter and stopped, out of breath. She hung her walking stick on a peg, put a bowl of dried fish and a cup of cold tea on a tray, and picked up her stick again. With the speed of a snail crossing a stone, the old woman moved across the room and placed the food and drink on the table. She slid it in front of Lin while falling onto the bench opposite, and then leaned back and put her hands on top of the cane resting between her legs. After a minute spent watching the old woman smiling at her, Lin sensed that her body was returning to normal.

"I'm looking for a doctor," she eventually managed to say.

The old woman leaned over, reached and unceremoniously took Lin's hands, and pulled them to the center of the table. She moved her head down close and examined the trembling palms, mumbling to herself. After a lengthy examination, she closed her eyes and leaned back in her seat. "You have no need for a doctor," she whispered.

"Oh, it's not for me. You see, my sister is..."

"You are, however," said the woman loudly, cutting Lin off, "in great danger." The woman continued to sit with her eyes closed and face up toward the ceiling.

Lin's pulse quickened, and for once she wished Ai were with her to tell her what to do. Suddenly, they heard horses rushing down the street in front of the building. Lin turned to the window and caught a glimpse of men rushing past.

"Violence is everywhere these days," said the old woman. Her eyes opened and she looked at Lin with an unnerving grin. "I don't think I would be running around dressed like that if I were you. Some men pay a handsome reward to anyone who tells them where to find young girls like you," she said, her chin lowering to her chest so that she looked upward through her thin hair.

"I trust you are not the type of person who would tell anyone," Lin said, the statement sounding more like a question than a belief.

"Oh no," said the woman in a ghoulish whisper, "I have no intention of helping them, but I am not the first person you have spoken to today. I'm simply warning you there are others in this town with fewer scruples than I who are hungry, and their hunger has overtaken their sense of right and wrong. Desperate mothers and fathers with hungry children are able to overlook the pain and suffering they cause by turning over someone else's child."

"Then will you help me get away from here?"

"I'm a feeble old woman. All I can give is advice."

"And what is your advice?"

"Wait until dark before trying to leave."

The old woman pulled some matches from a pocket, picked up a candle from the windowsill, and lit it. She turned the candle so that wax began to drip on the table and lowered her head close to examine each drop. She put the candle down and said, "You should leave this little town and never return. Soldiers, sometimes Chinese and sometimes Japanese, are starting to come around almost every night."

Lin inclined toward the window to see if anyone was coming. When she looked back, the old woman was dropping wax again, mumbling at the drops. It was entrancing to watch the methodical dripping process, and when she came to her senses several minutes later, she saw that it was already getting dark outside.

"I guess I should be going now. Thank you for your help." She stood and moved to the door and then remembered the old woman's words. Turning back to her, she asked inquisitively, "Why did you say I have no need for a doctor?"

The old woman glanced up from the wax with a puzzled look, as if she were surprised that Lin was still in the room, and said, "Because the child who needed one has already died, of course."

CHAPTER 9

Wednesday, July 14th, 1943: Late Afternoon
Changbai Mountains – Kenji

The sound of a charging horse halted the conversation. Kenji heard the rider pull up alongside the Manchurian and sensed from his manner of speech that it was a pressing concern. The Manchurian responded in a calm voice, which had no sense of urgency, and this seemed to infuriate the other rider as he became even more bellicose with his second flurry.

Although Kenji couldn't understand the words, there was no question that the rider had a serious problem with what Kenji's captor was doing. The Manchurian, in complete contrast, kept a tone of voice one would use in a quiet restaurant. The cool responses appeared to unsettle the new rider to a higher level with each exchange. It sounded as though the other went too far, and the Manchurian unleashed a severe reproach that ended the debate. The rider spoke again in a contrite voice before turning the horse and kicking it off in the direction from which he had come.

Kenji noted that, in addition to stealthy and competent, he could now add boss to the attributes of his new friend.

"What was that all about?" asked Kenji.

"No time to explain now. Just follow instructions and you be okay."

A moment later, Kenji felt the rope being cut from his hands and heard a brusque order to remove the blindfold and follow. By the time his eyes adjusted to the light, the Manchurian was already at a full gallop, his white hair engulfed in a cloud of dust. Kenji wasn't at all sure what was happening but thought his best bet was to do as he had been told.

In less than a minute they were off the beaten path and making their way through a forest without the benefit of a trail. The Manchurian piloted his horse sharply around brambles and thickets, over rocks and under low branches, having to pause occasionally for Kenji to catch up. It was obvious that he knew this terrain well. Kenji, on the other hand, appeared to catch every briar and branch the Manchurian missed. They reached a decent trail leading up a mountain and onto a summit that allowed a view of the valley where they had just been. The Manchurian mercifully came to a halt and watched as Kenji fell to the ground panting.

The two stared at each other, Kenji regarding the Manchurian as someone nearly superhuman, and the Manchurian looking at Kenji with something akin to fatherly pity. He looked at ease, as though he had just completed a stroll admiring the sunset, while Kenji, with a mixture of blood diluted by sweat streaked across his face, looked like a man lashed with a whip. The Manchurian breathed calmly as his horse circled Kenji on the ground, while Kenji heaved for every particle of oxygen.

"You look like horse ride *you* up the mountain, Kenji," he said with a smile. "In future, object is to miss trees."

"Was that necessary?" asked Kenji as he sat up and tried to catch his breath.

"You mean necessary to come here, or necessary to hit every branch on the way?"

"Any chance of you cutting the jokes and telling me what this is all about?"

The Manchurian hopped off his horse and touched the ground without a sound. "Come see," he said, and Kenji got up and followed him to the edge of the bluff. The sun was disappearing over the mountains, and the light on the purple horizon was fading. Kenji could make out about fifteen riders charging hard.

"You know who they look for?" asked the Manchurian without taking his eyes off the riders. "And do you know what they do when they find him?" He let those questions hang in the air for a few seconds before he commented offhandedly, "Someone must have seen you today riding around here and think you bring trouble. You tell me if this is necessary."

"Okay, I'm a little confused here Mr. – what should I call you by the way?"

"You call me Chang."

"Alright, Chang, I want to know what this is all about. You arrest me, tie me up, blindfold me, and now you claim to have rescued me. You claim to even know something about me. Who the hell are you?"

"Long story, Kenji, less you know is –"

"Don't say that again dammit. Surely you can give me some idea of what's happening here. I know you could have killed me if that's what you wanted to do, but you didn't. So why do you help me, if that is, in fact, what you're doing?"

Chang stroked his goatee and then turned and walked to a giant stone in the clearing and sat on it. Kenji, still not quite over the harrowing ride, stepped in front of him, resolute in his desire to get to the bottom of the situation. The Manchurian's weatherworn brown face, set off by his ivory white mustache and goatee, looked regal in the twilight.

"Where to begin?" Chang raised his hand and pointed in the direction of the riders. "You see, Kenji, those men have revenge and murder in hearts, nothing more. Hard to blame them. Japanese soldiers take their land. Sometime take their women. Kill their fathers and brothers. It's war."

"It's natural they should hate all Japanese, don't you think? Very few have any real education. They follow man from their village with strongest voice. He says, 'Kill that man,' and they kill Kenji without any thought because that is what they were told to do – no thinking required."

"Some of us – Chang is no genius mind you – have been around a long time and see many things, study a little bit about history. My opinion, we sometimes need good allies. Always help to have good friend."

"And where is it that you think I fit into this picture?" Kenji asked.

"Well, obviously, we hope Kenji be the good friend."

"Chang, since you seem to be a decent man, let me make something very clear to you. I have one loyalty, and that is to the Emperor of Japan. I will die before I ever conspire with an enemy or spy against my country. Is that clear enough?"

"Absolutely. In fact, Chang already know that."

"Okay, and that's another thing – if you think you know me, I'd like to know what it is you think you know because before today I have never seen you in my life."

"Okay," said Chang, in a tone suggesting he was accepting the challenge. "I think Kenji is a soldier for Japanese Army because life's circumstances make you. My guess, your father soldier too, so Kenji must be soldier. Chang is right?"

Kenji was intrigued but didn't reply.

"Actually, that was just a test. I know Kenji's father, but you do right thing by not answering. You don't know Chang yet – you can't trust Chang."

"I hope you're not going to try to tell me my father is a spy."

"Of course not, the great General Watanabe no spy – you right about that, Kenji. But why you keep talking about spy. Japan say they help us, right? Manchurian and Japanese working together for Heavenly Way, Asian Paradise here in Manchukuo, right? You've seen the posters. Japanese say we're brothers – have to fight to keep foreigners from destroying Asia."

Kenji eyed Chang skeptically but held his tongue. It was a bait.

"Right now, I have little advantage. I know Kenji, but Kenji doesn't know Chang. I know Kenji never be a spy against his country, and let me say this – I don't like Kenji if he did spy against his country. That kind of person is bad man. I stay away from traitors because you can never trust them, but your emperor give you some instructions to follow, no?"

Again, Kenji simply stared and waited for Chang to do the talking. This was his pitch.

"We Chinese know all about the advice emperor gave you long time ago. I believe you call them Five Precepts – very good advice don't you think?"

Kenji thought back over his own misgivings about the difference between how he had been taught to act and what he had actually seen occurring in China. But he certainly wasn't going to commit treason.

"Chang not asking you to spy against Japan, but following what your emperor say not a problem is it, Kenji?"

"What exactly are you asking me to do?" asked Kenji bluntly. "Just say it, then I can say no, and we can each move on."

"Tell you what – better if I tell you story. You have time for short story?" Chang asked rhetorically as he pointed for Kenji to sit down on the ground. Kenji was hesitant but complied. The imagery was clear – Chang was the teacher, and Kenji, the student.

"And I tell you before I tell story, the reason I talk to Kenji is Kenji's reputation in Changchun. Now, you call Hsinking, but it Changchun to me. People in Changchun watch carefully and tell Chang all about Kenji. I don't talk to everyone like this."

"So listen and see if Chang is right. Kenji doesn't like what he sees here in Manchuria. Some soldiers just join and follow and say, 'Everybody else is doing it, so must be okay,' but Kenji not like other soldiers. Kenji has a problem with what he sees but can't do anything to stop it because he's general's son. And those men," he pointed out to where the Chinese rebels had been riding on the plain a few minutes earlier, "they don't know Kenji. That is nature of war. You just kill man wearing wrong uniform. That's all the information you get – you don't know good person or bad – just other uniform and bam."

"That," said Kenji, "I understand. Them, I understand. What I don't understand is you – and what any of this has to do with me."

"I think Kenji doesn't understand the danger at the moment. Kenji think it's so peaceful here in the mountains and okay to ride around alone watching goshawks and breathing clean mountain air. Truth is, Chinese people around here not as peaceful as you thought when you rode this way from Changchun."

"Chang must be careful here because I also do not want to betray my country or my countrymen, but I think I can say, without harming anyone, that many Chinese are of the opinion that best is to attack and fight Japanese to the death. Chang is against this. Chang wants peace with you. Chang wants Kenji-san to stay alive, but you keep riding around like this, and you will not live long. Now you understand?"

Kenji didn't reply.

"Okay, let me tell you story, so Kenji can understand even better. This is true story about Chang. Maybe you can see why I want to talk to you."

"I was born in Liaoning, Port Arthur. When I was just a boy, six years old, China was at war with Japan. Before you think Chang hates all Japanese and think Chinese are perfect people, I tell you I know Chinese soldiers do many terrible things too. I'm about to tell you that. War can make any man a little crazy – a lot crazy even. So I'm not picking out only Japanese, this just happen to be my story."

"I was walking with my older brother one day trying to find something to eat one afternoon near the ocean. We see Chinese soldiers cutting something and think it's animals. We get a little closer and ask another boy what is happen, and he say it's Japanese soldiers. I saw so many dead Japanese and what those Chinese soldiers do to them was...just not human. Then we watch as they put stake in ground and put Japanese soldier's head on top. Chinese soldier yell to everyone that this is what happen to Japanese if they come back to Liaoning."

"My brother tell me we must get back to house. He know something bad about to happen. On our way home, we hear people screaming and crying – it was total chaos like I never hear in my life. We run to our house and hide. I was small, so I hide in basket in living room and my brother cover me with clothes. I want to cry but too scared. My mom and other brothers and sisters were gone, so it was me and my brother in the house that time. I could see through basket a little, and my brother come back to me and tell me to be quiet no matter what happen."

"My father come home and say we have to get out and run – Japanese soldiers coming. Before I could move, cries of the soldiers in the street got so loud that we know it's too late. A soldier kick the door open, and I saw his face, still scares Chang even now. That face I can never forget. My father picked up a knife and the soldier swung his sword, and I see my father's arm drop to floor. I had to close my eyes so I wouldn't scream. My brother come out of hiding and tried to attack, but more soldiers come in. I listen to my brother try to fight them. I cried hard but try not to make a sound. When shouting stop, soldiers left house, but I couldn't move. Still people yelling and screaming in streets."

"I finally open my eyes and see my father and brother dead on the floor. After a while, the screaming seem far off, and I climbed out of basket. I went to bedroom hoping somebody still alive, and I'm not all alone in the world. I found a doll my sister used to play with and curl up in a corner of the room. The smell of blood and death from that day will never leave me."

"Then I hear running and soldiers shouting again, but I didn't move. I hear footsteps in front room, and then a Japanese soldier come into my room with his rifle and bayonet in his hand and look right at me. I began to cry. I knew I was going to die, and I just hope it didn't hurt so bad. The soldier walk right up to me, and when he did, I could see his face. He was a young boy, same as my brother. I was so surprise to see he was crying too. He put his hand over his mouth, a sign for me to be quiet. Someone yell at him from the front door, and he spoke the first Japanese words I ever learn. '*Daremo inai*,' he shouted."

The Manchurian had been looking far off as he told the story, but now turned to look Kenji in the eye.

"He lied to save my life," Chang said.

Kenji was hanging on every word, motionless, imagining the scene and the sensations, unable to take his eyes off this stranger. Chang, as he relayed the story of his family's tragedy, looked like a philosopher staring off into the distance, his cadence rising and falling with the twists of the tale like an orchestra giving life and emotion to an opera. For Kenji, this day had taken on a fantasy-like quality, the magic and suspense hypnotizing him so that he was unable to speak or think of anything other than this enigmatic Manchurian and the secrets he was revealing.

"At just six years old, I learn very important lesson. Not all Japanese soldiers bad men. And over long life since then, that lesson has grown in many ways. Many bad Chinese – many good Japanese. Opposite is true too. Being good doesn't come from country where we are born. Comes from man himself."

Chang looked out over the darkening valley. A refreshing, gentle breeze cooled the drying blood on Kenji's skin, and the only sound he heard was the soothing voice of the Manchurian.

"Seem like no right or wrong that day. Everyone angry and attacking. But that Japanese soldier still did the right thing." He paused and thought.

"I've been searching for a man in your army like the one who saved my life." He turned back to Kenji. "Someone who knows right from wrong even in war. What do you think, Kenji? Was it wrong for him to help me?"

Kenji didn't want to speak. It was the dilemma he faced every day of his life in the army. He knew he wasn't like his father, that he wasn't like other soldiers, but he wasn't going to pour his heart out and discuss his personal struggles with this man.

"You've got the wrong soldier," said Kenji.

Chang studied him closely. It was as if the Manchurian could read his mind regardless of the words he spoke. Chang smiled, and Kenji knew the Manchurian didn't believe him.

CHAPTER 10

Wednesday, July 14ᵗʰ, 1943: Night
Changbai Mountains – Lin

Lin's hand drew up to cover her face. With the other, she felt behind her back for the door, terrified to continue looking at this witch, but even more terrified to take her eyes off her. When she reached the door, she pushed her way through and ran without caution straight down the middle of the street. There was an intersection she remembered, and she turned, hoping to find the road which would lead her to the mountain trail. But after the turn, she was halted in her tracks by the sight of a man in her path just a few steps away. Although there was very little light, she could see the Japanese soldier's face, a nasty scar on his cheek causing his wicked smile to look all the viler. She wondered if this might be some insane nightmare, first the witch and now this despicable figure of a man. As she stood staring, beginning to whimper, the man started moving toward her with a noticeable limp in his gait. She ran away from him down the street and started making random turns, so many that she was completely lost. When she became too exhausted to continue, she stopped long enough to see if he was gone. It was quiet, no one in sight, but she soon heard footsteps. She took off again without any idea of direction, just moving away from the danger.

As she approached a cluster of buildings, she heard voices and knew she needed to get off the road. The only cover at hand was an abandoned building with no doors. The floor inside was littered with debris and glass from broken windows. She went in and found a desk in a far corner covered with dust and dirt that she decided would do well for a hiding place. She crawled under and listened as the voices coming down the street grew stronger and was relieved to learn that they were Chinese men. As the sounds began to fade, she crawled out and walked over the crunching glass to the entrance and peered out, first toward the direction the men had gone and then behind.

The moment Lin turned to look back, she saw the scarred face and screamed. The limping soldier had been hiding, crouched outside the doorway, and was reaching to seize her throat. She pulled away, but his hand caught her by the hair and yanked. Her screams were now more from pain than terror, which she preferred. Lin felt better suited to fight back against the brute force than she had against the unknown. She punched hard into his groin and bit his hand. He let out a growl and lost his grip long enough for her to get to her feet and dart away. There was no time to think as she fled through the streets – adrenaline was all that carried her now. Lin knew she needed to gain a sizeable lead on him quickly because she didn't want him anywhere near her when she started up the mountain.

She made it back to the main street and saw the way was clear, and in a matter of seconds she had passed the last houses of the village and was closing in on the foothills of the mountain. When she reached the road leading upward to the barn, she turned one last time and saw him, still limping after, not giving up. Confident that she could outdistance him on the mountain, and having no other choice, she turned and ran toward the barn.

•   •   •

Everything was so different in the dark. Ai had told her to get back before the sun went down. The turn she needed to take had to be coming up soon, she thought. As she turned to look back, she stumbled over a root and fell. She heard insects buzzing and her own breathing, but nothing more. She rested for a few moments, continually searching the dark road to see if he was coming.

The thought of finding Ai, of not being alone to face this crisis, gave her the strength to get up and continue. She came to a road but couldn't remember if it was the right one. Lin decided to make the turn but soon realized that it was not the same road she had been on that afternoon and had to double back. She tiptoed as she neared the crossway again, then stopped to listen.

It was so faint that she didn't know if it were real or her imagination, but she heard what she thought was a footstep, followed by a dragging sound, and another step. She didn't wait to see if it was real or getting louder. She had a burst of power and ran as if he were right behind her. The thought of his hand reaching for her propelled her on, higher and higher.

At last, she found the road leading to the barn, and the discovery gave her strength – the finish line in sight. She found the path marked by the stone and struggled through the briars, ripping her favorite dress but not caring at all. She caught sight of the barn and let out a small cry of relief as she hurried to the door.

"Lin, is that you?" came a whisper from inside.

"Ai," she cried and ran to her sister in tears. "Ai, I'm so afraid. We have to hide. There's a man after me – a monster. I'll explain later, but we need to hide."

"I was so scared," said Ai. "Hurry but be careful on the ladder."

Ai was well practiced in shifting the bales of hay and replacing the flooring to its original state and completed the process in less than a minute. She climbed down in the absolute darkness and whispered, "Did he follow you here?"

Lin, still gasping for breath said, "I'm almost positive I've lost him. I haven't seen him since I left the town and he had a terrible limp. I don't see how he could possibly find us here."

"Just to be safe," Ai whispered back, "let's be quiet for now. Try to sleep, and we'll talk in the morning."

They felt their way down to the floor, lay down, and listened. It took a while, but eventually, Lin began to feel safe; she was with Ai, and there was no way for the man to find them here. She was so exhausted that, despite her fear, she began to doze.

On one side of them, the twins slept soundly, oblivious to the danger. On the other lay Jiao, wrapped tightly in a blanket, prepared for an eternal resting place.

CHAPTER 11

Wednesday, July 14th, 1943: Night
Changbai Mountains – Kenji

"Ah, Kenji," said Chang as if the two were just meeting. "You need a bath. Quick, follow me." He jumped off the rock and started for a nearby trail but stopped, thought for a moment, and looked back over the valley in the direction the group of riders had taken. "I think smart to keep horses close by."

The two led their horses to a trail and through a wood and came out beside a stream. Chang led his horse over for a drink, pulled off his clothes, tossed them on rock, and waded into the freezing mountain water without a flinch. Kenji did the same, the only differences being the exclamation he let out as he waded in and his teeth chattering. After the shock wore off, the water began to feel good on the lacerations he had received on the ride, but he was only able to take it a minute before he had to wade out.

The moon was up and cast a golden light over the cascading current, which thrashed and swirled its way down and around the stoic Manchurian. He sat with his back against a rock in the center of the stream, facing the oncoming current. Kenji put on his clothes and sat on a log near the water's edge, trying to imagine where the Manchurian had hidden his gun. Chang was singing softly with his eyes closed and, as far as Kenji could tell, not the slightest hint of discomfort, but suddenly he stopped and looked all around as if he had noticed something amiss. "Gang?" he called out.

Kenji turned with a start and saw an older man standing within reach, glaring at him with a look of hatred. He was stocky and had a queue of long black hair braided into a ponytail just like Chang's, which allowed a full view of his square jaw. He was dressed all in black, and Kenji thought he resembled a ninja. Of a more pressing concern for Kenji than his appearance at that moment, however, was the glimmering blade of a dagger in his hand. The man in black said something to Chang in a low, firm voice.

Chang rose from the midst of the stream, walked toward them, and spoke to the man in Chinese. Although Kenji couldn't understand, he guessed the discussion involved him, and that this was not a social call. Chang began to speak harshly, and the man reluctantly put the weapon away.

"We need a fire," said Chang in Japanese, switching to a cheerful tone, as if the man had not been staring at Kenji with a knife in his hand, as if they were hiking buddies. He spoke to the other in Chinese, and the man began bringing wood while Chang dressed. By the time Chang took a seat in front of Kenji, the newcomer had started a healthy campfire. Chang motioned for him to sit down beside them.

"Time for little talk, I think," said Chang, looking at Kenji over the burgeoning flames. "This is Gang," he said by way of introduction. "He would like to kill Kenji."

Kenji looked back and forth between the two men, paying considerably more attention to the man called Gang after the inauspicious introduction.

"He understand very little Japanese, but he hardly speak Chinese either – just not talkative man. He just came from meeting. That meeting about Kenji, so I need to tell a few things. Maybe a little history first. Okay?"

"Do I have a choice?" asked Kenji.

"A year ago," said Chang, ignoring the question, "I have great influence, at least, much greater than now. Men here were mostly united. Often disagree, but we want to keep our people safe – that much we agree. *How* we do that is big question."

"That time I have control over almost two thousand men. Also, have influence on other groups in Manchuria."

"In last year, all that change. Some men side with this or that Japanese officer. Some men join with this or that Chinese military group. We still have meetings, but men just shout insults. Nobody agree on anything. I have maybe twenty men now I can trust. Gang here is number two man, but as you see, even Gang has hard time to agree with me."

"What exactly," said Kenji, "is his problem with me?"

"Good question. Chang will answer."

"Gang's daughter is mother of children you spy on naked at pond today." Kenji shook his head but didn't interrupt. "Her name Nuan. Gang is children's grandfather. The children's father is," he hesitated, "I don't think necessary to go into details, but he is important man."

"About a year ago, Nuan took children to visit friends in Harbin, north of here. When she was on her way home from shopping with friends, Japanese soldiers stop them and take Nuan away for no reason. Friends ask what is problem, but soldiers don't say. Just take her away. They follow and see soldiers take her to Unit 731. You know Unit 731, Kenji?"

Unit 731 was known ostensibly as the Epidemic Prevention and Water Purification Department, but in reality, it was a scientific research facility for the development of biological and chemical weapons for the Imperial Japanese Army. Few people outside its walls knew the extent of what was occurring inside, but rumors ran rampant among the Chinese of horrific experiments conducted on human guinea pigs. Surgery without the aid of anesthesia, rape and forced pregnancies, using humans as targets for grenades and flamethrowers, and forced frostbite were just a few of the experiments rumored to be conducted at Unit 731. Not until after the war was over would the world learn the full story of everything that happened at the grisly unit.

"I've heard of it," said Kenji cautiously.

"It was two days before we were able to organize a rescue team to break in at night and get her out. She had been beautiful young lady, full of life, but she never said a word after that. Nothing. Not even to father. His daughter harm by your army. Can you see why he want to kill you now?"

Kenji thought it best not to argue the point. He hadn't done anything to the lady, didn't want anything done to her, and didn't order anything to be done, but he could see Chang's point.

Kenji asked, "Where is she now?"

"Perhaps now is not the time," Chang said, glancing at Gang. "He does understand some Japanese. But I have his promise, he will respect my decision. And I say no harm to Kenji. Gang knows his thinking not clear now. Other men though, they don't listen to Chang, so we need to get Kenji back to his men and all of you back to Changchun before something bad happen."

Kenji looked at Gang, who sat staring at the fire. Chang stood up and announced that they had to move now. He told Kenji to mount up on his own horse behind Gang and keep his mouth shut. Chang doused the flames and mounted his horse. Kenji followed the order, and within seconds they were trotting back down the path to the base of the mountain. When they reached the end of the trail, Chang paused and surveyed the open valley.

"What's happening?" said Kenji.

"Gang say several factions are ready for all-out war. Want to start with you. They will all be looking for you tonight." He pointed across the valley and added, "You must get over that mountain tonight and get back to Kenji's men. I recommend you return to Changchun tomorrow morning."

"We will meet again," said Chang. "You must go, no more time to waste. Take this road straight across valley, and make sure nobody see you. When you reach mountain, this road ends. Go south, to left, and you find path that leads up and over mountain. Once you get over mountain, continue west until you find your men. I assume you know they are camping by lake now. You not over that mountain tonight, I don't want to be Watanabe Kenji-san."

Kenji surveyed the flat terrain. All roads and fields, no trees for cover. "Not a problem Chang. That shouldn't be more than a five-minute ride."

"You do not understand. You not riding. You ride out in open like this, you never reach other side. I think best is trick them. They know Kenji is with Chang. We take your horse and ride south. They think Gang is Kenji. The men looking for you follow us and give you good start to get to that mountain. Stay low to ground and hide in fields if you hear anyone. Make sure to stay off roads."

The Manchurian handed Kenji his pistol and knife holster and gave his heels to the horse. Chang headed out into the valley with Gang riding Kenji's horse close behind. They heard yells and saw a group of riders off to the north starting toward them. Chang turned a hard left but slowed enough to let Kenji's horse pass so that he could shield Kenji from the view of the pursuing men. Gang slowed Kenji's horse, and Kenji slid off into thick grass as the two Manchurians took off without him. Kenji landed hard, rolled into a ditch, and lay motionless, holding his pistol out of the water. When his pursuers passed by him seconds later, Kenji had a good feeling they would never catch Chang unless he wanted them to. Soaking wet, and not wishing to waste a minute, Kenji rose, fastened his holster about his waist, and headed west under a glowing moon.

CHAPTER 12

Wednesday, July 14th, 1943: Late Night
Changbai Mountains – Ai

Ai hadn't wanted to speak about it. It could wait until morning. She heard Lin's breathing and knew everyone else was asleep now. She had failed her first test as a mother. The list of things she had done wrong in failing to care for Jiao grew every minute. If she had done any one of them, her little sister would not have died – irrevocable mistakes which would stay with her forever.

As she lay in that agony, a new terror began to grow from without. The sound was faint at first, but then she heard the barn door creaking open. It could have been the wind, or perhaps an animal.

But then there were steps.

There was someone in the barn above.

Ai's heart beat fiercely as she heard a heavy step, followed by a dragging sound and thump. Step, drag, thump; step, drag, thump. Lin awoke, and they squeezed each other's hands – it was the only thing they could do to keep from screaming. Ai prayed that the twins would continue to sleep. Perhaps Jiao was better off; after all, she had nothing to fear.

Above, for what seemed an eternity, they heard continuous movement of the distinctive step, drag, and thump moving about on the barn floor. The girls listened in their own private terrors, both wondering if the man above knew they were in the barn somewhere. *What was he doing up there, and where was Chang? Had Ai covered the trap door well enough?* They heard sounds as if heavy things were being dragged across the floor. They wondered if the mysterious person knew of the secret room or would find it in a matter of time. Their hearts leapt as the trap door above their heads began to shake. The intruder had obviously disturbed the bales of hay over the door. They closed their eyes and prayed that the door would not open.

And it didn't.

The shuffling feet were heard moving away; the noise growing fainter and fainter. The feet were no longer in the barn. The man was outside, and then they could hear nothing at all. They listened to the beautiful sound of silence but were still too afraid to speak for several minutes.

"I couldn't find anyone to help Jiao," Lin whispered at last.

"It's okay. I'm glad you're alright."

Ai told Lin to go to sleep, and they would talk in the morning. Lin eventually drifted away again, and Ai vacillated between grieving for Jiao and worrying about what would become of the rest of them.

CHAPTER 13

Wednesday, July 14th, 1943: Late Night
Changbai Mountains – Kenji

He dropped to the ground and held his face and body against the sloped bank of the field when another group of horsemen sprinted by towards Chang and Gang. He waited until the vibrations had faded to a safe distance, and as he lay in the field, the realization that he might not make it through the night struck him for the first time. Chang was telling the truth – these people really did want to kill him. Although he was a soldier, and his army was at war, this was the first real combat situation he had ever experienced. There had been whispers that this detail in Manchuria was for the kids of influential men who wanted to keep their sons out of danger. And he had indeed never been in danger thus far. He lifted his head to the level of the road, checked all directions, got up, and ran low toward his goal.

Occasionally, he was forced to cross roads running perpendicular to his course. As he was passing one such road, he heard voices but was unable to determine the direction. He jumped into a field of barley and crawled. While he couldn't discern the precise position of the sounds, he was sure they were getting louder. He moved well away from the road and lay still on his back. The voices faded away shortly after, but he decided to take a break just to be on the safe side. Surveying the night sky, he found the North Star shining near Cassiopeia and searched for other constellations as he had done on clear evenings lying on his back beside his grandfather and siblings in Nagano. He remembered his grandfather telling him that these were the same stars the Pharaohs of Egypt, Galileo, Napoleon, and the great samurai warriors had gazed upon for thousands of years unchanged.

As he lay gazing, he remembered Chang's advice and decided it would be prudent to get moving before his luck ran out. Given the short distance he estimated was left, he wondered if it might be worth the risk to finish it off at full speed. Surely he could make it to the forest within a couple of minutes.

Standing and turning, he listened and heard nothing. He walked to the edge of the field, climbed up onto the road and checked all around. He took off as fast as he could for the safety of the dark forest ahead, which he could see was now two or three minutes away. He glanced back and was relieved to see that he was still alone as he approached the base of the mountain. As he fought fatigue, he considered slowing his pace to conserve energy for the climb, but at that moment he heard a rumbling echo. There was no mistaking the sound. There was no need to turn and confirm his belief; several horses were rapidly closing in on him.

Where they had been, he couldn't say. It didn't matter.

Several shots were fired and missed. Kenji considered dropping down into the field but thought his best bet would be to try to reach the cover of the forest, which was now only fifty meters away. He grabbed his pistol and fired blindly to the rear to try to slow the assault.

With his pistol still in hand, he tried to search ahead for a barrier he could use for protection but saw nothing. He was totally exposed.

Kenji felt a sensation as though he had been punched in the left shoulder. Then it began to burn, and he realized he had been shot.

He was on the verge of turning with his pistol to make his last stand, but just before he did, he saw the flash of a gunshot being fired from the woods ahead of him. Whatever weak and dismal hope he still held out for survival vanished with the knowledge that several men were rapidly closing from the rear, and now at least one gunman was awaiting him at the spot where he had hoped to find cover in the forest.

But as he stopped and turned to fight his pursuers, he saw they had halted also. One of their horses had fallen. With feeble, but renewed hope, he looked back to the forest where a second discharge illuminated a man on horseback. The men who had been chasing him took off in the opposite direction with a velocity even greater than that with which they had been attacking. Ignoring what would have otherwise been unbearable pain, Kenji ran toward his benefactor, and at last he understood, as Chang came over and assisted him up onto the back of his horse.

CHAPTER 14

Thursday, July 15ᵗʰ, 1943: Wee Hours
Changbai Mountains – Ai

There had been countless odd noises through the night as Ai lay sleepless. It was possible, she thought, that the intruder might still be about. She briefly toyed with the idea of going up for a look, but prudence won out in the end.

At long last, the rays of dawn began to poke through the tiny cracks in the boards overhead. Ai felt as if the light bathed the room in safety. The barely perceptible warmth of the rays gave her reason to believe that today would be a beautiful summer day full of hope. The light also shone on the faces of the children and one by one they awoke – except for Jiao.

Ai told them to stay quiet until she had a chance to go up to the barn and have a look around. Lin sat up and noticed Jiao wrapped in her blanket. As she stared at the peaceful look on her little sister's face, the cruel image of yesterday's witch came howling back to mind. She turned to find Ai, and in an instant, she knew the truth.

"She went very peacefully," Ai said in an almost cheerful voice.

Lin had to look away from her elder sister, knowing how she had acted. All of the selfishness, the exact words she had used yesterday, and a thousand times before came to mind.

I'm not holding this sick child all day and night.

These brats.

Lin wanted to forget the words had ever been spoken – deny them and have them vanquished from memory, but they continued to play in her head one by one. She feared she wouldn't be able to get them out of her mind for the rest of her life.

Ai turned away to give her time to grieve in her own way, knowing that any attempts at comfort would be rejected. As she looked away, she noticed that the twins were staring at something on the ceiling. She moved over and glanced up but saw nothing of consequence.

"What are you staring at?" asked Ai.

This caught the attention of Lin, who was eager to divert her attention away from thoughts of Jiao. They were all staring at the iron grating on the edge of the room that Ai had uncovered the previous day, but it seemed to be covered again. There was no light shining through, so Lin went over and stood on the bench to get a better look. As she extended her legs and rose closer, she saw something on the bars but was unable to determine precisely what it was. Lin raised herself on her tiptoes and with her head inches away from the grating smelled a foul odor. It registered slowly, but she realized what it was – eyes. And then Lin saw the scar, and the gruesome smile spreading on the soldier's face just inches away. She backed away in silent horror, at first unable to utter a word, and then began to scream at him.

When Ai realized what was happening, she climbed the ladder and threw her shoulder against the door in full motherly attack mode, but it didn't budge. The door had been covered by something other than a bale of hay. Lin climbed the ladder to see if she could help, but both the door and boards could not be moved. They were trapped.

The soldier laughed as he stood and threw the board back over the opening. Ai climbed back down and put her arms around the twins. She looked at Jiao and thought how ironic it was that she was the only one who had escaped.

At that moment, she envied her.

CHAPTER 15

Thursday, July 15th, 1943: Early Morning
Changbai Mountains – Kenji

With the assistance of the two Manchurians – and two pints of whiskey – Kenji made it over the mountain during the night. Due to the anesthetic of the alcohol, he was even able to get some sleep. When he awoke, however, the throbbing of his shoulder was exacerbated by a pounding of his head. He put up his right hand to shield the rays of the sun and lifted himself up to a seated position. Chang was facing away from him, toward the sun, with his legs crossed and arms held upward in what Kenji guessed was a pose of meditation. Without turning around Chang said, "*Ohayo gozaimasu, Kenji-san.* It look like you fall off your horse and land on sharp rocks last night. We take out bullet and clean it while you sleep. You take care and no infection, it will heal quickly. I think it best you not tell your superiors what really happen – you say you fall off horse. Many innocent Chinese die if you tell truth."

There was no doubt that if the Imperial Japanese Army learned Chinese locals had dared to attack one of their officers, the repercussions would be swift and disproportionately severe. At the moment, however, Kenji was having trouble focusing on that matter because of the competing complaints of his head and shoulder.

"Other than your shoulder, Kenji, everything just same as when I met you yesterday. You need get back to your camp before they come looking for you."

Kenji saw Gang working over a campfire and could smell the fried meat. As he was famished, he tried to get up, putting weight on his left side but cried out and fell back to the ground.

"Confucius say don't put weight on fresh gunshot wound," Chang said, turning with a grin. Kenji rolled on the ground and writhed in pain, and Gang showed the first sign of genuine humanity by smiling at Chang's joke.

Gang helped Kenji up and put a plate in his lap with several strips of bacon and a heap of boiled rice packed into a ball.

"I suggest using your right hand to eat," said Chang. The two Manchurians smiled at each other as they watched Kenji attacking his food.

"Slow down, Kenji," said Chang, "nobody steal your plate. You get sick eating like that." Kenji did not heed the advice.

"When you supposed to be back to your camp?"

"I'm supposed to meet my men today," said Kenji with a mouth full of food, "at the lake."

"You can get there very quick."

"I hope you don't expect me to walk like this."

"Why you walk when you have good horse?" said the Manchurian, pointing behind Kenji to where his horse was grazing. Chang nodded to Gang who got up and began saddling Kenji's horse.

"What happened last night?" asked Kenji.

"I guess we were too fast for them. We notice they stop and return, so we rode across valley and double back to see if you make it to mountain. Lucky thing too. I told you stay low and off the road."

"I did stay low," said Kenji.

"Not low enough."

"I know Kenji still have questions," said Chang. "You don't think you should trust Chang. I understand – risky, I know – just don't say anything for now. I ask you, maybe you don't think me as friend, but I ask you to keep everything you see yesterday and today as secret. If you are person I hope you are, you be happy to know that your silence keep children you saw yesterday safe. You talk and – who knows?" he said with a shrug of the shoulders.

Kenji took a long look at Chang's smiling face. The face of his father's driver, Kazu, came to mind as the only other person he had ever met who had that degree of trustworthiness. The Manchurian exuded such a keen and earnest likeability that Kenji thought he could believe every word he said. He had the gift of gab. Just like Kazu, the Manchurian had the talent of making friends with anyone he met.

"Why would I lie about my injury?" asked Kenji.

"Because Chang ask you."

"And why would I do what a perfect stranger asked me to do?" said Kenji, setting down his empty plate.

"Well, perfect stranger ask nicely. And perfect stranger did save Kenji's life last night. Maybe for that, you can tell little white lie."

"Anything else?"

"That's all. For now, just don't tell anyone about us. If you can't do it for Chang, do it for children."

"I'll think about it."

"That's all I can ask."

"And who shall I say did such a fine job of cleaning and dressing my wound – that I got from falling off my horse?"

"Kind Chinese man, of course; that no lie."

Chang helped Kenji to his feet, putting Kenji's right arm around his neck, and the two Manchurians helped him onto his horse. Kenji studied the faces of the two men judiciously, men he could not have dreamed of a day earlier, men who had saved his life for reasons unknown, and shook his head in disbelief that he was actually considering going along with their scheme.

"And I get answers the next time we meet."

"You have my word. You will not be disappointed if you trust Chang. I promise you; no dishonor to your country and great emperor."

Kenji turned his horse and lightly prompted it in the direction of the lake.

"Wait a minute," said Chang motioning for Gang to get something. Gang returned with a sling. Kenji slid it over his head with his right hand and worked his left arm in gently.

"You see doctor right away, Kenji," called Chang as Kenji began to leave.

Kenji held up his right hand in acknowledgement without turning around and rode away, thinking *What a difference a day can make.*

CHAPTER 16

Thursday, July 15th, 1943: Early Morning
Changbai Mountains – Ai

It took a few minutes to recover from the initial shock. Ai got up and told Lin to climb the ladder with her. They stood together on the same rung and pushed but couldn't budge the door.

They both felt around and pushed on the boards beside the door with no luck. It was clear the soldier had covered them with something weighty.

"How about the grating?" said Lin.

They went over, stood on the bench, and pushed. Nothing.

"We have to think," said Ai. "Where has he gone? How much time do we have?"

Over the next hour, the girls ventured back up the ladder numerous times with renewed strength and confidence to try a new plan, only to be disappointed and discouraged with each additional failed attempt. Ai sat down beside the twins and tried to think of words of encouragement.

"I know you're scared, and things don't look good at the moment, but we have people looking out for us. They *will* rescue us. You mustn't lose hope." Then she moved beside Jiao and sat, softly lifting her head and laying it in her lap. As she stroked her little sister's hair, she began to sing a Chinese lullaby, one which their mother had sung to them all as children.

The children wept as they listened. They each remembered the happiness of their youth, the warmth of their mother's voice, and the safety of their home and bed. When she finished, they all sat in silence wondering who would open the door.

CHAPTER 17

Thursday, July 15ᵗʰ, 1943: Early Morning
Nagano, Japan – Ami

The yellow hue of morning sunlight spread throughout the *tatami* room where Ami sat in the formal, customary *seiza* style, on her knees with her calves folded under her thighs and her back straight and tilted ever so slightly forward over a low, hand-carved oak table. It was her habit, as it was for all well-bred and properly trained girls of her generation, to obey customs, even when alone. She had already changed from her nightclothes into her kimono, a splendid garment from Kyoto made of the loveliest Chinese silk and adorned with silver hand-stitched cranes flying over a wide blue estuary. Thanks to years of training, she could fold and wrap the kimono onto herself without assistance.

Even before troubling with her hair or putting on makeup, of which she used little, Ami was still uncommonly attractive. Her eyes were mesmerizing. With her small, delicate nose and thin red lips, she resembled the Japanese dolls sold by merchants along the busy streets of Tokyo, only the breath of life and animated features making her infinitely more breathtaking.

She had been raised by a wealthy, although mostly absent father, and a mother whose beauty was matched only by her heartlessness. The sole purpose in her upbringing had been to hone her feminine skills and charm into a Venus flytrap inescapable by any male of her choice, and she had succeeded far beyond her mother's expectations when she had closed her lobes around the highly sought-after Watanabe bachelor.

The Watanabe family owned several houses in the mountains of Nagano, far from the dangers of air raids feared by many in the Tokyo area after the American bombings in the spring of 1942. With no ports, strategic railways, weapons manufacturing facilities, or military bases, Nagano was virtually untouched by the war. The house in which Ami sat had been given to her and Kenji as newlyweds to be used as their summer retreat in the years to come.

Ami sipped her tea as if she were engaged in a formal tea ceremony, the handcrafted black *raku* pottery held just so in her right hand with the left supporting the bottom of the cup. In spite of the formalities, her head was filled with happy thoughts of the life she would have after the return of her husband. She had set aside a full week to decorate the house with special touches that Kenji would surely prize when he returned from the war. She studied the walls of the room to find the most favorable spot to hang the stunning portrait of Kenji's father, the general in full-dress uniform, which she had prepared in secret by a renowned artist from one of his old photos. The southern wall at which she gazed, she had chosen as the perfect location because of its prominence, without a doorway or window on its length. When the general came to visit, he would be seated beneath the portrait, and she would keep his cup full of green tea in the mornings and *sake* in the evenings. She no longer felt the intimidation she had experienced in his presence at first. Now, she simply wished to keep the patriarch of this powerful family happy, both for altruistic ends and more selfish ulterior motives. Nothing, she thought, would stroke his pride and ego more than being seated at the head of a table with his immortal likeness behind, hovering like a specter for all to admire – and fear.

Ami had also brought many pictures of Kenji, his mother, and siblings for which she would need to find suitable positions of honor within the room and house. Placing her cup in its saucer, she stood and walked about the room with the shortest of steps. In her mind's eye, Ami saw bamboo water spouts tipping full with their weight of liquid, guests laughing, and wooden cups continually replenished with *sake*, children running and singing delightful songs, and herself as the gracious host at the perfect family summer evening party. She could smell the lavender, lilac, and lilies, hear the men laughing and refilling each other's cups while regaling each other with tall tales of glorious battles won, see the women playing with their children and telling stories about how awful the men were but laughing all the while. And she felt a shiver as she saw Kenji smiling at her from the table beside his father, nodding and raising his glass in her direction to let her know how pleased he was with her.

CHAPTER 18

Thursday, July 15th, 1943: Morning
Changbai Mountains – Ai

The stillness was broken minutes later by a commotion of horses and men. The children sat in anticipation, not knowing whether the news would be good or bad. Seconds later, their hopes were dashed as they heard the rough language of Japanese soldiers entering the barn above. Dirt fell through the cracks as heavy objects were moved overhead. At last, the door they had so desperately attempted to break through opened to reveal three terrifying, smiling faces peering down on them. One of them said something in Japanese, and after a moment of silence began to yell it. Although the girls had no idea what the man was saying, it was clear from his gestures that he wanted them to get out.

Ai picked up Jiao and started up the steps. She told the others to follow her and try to do what the soldiers instructed them. The looks on the faces of the men were enough to make her sick, but she decided to set an example she hoped Lin would follow. The twins followed right behind her and once they were out clung to her waist on each side.

Lin was the last out and did not hide the loathing she felt toward the men. Two of the soldiers began oohing when she stepped into the barn in her tattered red dress. One of them reached up to touch her face, but the third man, apparently the one in charge, slapped him.

The leader was the shortest of the three and had a habit of shouting everything he said. The soldier who had tried to touch Lin had a dark complexion and thin mustache. The third soldier was tall and smiled wickedly at Lin. The leader gestured for everyone to leave the barn.

Lin was the first out and saw the limping man from the night before among a group of Japanese soldiers on horseback. He wasn't frightening at all now, and Lin wished she had tried to kill him at the abandoned building when she had the chance.

They were loaded into an open carriage, Ai still holding Jiao. They all sat down on the wooden planks of the carriage floor, and the leader climbed in and stood over them taking a long look, seeming to notice Jiao for the first time. He grabbed her face roughly and realized that the child was dead. He tried to take her from Ai, but she held tight and begged him for compassion. A quick order to the tall soldier brought him bounding into the carriage where he ripped Jiao from Ai while the leader pulled her arms behind her back.

Fan stayed seated, understanding the futility of attempting to prevent the inevitable, but Shou and Lin tried to intervene. They only succeeded in getting themselves abused and having their hands tied behind their backs while the soldiers looking on laughed at their vain attempts.

The children pleaded as the tall soldier, upon shouted orders from the leader, carried Jiao's body into the barn and threw it headfirst back down into the cellar, the body landing with a sickening dull thud on the boards where she had died peacefully. The cellar door was slammed shut, the tall soldier returned, and off went the caravan through the high grass. The leader was out in front followed by the tall soldier, both on horseback. The dark soldier drove the one-horse carriage with the children, and the other soldiers brought up the rear.

The group proceeded down the road they had traveled the day before, past the spot where Chang had found them hiding, and then past the old grandmother's house near the bluff. Ai had nothing to say to lift the spirits of her younger siblings. Jiao was gone, and the rest of them might as well be with the life which faced them now. She could see the looks in the eyes of the soldiers, the nauseating smiles, and knew these men could do anything they wanted to her. Although Ai was only seventeen, she had a very good idea what that *anything* might be. As bad as it would be, she thought she could bear it if that were the worst. What she couldn't accept, however, was the great unknown of what would happen to Lin, Shou, and Fan.

Her father, she had never known. She hadn't seen her mother for over a year. Her youngest sister was dead, and now the remaining children were captives of the Japanese army.

The looks of the soldiers had not escaped Lin's notice either. The thought of one of these men touching her was beyond sickening. She had been treated so well, too well, all her life, and now these men, these soldiers who had taken over her country, treated her like a miserable criminal. No boy had ever been allowed to touch her, even to look at her in that way, and now these soldiers laughed at them and looked at her with their vile, perverted grins.

Fan and Shou were not old enough to understand the full ramifications of their predicament, but they could read enough from their elder sisters' faces to know the situation was grim. The specifics of what was to come were fortunately vague in their minds. Shou had lost much of his bravado, but Fan was careful to take mental note of every face and injustice just in case she was ever afforded the opportunity of retribution.

They rode across a plain with just one mountain left to negotiate before they would be on the outskirts of Hsinking. The leader's head was consumed with thoughts of magnificence as he contemplated his superior's gratitude for such a rare find. Surely this would merit some promotion or benefit, or both. Given that he was the point man, this preoccupation could have proven fatal.

Because on the slope of the steep mountain ahead lying in wait were Chang, Gang, four of their best fighters, a doctor they had brought to see Jiao, and one femme fatale. Behind a cluster of boulders on an elevated position beside the road, partially blocked from view by a few healthy spruce trees, Chang's group surveyed the approaching caravan.

•   •   •

"I say we kill them all," said Gang, as if he were making a menu decision.

Chang looked as though he were calculating a complicated geometric sequence, which was in a sense what he was doing.

"We can't take that chance," replied Chang. "It would be risky with just our own bullets to worry about, but with their return fire...we just can't take that chance. If a stray bullet were to hit one of the children...if the boy were to be hit...no, we have to use our heads."

"Everyone listen," Chang said to the group. "Ju and I will go down and be captured. You are to stay here and watch until they are gone. You are not to attack unless the children's lives are in danger. Ju has been trained for this, and we must rely on her skills. After she is captured, we will follow and see where they are taken."

Ju, whose father had named her to be his *daisy flower*, had been trained as a spy by Chang personally. Many girls had been forced into prostitution or other roles to help their families, but Ju had asked Chang to teach her a craft she could use to help her people. She had been refused by all others, but Chang recognized the usefulness in having such a weapon in his arsenal. No boy or man he had ever trained had worked harder at the craft than the beautiful *daisy flower*. She could speak Japanese fluently, and was competent with a variety of weapons.

"And what if they kill you?" asked Gang.

"Then I've had a good life and a good death. I'm an expendable old man. You will not attack to save me – understood?" he said to the group.

The others nodded with genuine and reverential awe.

Gang did not.

"I'll go with Ju," said Gang.

"Thank you, my friend, but this job may require some Japanese. Ju, we can't take any weapons." He continued to instruct her as she lay down her rifle and began removing weaponry from under her gown. The doctor and other men watched in amazement at the number of concealed weapons the beautiful girl had hidden on her small frame.

"Perhaps it would be okay for me to keep just *one knife*?" inquired Ju.

"Yes," said Chang. "Perhaps you're right. As long as they don't find it."

She nodded and concealed a dagger under a strap on her upper thigh.

"It's time," said Chang.

As the two walked down, careful to remain hidden from the view of the Japanese, Chang explained they would walk out into the valley as if unaware of the Japanese presence, and once they were sure they had been spotted Ju was to take off and try to hide. After her capture, she needed to make sure no harm came to the children and try to keep in touch through any reliable channels so Chang could monitor their whereabouts and rescue them. She would pretend to be his daughter, and, unless she deemed otherwise depending on the circumstances, it would be best not to let them know that she spoke Japanese.

All went as planned as they walked out into the open with their heads down until they were in plain view of the oncoming caravan. Ju turned and ran in the opposite direction, and two men broke away from the detachment and flew past Chang. It took very little time for them to return, each soldier holding one of Ju's wrists as she was suspended in air between their horses. All of the soldiers laughed watching the girl struggle.

The carriage pulled up alongside Chang about the same time the two soldiers returned with Ju.

"Please don't hurt my daughter," said Chang in Chinese, but using the voice of an older man. Ai saw him and knew he was acting when she heard the strange speech. She caught Lin's attention and told her with her eyes and quick shake of the head not to say a word. She huddled with Fan and Shou and whispered for them not to react or speak to Chang.

"Could it be that you don't like us?" said the Japanese leader with feigned hurt feelings, drawing laughter from his men. Ju kept up her token struggle, and Chang continued to plead in Chinese for the release of his daughter.

"What shall we do with her, sir?" asked one of the soldiers holding Ju.

"Put her in the carriage with the others," said the leader. "Today must be my lucky day." They hoisted Ju into the back, ignoring Chang's pleas.

"Forward," said the leader.

"What about the old man?" asked the tall soldier.

The leader turned and looked at Chang first and then smiled at his men.

"You haven't fired your weapons all day. Use him as target practice," he said as he kicked his horse into motion.

"Papa," pleaded Ju in Chinese. "I'm okay. Please look after yourself."

None of the children spoke Japanese and had not understood the words of the leader. Gang and the men on the mountain also couldn't understand what had been said.

The Japanese soldiers looked at each other, each hoping someone else would carry out the order. The pitiful old man was unarmed – all he was doing was pleading for his daughter. Even the tall soldier reached for his weapon but couldn't bring himself to shoot a defenseless old man.

Chang understood the order but continued to play the part of a grieved farmer who couldn't speak Japanese. He followed a few steps with his arms outstretched to Ju even as she pleaded for him to turn and run.

The leader pulled his pistol, spun his horse around and fired straight through the carriage. The bullet passed between the children and hit Chang in the stomach, dropping him to his knees. Ju screamed, and Ai caught Shou's mouth just in time to stifle his cry.

"Cha…"

"You," the leader shouted at the men, "are without a doubt the worst soldiers I've ever seen. How the hell did any of you make it into this army?"

Gang fought hard the impulse to attack and kill the man. He could do it, and he knew it would gnaw at him for the rest of his life if he didn't, but he honored Chang's order.

He had known from the beginning it was suicide, but there was no stopping Chang when his mind was set – not when it involved the children.

CHAPTER 19

Thursday, July 15th, 1943: Late Morning
Changbai Mountains – Kenji

Kenji found his men where he had told them to wait and instructed them to mount up for the return trip to Hsinking. The Manchurians had done an excellent job bandaging his shoulder, but it was nevertheless torturous making it back over the mountain.

As soon as they made it back, Kenji released his men and headed straight for the hospital. One of his best friends, Yuta Uchibori, was a doctor there. He had known Yuta since childhood, and Yuta was one of the few people in the army who he knew he could trust with a secret. They had spoken about the war privately in the past, and both had reservations about the war in general, and about the conduct of the soldiers and doctors in Manchuria specifically.

The medical unit for the Japanese was far superior to the facilities where the Chinese were treated. The Imperial Army had requisitioned the Chinese hospital for its own use, and the Chinese were not permitted entrance; they were forced to seek medical assistance from healers of their own race. Kenji moved as swiftly as his injury would allow him in hopes that he would arrive before Yuta left for the day.

As he was dismounting and hitching his horse to a post outside the hospital, he saw Lieutenant Kanta Fujii, who he considered to be a major pain in the ass, approaching on foot. Fujii was boisterous, contemptuous, and arrogant, and he had never encountered a rule or law that he believed pertained to his high status. Much like Kenji, he came from an influential family and was given preferential treatment because of his name, and he liked to let everyone know that he was not to be taken lightly. Whenever possible, Kenji avoided him, but there was no escape now.

"Kenji, my friend, I heard you were out chasing Genghis Khan all over hell and back," yelled Kanta, who, as usual, was flanked by several of his flunkies. "I'm *ecstatic* to see that you've been returned to us safe and sound," he said before turning to share a hearty laugh with his entourage.

"Friend my ass," mumbled Kenji.

The two lieutenants were part of a small unit which was responsible for patrolling the city of Hsinking and the surrounding area. It was generally considered to be one of the safest details in the Japanese army. Both of their fathers were well-known generals, and it did not appear to be a coincidence that the two sons had received relatively easy assignments in the war effort. The captain overseeing their unit required of them minimal duties, and Kenji did his best to bifurcate their company so he would have as little contact as possible with Kanta. However, given the small size of their group, the two men were forced to deal with each other much more frequently than he would have preferred.

"I trust you're not in need of medical assistance, are you, dear friend?" said Kanta, glancing at Kenji's sling and then at the hospital.

"Is that you, my good friend Kanta?" shouted Kenji mimicking Kanta's volume and style of speech. "I swear, my brother, I just can't recognize you these days without your twelve-year-old girlfriend." The low blow, far out of character for the usually mild-mannered Kenji, erased every smile at the gathering save Kenji's.

The reference to the young girl was about a night, only a week earlier, when Kenji had been returning home after dinner and drinks alone at Lu's. As he had passed through a street in town renowned as the drinking district, frequented by both enlisted men and officers, he had found a chair in front of a closed grocer and sat down to finish his beer, have a cigarette, and watch the men make fools of themselves. Prostitutes, some who had voluntarily chosen the lifestyle, and others who had been forced by hunger, circumstances, or family to make money the only way they could, stood in the shadows along the rough-and-tumble road. A commotion had erupted in one such alleyway near him beside a crowded tavern, and several of the girls were screaming frantically for help. Curious, he had walked over and pushed his way to the center of the chaos where he found a young girl lying on the ground in a tattered white dress soaked in blood about her waist, barely conscious. He remembered picking her up and running with her the two blocks to the hospital – this hospital – followed by hysterical Chinese women and girls. The Japanese guards at the door had allowed him to pass but blocked all the Chinese women behind him. He remembered then, and would never forget for the rest of his life, the feeling of her small body in his arms and her confused expression, weakly asking for her mother. The Japanese nurses told him to stop, but he had shouted for a doctor once inside. He had reached what looked like an emergency room and called out again. The head nurse ran to him and asked what had happened. Kenji explained all that he knew and said the girl was losing blood and needed to be cared for immediately or she would die.

"Sir," the nurse had said, "you know that we do not treat those people in this hospital. Take her to the Chinese section."

"There's no time," he had said. "Besides, there are no doctors there this time of night. She's in shock you imbecile. She's losing blood. Are you blind? She needs to be treated this minute."

"Sir, please keep your voice down or you'll wake the doctor," the nurse had whispered.

Kenji pushed her aside and began walking down the corridor. "Doctor, I need a doctor now!" He reached the end of the hallway, turned, and came back toward the nurses, continuing to call for a doctor all the while. At last a door opened near the nurses' station, and a man in a white smock emerged. The nurses began to bow and apologize for the interruption. Armed guards had also come through the front door and were approaching with their weapons trained on Kenji.

"Doctor, this girl has serious injuries. She's bleeding to death," he had said, out of breath.

The doctor looked at the girl first and then at Kenji's insignia. "Lieutenant, is that a Chinese whore that you've brought bleeding all over my hospital floor?"

"Doctor, this child will die without immediate attention."

The doctor looked down at the girl once more and then into Kenji's eyes with no more emotion than if Kenji were holding an injured animal. "I do not waste my skills on Chinks, Lieutenant. And besides, that girl is already dead."

In his fury, Kenji hadn't noticed that she had gone completely limp and had stopped asking for her mother. Stunned and confused by the doctor's soulless response, it took a moment for him to look down at the girl he held. Her left arm had fallen off her stomach and dangled lifelessly by her side. Her mouth was open, and a pitiful, melancholy expression was on her face and in her eyes. It was so dreadful that he had to look away.

"Get that bleeding corpse out of this hospital immediately before I change my mind and have you arrested," the doctor had said as he turned and entered his office to go back to sleep.

Kenji had looked up and stared after the man, unable to comprehend the inhumane response of his compatriot. This war was changing everyone. *This is not how we were trained,* he wanted to shout after the man.

Eventually, he turned and carried the girl back down the corridor and through the door outside into the waiting crowd, walking like a zombie among the girls who still waited in tears. For the first time, he was ashamed to be part of the Imperial Japanese Army. This monstrosity, of which he was part, had grown into something evil which Kenji could never have imagined when he first dreamed of becoming a soldier. When they saw the dead girl, the crowd became silent, the only sound being that of Kenji's feet shuffling in the dirt. He had no idea where the girl was from, so he just made his way back toward the tavern and alley where he had found her. As he approached the bar, Fujii and his sidekicks were just coming out of the front door laughing, quite drunk.

"Kenji," Fujii had yelled, slurring his words, "what are you doing with my date?"

Everyone in the crowd stared at him, mostly loathing his arrogance and heartlessness, but also with a sense of bewilderment. Kenji attempted to move on, knowing there could be no meaningful discussion with the group and that any confrontation would end up hurting other innocent Chinese.

"Well, be my guest, Kenji," said Kanta. "She was certainly a peach earlier, though I must warn you that she's no longer a virgin." The whole group of drunks broke into laughter and slapped their knees at the sick joke.

A woman came running, issuing stomach-turning shrieks of fright and despair, from somewhere up the dark street. "Jie," she yelled between sobs. "Jie, oh my god, Jie." When she reached the group and saw Kenji holding her daughter, she dropped to her knees and shook her head violently, screaming *no* over and over. Kenji realized she must be the girl's mother and tried to walk to her to give her the child, but she backed away as if her daughter could not be the girl in Kenji's arms and the nightmare could not become a reality if she could stay far enough away from him. The other ladies around her tried to hold her up and give her comfort but she continued to try to deny what was happening. Her voice had a bone-chilling shrill to it that Kenji found agonizing. People began muttering that the child's father was approaching, and a path opened up to a gaunt man in his nightclothes hurrying toward his wife. When the man reached her, he appeared confused about his surroundings as if he had just awoken, and then he turned and saw Kenji holding his daughter. His arms went out instinctively, trembling, a few steps away. His head tilted to the side to see her better as he walked mechanically the last few steps it took to reach her, staring down at the girl and never looking up to see Kenji. With the same care and caution he had used when she was an infant, the child's father lifted her out of Kenji's arms and embraced her, pulling her close to his chest before turning and walking back down the street into the darkness as his wife continued to shriek and try to tear herself away from the grim reality of death.

•   •   •

And now, here was Lieutenant Kanta Fujii before him again at the very hospital where the girl had been denied treatment and died. The comment about his twelve-year-old girlfriend had frozen Fujii. Kenji was the only contemporary who would dare speak to him with such insolence, an officer with such a pedigree that even senior officers avoided any dissension with him. Kanta had a reputation for causing people trouble, but he usually steered clear of Kenji because of the Watanabe name. And in the present case, he had no desire to bring light to the fact that he and his men had been responsible for the death of a pubescent child.

The ironic truth, which Fujii would never admit, was that he admired Kenji for his independent thinking, integrity, and self-confidence, all of which he lacked. Yet he hated Kenji for the same reasons. His flunkies provided nothing more than prosthetic integrity, and everyone knew it.

"You know, Kenji, someday, *some day* you are going to regret the way you speak to me. I have better things to do today than waste my time with you, but your time is coming. When I outrank you, and my father says that I will soon, I'll make your life a living hell."

"Now boys," Kenji said addressing Kanta's group, "I'm sure there must be other old women and children you haven't molested yet." He then turned and entered the hospital.

Luckily, the nurse at the reception desk was not the same one on duty the night the girl had died. Kenji lied and said that he had an appointment with Dr. Uchibori.

He couldn't help thinking about the girl as he walked down the same corridor. He looked through the window of the door where the doctor had emerged, realizing how much his heart had hardened since becoming a soldier.

He continued around the next corner and up the steps to the third floor. He was surprised to see such a large contingent of doctors and nurses milling about because Yuta had told him that they had very few patients these days. There was a spacious waiting room, but he was the only patient there.

"Kenji," said Yuta in a voice reminiscent of a grade-school teacher directing a pupil to the principal's office. "Come with me."

"Am I in trouble?" said Kenji, standing and following.

"I hope this is just a social call," said Yuta as he led Kenji to his office, glancing at the sling on his arm.

"Of course it is. I'm fine. Just came for a cup of tea and a chat if you have the time."

Yuta opened the door to his office and ushered Kenji in, the apprehension he felt showing clearly on his face. He told a nurse to bring some tea and snacks before closing the door.

Yuta wore thick, black-rimmed spectacles, and his short hair was always precisely parted off center and combed just so around a chubby, clean-shaven face. He always wore his white smock whether in the hospital or in public. As with most of Kenji's friends, Yuta was good-natured and convivial, except on those rare occasions when Kenji brought his singular type of mischief into their lives.

The office furniture consisted of the doctor's chair behind a steel gray desk, two visitors' chairs, and a worn greenish sofa against a windowless wall. The sofa was the one object in the room not covered with books or research papers. Kenji cleared off a chair and sat down, surveying the room with a condescending smile.

"This place has all the ambiance and charm of a public toilet, Yuta. Is this the best you can do – aren't we winning this war?"

Yuta ignored the remark and began his reprimand with index finger pointed firmly on target. "The word going around is that you brought a Chinese girl into the emergency room last week. Have you lost your mind? The chief physician somehow found out you're a friend of mine and hasn't let up on me for days. What the *heck* were you thinking?"

Heck was strong language for Yuta.

The nurse opened the door with one hand, holding a tray with teapot, cups, and crackers in the other. Yuta's smile was back in a flash before the nurse could see and become suspicious of their meeting. She placed the tray on the desk and carefully poured, first for the guest and then for the doctor, and left without speaking or being spoken to.

As soon as the door was shut Yuta's previous demeanor resumed. "If you want to get yourself kicked out of the army, or worse," he whispered, "that's your business, but I'd prefer you leave me out of it."

"I didn't involve you in the least – never mentioned your name. I simply made the idiotic mistake of bringing a dying girl to a hospital. That's all. I suppose I should've taken her to a bakery. That would have been about as useful as the doctor on call. No, actually, at least a bakery would have had a pleasant smell and atmosphere."

"You brought a dying *Chinese girl*," he whispered with ferocity, spittle discharging from his red lips, "to a *Japanese* hospital for *Japanese* people, run by *Japanese* doctors and nurses, for the *freaking Imperial Japanese Army*."

Freaking was off the charts for Yuta.

"Calm down before you have a stroke," Kenji said matter-of-factly. "Unit 731 has completely changed you, and not for the better I regret to say."

Yuta's eyes bulged to the point of bursting, and his head swiveled around the room looking for eavesdroppers as if Kenji had spoken words that would cause both men to be decapitated. He stood with a frantic motion, almost overturning his chair in the process, and went and put his back against the door to deny entrance. After scanning the room again, he pointed his finger at Kenji, his mouth twisting but unable to form any words.

"Is there a problem?" asked Kenji.

"You know nothing. Never say that again," said Yuta.

"You mean about calming down or Unit 731?" said Kenji as though he were administering lashes.

"*That!* Stop saying *that*."

"We're alone, Yuta. What the hell are you so paranoid about?"

Yuta locked the door and returned to his seat. "What I, or better said, what *we* did there was experimental medical research in the cause of glorifying the Emperor and helping the people of Japan. And I spoke of those things to you as a friend, to help clear my conscience, not to have you fling about to embarrass and annoy. I told you never to speak of it."

"As I recall, Yuta, you swore me to secrecy prohibiting me from spreading the information to others, but you never said that you and I should not speak of it. And I think we need to discuss it because it appears it is still tormenting you quite severely judging from your actions." Kenji paused, drank some tea, sat back in his chair, and took a bite of rice cracker.

"I heard from someone yesterday," Kenji said, "that you guys impregnated young girls just so you could perform abortions and do research on the fetuses." Kenji knew he was being sadistic with his friend but felt justified in trying to shake Yuta free from the callousness the army had caused to thicken around his conscience. The truth was he valued Yuta's friendship immensely and knew that Yuta would never have done what he did if not forced by his superiors.

"What I did was research," said Yuta in a feeble voice.

"Yes, I can see that. I guess what Kanta did to that little Chinese girl last week was kind of a research project as well. I think I'll suggest erecting a shrine in his honor."

Yuta sat gazing down at his desk, unable to look Kenji in the eye any longer, his smile and good nature defeated.

"Speaking of Unit 731, do you ever remember if anyone ever escaped from there – like people breaking in and rescuing one of the patients – prisoners I should say?" asked Kenji.

"Why do you ask?" said Yuta, quickly looking up, and clearly hiding something.

"Just answer the question."

"I will not just answer the question. That was supposed to be top secret."

"So it *did* happen," said Kenji.

"I didn't say that. Quit putting words in my mouth."

"Was she your patient?"

"No. How did you know it was a woman?"

"You just confirmed it."

"No, I didn't," protested the doctor. "I haven't said anything. You keep putting words in my mouth."

"What did you do to her?"

"Nothing, I swear. I told you she wasn't my patient. I never met the woman. I just remember a huge deal being made of our security when it happened, and we were all sworn to secrecy."

"So you don't know what the others did to her?"

"No idea."

"That sounds like a pretty sick place, Yuta."

"Is this why you came today, to rub salt in the wound?"

"Oh hell, speaking of salt in the wound, I almost forgot," said Kenji putting down his tea and cracker. "I have a little situation here. I hurt my shoulder and need you to take care of it without letting anyone know, if you don't mind. Say, you're almost finished for the day, aren't you? How about grabbing some disinfectant, some gauze, and you might need a needle and some thread – whatever you use to stitch people up. It's actually already been stitched a little, but I'm not sure I trust the man who did it because he's not a doctor. And as I said, I need this to be our little secret, so don't let anyone see you gathering all this up."

Yuta lumbered up like a man being forced to the gallows, shaking his head in denial. "I'm not even going to ask. You're going to be the ruin of me; that much is clear. First, you bring a Chinese girl in here, then you...Do you hate me, Kenji?"

"Don't be silly, Yuta. You're my best friend."

"That's what I thought you'd say," said the doctor. "What do you do to people you don't like?" he muttered as he rummaged through his medical bag checking off supplies.

"That's my good friend, Yuta. I owe you one."

Yuta laughed at the comment. "Tell you what, Kenji – here's all I want from you. Just leave me out of all your little schemes until this darn war is over."

CHAPTER 20

Thursday, July 15th, 1943: Noon
Changbai Mountains - Chang

There was an island Chang could swim to as a young boy. After he lost his family, he would go there, climb the tallest tree, and watch the ships sailing out to sea. They could go anywhere in the world – there was freedom – and the little boy with no family imagined himself on board, destination unknown.

Chang was there now. On a high branch. Aware of people talking around him. Moving him.

He was still lying face down in the street when they had reached him after the carriage was out of sight. The doctor had them gently move him into the shade and remove his tunic. Chang's stomach wasn't bleeding badly, but the intestines were visible. The doctor went to work dressing the wound, and Gang gave instructions to the others.

"Still with us, old man?" said Gang.

Chang opened his eyes, and Gang could see immediately where his thoughts were.

"Don't worry, I sent someone to track them. It will be no problem to follow that carriage."

Chang tried to talk, but the doctor shut him down and told him if wished to live until tomorrow he'd keep his mouth shut. Gang walked away to make it easier to follow the doctor's advice.

Chang closed his eyes and went back to his meditation – the thoughts of the orphan boy, how it felt to have a large family one day and be alone the next. To have parents supply things that one took for granted, and then be forced into having to try to find them on your own. Shelter, food, and water;

difficult at times, but possible. But the touch and love of a mother? That was gone for good.

Crying did nothing, he learned that quickly, and hating those who had done it served no real purpose. He would have to move on from those memories somehow, but sometimes he just needed to escape.

And looking off into the Yellow Sea, on top of that tree on the island, would always be the place he went for peace and comfort, even now.

CHAPTER 21

Thursday, July 15th, 1943: Afternoon
Changbai Mountains – Ai

The carriage rolled toward its destination. An hour earlier, the children would have found it difficult to believe their spirits could sink any lower.

Yet they had.

Their most devoted and dedicated servant and friend had been shot.

For no reason.

Possibly their last hope, one of the few men they could rely on to help this nightmare end, was shot and left clutching his stomach under a hot sun. They had all watched him struggle as he fell to his knees and then hit the ground face first, a hollow feeling settling in their stomachs as the carriage turned, losing sight of him.

Ai knew Chang had done it for them – for her – and that made the feeling worse. The loss of the luxury and comfort, the servants, the fine meals served on the best china – none of that mattered any longer. But the deprivation of their safety and well-being, the absence of affection of family and friends, those losses were real.

They were priceless.

The carriage shook and bounced over the rough terrain which led around the mountain. Ai realized she had nothing now. She had no possessions, and her family was slowly slipping away to nothing, as were her friends. She and the others were now the property of the Imperial Japanese Army to be used and disposed of as they wished.

Lin, whose contempt had been funded by a sense of superiority and a belief that she would forever be surrounded by a fortress, now faced the reality that she was powerless. It tortured her soul to think of one of these men violating her, something so fervently against her will. If her ancestors, if the gods would give her the strength, she would rip every one of these barbarians limb from limb and let the wild animals and insects feast on their rotting flesh. And when she saw the limping soldier smile and mouth something at her, using his tongue in such an obscene manner, she knew exactly which one of the odious cretins she would start with if given the power.

Shou cried silently as he clung to Ai's waist. No one had spoken a word since watching Chang fall. Shou had not an ounce of the defending spirit which had been his hallmark remaining.

Fan was the only one who hadn't lost hope. She was free of emotion – the pragmatist. She stared at the new girl and tried to imagine why she had come with Chang, who she knew didn't have a daughter.

And then the new girl began to draw Chinese characters in the dirt on the planks of the carriage. All the children leaned over to see what she was writing.

Chang sent me to help you. Everything will be alright.

Then she erased it with her hand and smiled at them.

CHAPTER 22

Thursday, July 15th, 1943: Early Evening
Hsinking, Manchuria (Changchun, China) – Kenji

It seemed to Kenji that there was a perverse happiness amongst the Japanese soldiers, especially the higher-ranking officers, as they went smiling and laughing through the streets of the somber Manchurians. As he and Yuta traveled the four blocks toward Lu's, Yuta walking and Kenji on his horse, he noticed that even without uniforms, there was a distinct difference in mannerisms between the Japanese and the locals.

The sun was lowering over the mountains to the west of the city, and the air was hot and humid. Sweat under the bandage on Kenji's shoulder oozed into the wound, burning. A few unsuspecting Manchurian children, covered in dirt, risked playing in the streets, not yet having learned the consequences of impeding the progress of a Japanese soldier.

Even in this oppressive atmosphere, however, the aroma filling the streets every evening brightened Kenji's spirits. A new scent could be detected on every block in town. Their mouths watered as they picked up hints of basting ducks, roasting chickens, and boiling rice wafting through the streets on the evening breeze.

As the two of them moved along the main street away from the hospital, they passed in front of the Officer's Club. It had once been a hotel but now served as a restaurant downstairs and a house of prostitution above. The first floor was a five-star restaurant with the best Chinese chefs the Imperial Army could commandeer from the region. The second floor had numerous rooms that could be used in the standard hotel sense by visiting officers but generally served as a brothel. After officers had their fill of food and spirits on the first floor, they could climb the stairs and choose from a wide range of Chinese, Korean, Thai, or Filipino girls – *comfort women* – some of whom had volunteered for the position and others who had been coerced or even forced into service. Regardless of how the women had gotten there, they all now begged for the opportunity to please the officers as they ascended the staircase.

As Kenji and Yuta glanced over, they could see officers they knew through the many open windows but continued on toward Lu's, which was just a block further. Lu was actually a better cook than any in the Officer's Club but had avoided induction by astutely sabotaging his cooking whenever any top brass visited his establishment. It was not unusual to see dog carcasses hanging above his entrance, or to find assorted eyeballs floating in the soup of anyone he didn't trust.

For Kenji, however, Lu was at his best. Kenji's acts of kindness to the locals were widely known. He was one of the few Japanese officers in Manchuria respected and admired by the Chinese. Kenji had won their trust some months earlier one evening when he had come alone for dinner. Several enlisted men had been drinking heavily and began complaining about the food and service. They hadn't noticed Kenji sitting in the corner. One of them had overturned a table and spat over the counter where Lu was busy cooking. The inebriated soldier had been shouting and speaking in such a base manner that even Kenji couldn't understand, much less the poor Chinese cook.

The best Kenji could decipher from the belligerent was that he was calling Lu a dog and threatening to shoot him. Throughout the tirade, Lu had never looked up from his pots and pans and showed no emotion. When all of the soldiers stood to leave, Lu's wife handed the drunk soldier a piece of paper on which she had written the cost of their meals and drinks. The soldier crushed it in his hand, put it in his mouth and chewed it for a moment, took a large swig of beer, and then spat the concoction into her face, drawing a roar from his friends. Again, Lu continued with his work without the slightest hint of awareness. The group remained in a fit of laughter for a full minute, slapping the table and walls and pointing at the old woman whose face and hair dripped with spew until Kenji got up, walked over, and stood in front of the group. The laughter, which had been hysterical, subsided with each deliberate step of Kenji's boots across the floor until there was total silence.

"Is this how you've been taught to treat our hosts, private?"

"They fed us dog meat, sir," said the soldier with instant sobriety.

Kenji looked at Mrs. Lu, who had yet to move, still dripping beer and saliva from her face. "Dog?" he asked in Chinese, pointing at the table. She shook her head and said it was beef.

"There you have it, men. Now, you weren't planning on leaving without paying your tab, were you? We wouldn't want to give Japan a bad name."

The soldiers talked among themselves as if they thought one of them had already paid the bill and began to gather funds and affably place them on the counter in front of Mrs. Lu with compliments to the cook. Kenji returned to his table and continued with his *sake* and meal, pretending to ignore their conversation.

Kenji and Lu had never spoken about that evening, neither being fluent in the other's language, but there had been an unspoken understanding between the two from that day forward. Lu knew of at least one decent person in the Imperial Army who he could trust, if only a little, and Kenji knew where to go for the best Peking duck in all Manchuria. Lu's wife also never said a word to Kenji, but no mother ever doted on her son any more than she did over Kenji after that day.

When Yuta and Kenji entered Lu's, Mrs. Lu shooed away two Chinese men who were sitting at the corner table which she had decided was a place of honor for Kenji whenever he visited. She scurried into the kitchen and returned with a bottle of fine *sake* that some brave Manchurian had purloined from a Japanese general, and proudly poured for them, searching their faces to see if they recognized what fine spirits she served for them.

"What's on the menu tonight?" asked Yuta in Japanese.

"Yes, we've been saving it for Kenji," Mrs. Lu replied in Chinese. "Do you like it?"

"I'll have ramen," said Yuta.

Kenji smiled at Mrs. Lu and she at him.

The interior of Lu's place would never win any five-star restaurant awards. It resembled a dilapidated bar from the scene of a gunfight in the old west. Neither the building nor any piece of furniture in it looked a day younger than Lu himself. There were sizeable cracks, and in some spots large holes, in the interior walls, many no doubt from similar incidents with drunken patrons.

Lu's wife left the bottle on the table and returned to the kitchen. After finishing off the first cup, Kenji, being slightly younger than Yuta, was obliged to pick up the bottle and pour first for his friend, and Yuta completed the protocol by returning the favor.

"*Kanpai,*" they said in unison, touching their glasses.

They both downed the second measure, and the wine began to take effect – warming their stomachs, putting them both at ease, and signifying that the workday had officially ended – and the anesthetizing process had begun.

"How is your mother?" asked Yuta.

"Actually, she often asks about you, Yuta. She worries that you won't adapt to military life."

"Tell her I'm handling it better than you. At least I know which side I'm on," Yuta replied, an explicit reference to Kenji's assistance to the Chinese girl.

"Take it easy, Yuta."

"How about your father, is he in Tokyo?"

"Couldn't say," said Kenji. "He's not much of a writer. Wherever the battle is most ferocious, I'm sure."

The two repeated the pouring ritual again and drank at a more leisurely pace. For Yuta, who drank infrequently, the effects of the *sake* came on rapidly. He began to chuckle at things which weren't the least bit funny, and as he often did when he drank, he laughed silently with his shoulders, moving them up and down with his laugh held in his mouth. This had always amused Kenji; he enjoyed it the way others enjoy taping a cat's feet and watching them run on a slick surface.

Mr. Lu brought out a duck and some sweet sauce personally and started serving – first the skin – to both Kenji and his friend. Kenji began eating right away and had a good laugh when he saw Yuta examining his dinner.

"How's the ramen?" Kenji joked as he picked up another piece of skin and dipped it in the sauce. Yuta continued watching the Manchurian with a bemused look.

"Have you still not picked up on the fact that they understand absolutely nothing you say?" said Kenji. "Just eat it – I promise you'll love it."

Lu finished slicing the bird and left them.

"So, Kenji, I'm sure I'll regret asking, but how did you manage to injure your shoulder?"

"Long story," said Kenji, mimicking Chang's voice and accent. "Less you know, better for you."

"What?" Yuta asked. "Why are you talking like that?"

"Sorry, that was just a joke."

"So you're not injured?"

"Oh no. I'm injured. The funny talk was a joke. My shoulder...well, I was...you are going to keep this to yourself, aren't you?"

Yuta took a large gulp of wine and nodded.

"I was shot by Chinese rebels."

Yuta coughed up some of his drink. "Okay. I forget. Life's a joke for Kenji."

"Seriously," Kenji said.

"Quit joking around."

"Okay. I fell off my horse and hit a sharp rock."

"That's it? That's your big secret?"

"Well there's more, but you wouldn't believe it."

"I'll need to take care of that soon. You don't want it to get infected."

"So I've heard. I'm hoping you can do that right after we eat, so go easy on that *sake*."

As they ate, Kenji noticed a man come through the back door into the kitchen. The man spoke in hushed tones and appeared to be imploring Lu to take some unknown action. More than once he noticed Lu turning and looking directly at him. Lu eventually nodded his head toward their table, and the man walked over and stood before them with his hat in his hand, addressing him in Japanese.

"I'm sorry to bother you, but are you Kenji-san?"

"Yes," said Kenji with piqued curiosity, wondering who this man might be and how he had come to find him here. Kenji was quite sure he had never seen the man before.

"A mutual friend of ours needs to see you – now. There is no time to waste."

"Who?" said Kenji.

The man cast a troubled look toward Yuta and then turned back to Kenji. "He said to tell you he was born in Port Arthur."

Kenji's eyes narrowed on the curious visitor. The clue was obvious, but how could this person have found him here, and what was his connection to Chang? Yuta's eyes darted back and forth between the mysterious peasant and Kenji. Lu shuffled about in the kitchen, moving pots and speaking quietly to his wife who had begun to wash dishes, both nervously trying to act as if they weren't aware that something was amiss.

"I guess you won't be operating tonight after all," said Kenji as he stood.

"Should I come with you?" inquired Yuta.

"Kenji-san alone, if you please," said the man. Kenji nodded and followed him out through the kitchen but stopped at the door and called back to Yuta.

"Thanks for dinner, Yuta. I'll come see you as soon as I get back."

"You're welcome. Let me know if you need anything," Yuta said as he watched his friend walk out. He picked up the bottle of *sake*, poured and drank, and shook his head when he realized he had been left with the tab. His shoulders began to move up and down.

CHAPTER 23

Thursday, July 15th, 1943: Evening
Outskirts of Changchun – Ai

The leader's horse broke into a canter, and Ai looked up to see him ride to a car where a man stood waiting. When the carriage pulled alongside, she could see he was an officer of the Imperial Japanese Army. Smoking a cigarette, he walked over and began his survey of them as if he were examining sides of beef, smiling smugly.

As he walked and stared, Ju tried to imagine what would be most appealing to the man. If he was going to do anything sinister, she wanted it to be done to her instead of the others. She tried to catch his attention, deciding to go for the weak and helpless damsel in distress.

"I hope I did the right thing sending a messenger ahead to have you meet us here," said the leader.

"Oh yes, Sergeant, you did the right thing. Outstanding work."

"I thought you might like to see them as soon as possible, sir," he said obsequiously.

"And you were right."

The officer walked around past Ju and focused on Lin. She still had her hands bound behind her back, and she glared hatefully at him. He reached up and tried to touch her hair, but she jerked away and spoke harshly at him.

"Better watch that little minx, sir, she's a feisty one," said the sergeant.

"Is she now?" the officer asked with satisfaction. "I like girls with a little spunk."

Ju regretted her damsel-in-distress decision, but it was too late to change mid-stream.

"And do any of you lovely young ladies speak any Japanese?" said the officer in a silky voice, as if he were an uncle picking up relatives at a train station.

"They don't speak a word, sir. We've tried all the way over the mountain – they don't understand a thing," said the sergeant.

Ju saw an opportunity to get herself noticed. "Help, please," she said in Japanese, trying to butcher the pronunciation as much as possible.

"Why look there, Sergeant. She speaks the language beautifully. My dear, please let your friends know that we mean you no harm. We will take good care of you. You have my word as a gentleman."

Ju told him with her eyes and a shaking head that she didn't understand.

"I don't think they know each other, sir. We picked her up separate from the others. I'm telling you, sir, I don't think she understands a thing you're saying. But they don't need to talk for what you got planned," he said, poking his elbow at the officer. A condescending stare from the superior made it clear to the sergeant that he had crossed a line.

"Sorry, sir. Where would you like me to take them, sir?"

"You've done enough, Sergeant. I think I can handle it from here. Just put them in the back of my car."

"Yes sir." The sergeant barked out the orders, and the men pulled them out of the carriage and loaded them into the waiting vehicle.

From his vantage point, Gang's spy watched and knew this transfer was not good. He would not be able to follow them any longer, the trail would go cold, and his bosses would not be happy. But there was nothing to be done.

The officer handed a few bills to the sergeant and got in the front seat beside his driver. As they began to pull away, the officer held out his hand and told the driver to stop. He stepped out again and spoke to the sergeant.

"I trust that the merchandise has not been damaged."

"Sir?" said the sergeant with a perplexed expression.

"Idiot," he said under his breath. "No one has touched these girls I presume."

"You have my word on that, sir."

The officer sat back down, and the car took off. He turned to the back seat and smiled brightly, just a friendly officer giving them a lift. There was a definite preference in his attention toward Lin, who continued to scowl at him.

Ai stared out the window and held Shou and Fan tightly. Ju tried once again to see if she could get to the forefront of this officer's attention.

"Ju," she said, pointing to herself.

The officer was in a trance, staring. It took a moment to register. He looked away from Lin and turned to Ju. "Excuse me?"

"Me. Ju," she said, using the worst Japanese she could manage.

"Ah, I see. Nice to meet you, Ju. My name is Kanta. Lieutenant Kanta Fujii at your service."

CHAPTER 24

Thursday, July 15th, 1943: Evening
Hsinking, Manchuria (Changchun, China) – Kenji

The man had a horse waiting behind the restaurant and brought Kenji's around for him. Within minutes, they were out of town and entering a forest. Night had fallen, and a stiff breeze blew among the high branches as the two rode along the trail faster than Kenji thought prudent. Foreboding dark clouds rolled in, hinting of a storm. Thunder rumbled in the distance, and Kenji knew heavy rain was on the way soon. When they reached the foot of a hill, the path turned left and the peasant went right without breaking stride.

"Be careful of your head," he shouted as he rode beneath low-hanging branches. The rain began softly, tapping the leaves, and then came the deluge. Lightning ripped through the sky as a simultaneous crash of thunder shook the earth. The lightning lit their way occasionally, but when it vanished, the forest turned black.

"Over there," yelled the peasant as he drew in the reigns and brought his horse to a stop.

Kenji saw a light at the entrance to a cave in the side of a hill. He dismounted and ran inside shaking off the rain. He was met by Gang, who characteristically said nothing but pointed him in the direction he would have him go, holding a lamp to light their way. They entered a long corridor and Kenji saw a room lit with lanterns and armed guards who stood aside to let them pass. He went in behind Gang and saw Chang sitting on the floor with his back against the wall, a bandage around his midsection soaked in blood.

"What happened?" asked Kenji, kneeling down beside him.

"Don't worry about Chang, but I do need to speak with you about something a bit more urgent." Kenji could see that his speech and breathing were labored.

"Kenji," said Chang, "I have favor to ask." Kenji thought of how strong this man had been just this morning. "It's about children. Japanese soldiers find them – take them to Changchun."

"If that's true," said Kenji, "there's nothing I can do."

"I have strong feeling, a sixth sense perhaps, which I have found most reliable in this short life. I think – I hope that Kenji understand right from wrong – even in war."

"There are some," Chang paused for a moment to catch his breath, "secrets, which I was not at liberty to tell you, and, unfortunately, do not have time to explain now. Take Chang's word that it is very important those children should not be harmed. I hope you will help me because you know it is right thing to do."

Chang held his hand out, and Gang handed him a necklace. Chang held it out proudly for Kenji to see.

"This jade necklace was Empress Dowager Cixi's favorite. It is priceless. It was taken from Forbidden City."

"I told you before, Chang, I have only one loyalty. And it's not for sale," said Kenji.

"This not a bribe, Kenji. There is another reason I show you this. Not for money – I know Kenji is loyal to Japan."

"Then what's it for?" asked Kenji.

"I ask you to return now, quickly, and talk with someone you know better than Chang. We have many friends who are aware of this situation and understand importance of my request to you."

Kenji did not reply.

"Just do it because you know it's right thing to do."

"I keep telling you – I have no idea what you're asking me, Chang. What do you want from me?"

"The children you saw yesterday. Japanese soldiers capture them today. You're the only one that can help them. I can't do anything. We don't have manpower. Too many Japanese soldiers – not enough of us."

"Where are they?"

"That's what I need Kenji to find out."

"How do you know they're here?"

"Children were taken in mountains by Japanese soldiers, put in carriage. We followed but could not attack. That's when I was shot. One of our men followed and saw them travel all the way to Changchun, put in car with

Japanese officer. That's the last we know. All Manchuria looking for children now. Fortunately, I don't think Japanese know who they are yet."

"And who are they?"

"Their importance," said Chang, "to Chinese cannot be...well, Kenji cannot understand now, but soon will."

"Chang, you seem like a good man. In other circumstances, I'm sure we could be friends. But I have no intention of going along with this secret mumbo-jumbo regardless of the fact that you saved my life. Either you give me some real answers, or you can find someone else."

"There is no one else I tell you. You are it. It is time for answers, but best you hear them from someone you know better. Go, now. Gang will lead you back to Lu's. Wei will be waiting for you and give answers to Kenji's questions, but please hurry. I promise you, even Kenji's father would approve of what I'm asking you."

"Wei?" said Kenji. "My father?"

"Long story – little time."

"That's the second time you've mentioned my father. If you know him, I want to know how."

"Sorry to tell truth, Kenji, but I don't like your father."

"Well neither do most people who've met him, but what the hell does that have to do with this conversation?"

"Wei has answers. I will pray that the spirit of my ancestors guide Kenji." With this, the Manchurian closed his eyes, leaned back against the wall, and gave his final instructions to the others.

The doctor who had been looking after Chang took Kenji's arm out of the sling and had him remove his shirt and undershirt. The bandage came off easily, and he congratulated Chang on doing an excellent job of cleaning and stitching the wound. He applied an ointment that, in addition to stinking terribly, burned like fire. Kenji put his clothes back on but decided to forego the sling.

Gang motioned for Kenji to follow and led him back to the entrance. The pair emerged from the cave to the winds and rain of the thunderstorm. Kenji ran to his horse, found a poncho in the saddlebag, and mounted up. The rain fell in torrents, angling into their faces as they maneuvered their horses through the forest. In the darkness of the wood, with no moonlight to help guide the way, Kenji was forced to rely on the instincts of the animal, and it did a remarkable job. They exited the forest and made directly for Lu's. As he rode, Kenji tried to imagine what connection his father could possibly have with this group.

When they reached Lu's, the wife held the back door open for them, handed them towels, and took their ponchos. Wei was also waiting for them at the door and guided them to a table where Mr. Lu was already seated. Gang spoke softly to Wei, giving him the news of Chang's situation and instructions for Kenji.

"It appears China may lose one of its proudest warriors tonight," said Wei, "and our ancestors will gain a great martyr."

"Chang said you would give me answers," Kenji said.

"I will. And I must ask you to take quick and decisive action."

"I doubt it, but I suppose that depends on what you have to say."

Wei looked at Gang as if seeking permission. The elder nodded.

"We have spoken in this room many times about the histories of our countries. I have not told you any direct lies, but I have not been completely honest either. The truth is that I have withheld a great deal of information from you for obvious reasons which you will soon understand."

"The last time you were here, you asked me about Emperor Pu Yi, and I told you some things about him – that he was the last of the Qing emperors, the Manchurian Dynasty that had been in power for over two hundred and fifty years until the revolution in 1911. What I chose not to tell you *until the appropriate time* is that Chang, Gang, and I were members of his Imperial Court, and remain loyal to the cause of reestablishing the throne to His Imperial Majesty as soon as practicable."

"That's very interesting, Wei, but hardly earth-shattering news that..."

Wei closed his eyes and held up his hand in an imperious manner and continued. "Do not interrupt me, Lieutenant Watanabe, as it will delay your answers, and we have no time for delays."

The arrogance was annoying, but Kenji decided to let it go. Mrs. Lu brought in a tray with cups of hot tea for Kenji and Gang.

"At that time, you glibly commented on Emperor Pu Yi's sexuality," continued Wei, "but what I am about to tell you will put those rumors to rest. We have very few Japanese who we can trust. In fact, we can't trust many Chinese with this either. Only a handful of people know what I am about to tell you."

"I believe Chang has already mentioned something about this to you, but we have had contact with your father in the past. And I'm sure you know of

Kawashima Yoshiko."

Everyone in Japan was aware of the celebrity Kawashima Yoshiko. Born into the royal Aisin Gioro clan of the Qing Dynasty, she was given to a Japanese man who had been loyal to her father in China after the fall of the Qing in 1912. The adoptive father had taken her back to Japan and raised her to return to her homeland someday to help reestablish the reign of the Qing. Somewhere along the way, she had adopted a male persona and was fond of being photographed as a man, but had maintained enough femininity to carry on several affairs with high-ranking Japanese officers in Shanghai, Manchuria, and elsewhere. The *Chinese Joan of Arc* was frequently in the news in Japan.

"She is Emperor Pu Yi's relative," said Wei, "a Manchurian Princess, who grew up in Japan – in Nagano, to be more specific. She has been used by the Japanese to further their goals and purposes here and is good friends – perhaps more than just friends – with your father."

"Yes," said Kenji, "of course I know of her. Never met the woman and wouldn't be the least bit surprised to learn that my father slept with her, but can we get to the *Kenji* Watanabe part of your story."

Wei took a deep breath, clearly annoyed by Kenji's interruptions. "You, Kenji, have done many things to earn the gratitude and respect of the Chinese people since arriving last year. Your actions, in addition to my private conversations with you, have given cause to many of us to put some faith in the Japanese rhetoric that your country does actually have some intention of helping us. But believe me, with all the lies, atrocities, and evil we have witnessed at the hands of the Japanese, it is a paper-thin trust. So, when we began to ask ourselves if you were a man we could truly trust, we began to look into your background and found the connection to your father. Although he does not, in our opinion, have the same level of integrity we see in you, he nonetheless has been willing to assist us where he could. He is a frequent visitor to this region, or at least he was before you arrived."

"Let me get this straight," said Kenji, clearly not buying the story. "You're trying to say my father is a spy?"

"No. There is a difference between high-level officials who work back channels, and spies. The interactions he has had with us, I'm sure they were all approved at the highest levels by your government."

"But you've been spying on me all this time?" said Kenji. "Acting like we were friends."

"That is not the word I would choose. Spying has such a negative – what is the word?"

"Connotation."

"Yes. That's it. But I suppose I am a spy – if that's what you would like to call me. I want the best for my country. We were simply being cautious before placing our trust in your hands. However, circumstances have now forced us into a decision."

"And what are those circumstances?"

"First of all, I must tell you it was not exactly an accident that you met Chang in the mountains. He has wanted to meet you for some time now. So when I learned you were going on a reconnaissance mission, I decided to arrange for the two of you to meet."

"You set that up? You almost had me killed? And now you want to ask me a favor?" he said, his voice rising with each question as the pieces began to fall in place.

"I only told Chang you *might* be heading into the Changbai, which was where he had been hiding the children. I had nothing at all to do with the rebel attack. That was a complete surprise to both of us and was not in the plan at all. We would never do anything to endanger the life of one of the few Japanese officers we think we can trust."

"This is unbelievable. And you honestly think I'm going to help you?"

"I will now complete my story and leave that to you. We have nothing else to lose now, so I have to tell you and just hope for the best. The family you saw, the girls and the boy at the lake, do you remember?"

"Are we getting to the point, Wei?"

"Yes. We are to the point. Those children are the son and daughters of Emperor Pu Yi. The boy is the heir to the throne, if we are ever able to reestablish the Qing Dynasty."

Kenji was silent as the wheels turned; his thoughts went from considerations of believability to how this could possibly be his concern.

"We, Chang and I, who are the protectors of these children, Sons and Daughters of Heaven in their own right, have no one we can trust. The Chinese are deeply divided between Chiang Kai-shek and his fighters, the communists who are gaining strength day by day, too many warlords to number, foreign armies from around the globe, and, of course, the Japanese. I would have told you, but it was too much of a risk. We have no crystal ball to tell us who will be victorious in this war. We just have to keep the children safe until it is time for the Qing to reclaim what is rightfully theirs."

"How am I supposed to believe any of this? Why would the Emperor's children need to go hiding in the mountains?"

"Think about it for a moment. If the Japanese lose this war, something you may not be willing to consider but something we must, Pu Yi and his family will either be killed, or tried as traitors and then killed or jailed, depending on who captures them. If no one knew of the children, they could be spared. Our hope has always been that Japan will win and need the Emperor to keep order in the land, similar to what he is doing for you now. But he has never really trusted the Japanese government either. He wanted to keep the children a secret until the right time. Unfortunately, we no longer have the luxury of waiting to see who wins. We have to act now, but we don't have anywhere near enough manpower to attack the men who kidnapped the children and don't wish to begin a war with you. We need help, and you are our only real option."

"But how could it be possible for the Emperor to have children without us knowing? It's..."

"It's quite simple. If I can explain to your satisfaction, will you at least help us find the children?"

"If they are who you say they are," said Kenji, "I think even the Emperor of Japan himself would approve."

"That's what I'm trying to tell you. It is not treasonous for you to help us," said Wei.

"So, convince me," Kenji responded.

"First, the necklace Chang showed you tonight belongs to His Majesty. He said to offer it to you to get you to help us, but Chang and I knew you would consider it a corrupt gesture. The Emperor would do anything for his children."

"I'm not an expert on jewelry, Wei. I have no idea where it came from or its value. You'll have to do better than that."

"Also, you should know that I have been a personal attendant of His Majesty since I was very young. I helped take care of him as a child in the Forbidden City."

"You were in the Forbidden City," said Kenji with derision.

"Yes, that's right."

"Well right there – that's already a lie, because men weren't allowed in the..." And then it hit him. The lack of facial hair, the feminine voice.

"You mean, you don't have any…"

"Oh, I have them." Wei said. "But mine are preserved in a jar to be buried with me when I die – to make me whole again."

Kenji was dumbfounded.

"Do you doubt me?" asked Wei.

Kenji was too shocked to speak at the moment and sat staring.

Wei stood and began lifting his gown. Gang and Lu, seeing what he was about to do, looked down at the floor out of reverence and respect for the man and his sacrifice. Wei lowered his undergarment.

Kenji was speechless. They were telling the truth.

Wei put his clothing in order and sat back down. "So, you see, it's not a lie, Kenji. I was one of His Majesty's eunuchs in the Forbidden City. I was with him when he was forced out in 1924. I was with him in the Japanese Concession in Tianjin until he agreed to come here to be the Emperor of Manchukuo. I was there when Kawashima Yoshiko snuck his wife out in the middle of the night to join him here in Changchun. I am able to see him anytime I wish."

"But the children," said Kenji, still in a fog. "How could we not know? His wife has never had a child."

"That is right. Empress Wanrong is addicted to opium and is more likely to spit on His Majesty than to have relations with him. She has lost her mind."

"Then how?"

"Gang is a cousin of His Majesty. When we began many years ago to help the Son of Heaven in his desire to have an heir, we knew the Japanese would be watching closely. They encouraged him to have a son, but they made it clear the boy would be taken to Japan to be raised, just like they took His Majesty's brother and forced him to marry a Japanese girl."

"Gang's daughter was chosen and agreed to by all concerned – all *Chinese* concerned I should say. She was able to visit, as she was family, and then allowed to leave and return to Changchun where she lived with Gang. Her visits to His Majesty were carefully timed – she went when she was ovulating."

"And they…and no one knew?"

"That's right," said Wei. "Emperor Pu Yi is very much a king – not a queen."

CHAPTER 25

Thursday, July 15*th*, 1943: Evening
Hsinking, Manchuria (Changchun, China) – Kanta Fujii

The levels of detestation humans are capable of achieving are well-known. Examples of ignominious, repugnant treatment by barbarous characters against their fellow man dates back to the beginning of recorded time. The reasons for such behavior are countless, but one such reason is hatred, and of all the roots of hatred, perhaps the one core cause that produces the most toxic results is jealousy. And Kanta Fujii had suffered not only from his own covetousness of Kenji Watanabe, but he had also had to endure a lifetime of bitter vitriol from the mouth of his father. *You had damn well better beat that damn Watanabe boy. You will not show your face in public if that son-of-bitch beats you in as much as a game of cards.* It was second-generation malignity.

And he always felt as though he was losing.

Just like Kanta, his father, Lieutenant General Shunko Fujii had always lost to the great General Tatsurou Watanabe. Always one step behind in moving up the ranks. Always a day late with the ideas that the superiors loved. Always in the shadows when *that damn Watanabe* was in the spotlight.

Kanta had a strange love for his father. He had hoped that his father would finally get his revenge, that he would be promoted over his rival, and that they could look down on the Watanabe family the way the Watanabes had looked down on them. But it had never happened, and the bitter, old soldier was nearing the end of his career, still one step behind. His old man had pinned his hopes on him, and he was letting him down.

It was in his head daily, hourly, the obsession to be better than Kenji Watanabe. The monomania consumed his life. Murder had never been outside the range of possibilities if he could get away with it. No price was too high to reach the goal of besting *those damn Watanabes*.

Yet those arrogant bastards still walked with their heads higher than the rest, as if there was no question of their superiority. They pitied the lowly wannabes. They never even considered the Fujiis to be rivals. They had never spent a single minute in his hell, trying to come up with schemes to get ahead. They viewed themselves as so superior that there was no competition.

But in his hand was something that could change all that. The confluence of events had finally, *finally*, come together to bring dishonor to the enemy.

Karma.

It was within reach. Everything he needed to know was right here – in the letter.

•　　　•　　　•

Any officer could get into the Officer's Club. There was no great standing in that.

Getting into The Ranch, however, that was something to brag about. It was so lofty that most soldiers didn't even know of its existence. Only a small brotherhood of officers knew of it, and only the most prestigious were allowed to enter. It was an exclusive, members-only type affair.

Up until now, Kanta had never received an invitation to join the group. Today, however, that had all changed. His father had put in the calls, and Kanta had supplied some of the entertainment for the incoming VIPs. Tonight, he was on the list of invited guests. And he had arranged for his good friend to be on the list as well.

Now, he just needed to find Kenji and get him there.

CHAPTER 26

Thursday, July 15th, 1943: Night
Hsinking, Manchuria (Changchun, China) – Kenji

There was the sound of a car sliding to a stop and then footsteps running into the restaurant. A man hustled through the door and went to the table where the men sat.

"What is it?" said Wei in Chinese.

The man turned to look at Kenji, the angst he felt in the presence of a Japanese soldier evident on his face.

"It's okay, you can talk," said Wei.

"But it's about...that matter."

"Out with it. Hurry," he said.

"They were seen north of town traveling in the officer's car this evening, about 7:30. They stopped at a house to use the facilities, and Ju had a chance to speak to the lady of the house."

"And?"

"I have the officer's name."

"Anything else? Any idea where they went after that?"

"No sir. We've got people asking everywhere, but nothing more for now."

"Very well. Whisper the name in my ear and get back to work."

The man did as he was told and left.

"Can we count on your assistance, Kenji?" Wei asked, reverting back to Japanese.

"I suppose I can try to help you locate them. There shouldn't be any harm in that."

"Excellent. I have the officer's name. I need you to find him and see if you can get any useful information."

"Who is it?"

"All we know at this time is that his name is Lieutenant Kanta Fujii and that he is an officer in your army. Do you know of the man?"

Kenji shook his head, imagining his despised fellow officer being at the center of this. But, of course, it was not surprising. It all made sense.

"You don't know him, then?" said Wei, not knowing how to interpret his reaction.

"Uh, no. Yes, I know Lieutenant Fujii quite well."

"But you were shaking your head."

"I was shaking my head because...Don't worry about that. I definitely know him."

"Can you find him?"

"He usually eats dinner at the Officer's Club and then drinks with his friends."

"Good. How best to proceed?" Wei asked. "We need to move as quickly as possible. As you are in pain, shall we have someone transport you?"

"Getting to the club is no problem. Do you think the children are there?"

"No. We have many people working at the Officer's Club. We would have heard by now if they are inside the city."

"Then we should have a car just in case," said Kenji.

"Gang," Wei said switching back to Chinese, "take him in the auto. I'll wait here to coordinate the search effort. Once they're located, we will formulate a plan to extricate them." Wei then translated the same information for Kenji in Japanese.

"One more thing, Kenji. The youngest sister was not with them. We fear that she succumbed to illness. So that leaves the boy and three sisters. However, Chang successfully had another young lady added to the group. She is a spy. If you should encounter her, understand she works for us and is very good at what she does."

Shortly thereafter, Kenji found himself seated beside Gang in a car, both men wearing wet rain ponchos with hoods over their heads. He thought Gang looked rather comical in the driver's seat. It was surreal watching a man he had only seen riding a horse operate a motor vehicle. The car stalled several times as he tried to get moving, and it was apparent that Gang's skills on a horse had not translated to aptitude behind the wheel of an automobile.

"You know, if you push that little thing down there," said Kenji pointing at the clutch, "the car won't stall." Gang ignored him.

They made it to the Officer's Club and Kenji motioned for Gang to pull over. Gang hit the brakes, rather too abruptly, which aggravated Kenji's shoulder pain. After he got out, he gestured for Gang to wait.

As he walked toward the entrance, he heard a familiar voice. Kanta strolled out of the Officer's Club, bellowing as usual.

"Kenji! Just the man I've been looking for. Where have you been hiding? I have a surprise for you my friend! You will never guess," he said as he waved his hand through the air to emphasize never, "who is here."

"You've stumped me. Who could it be?"

"Come on in and have a drink, old buddy. I swear, sometimes I get the impression you don't even like me," said Kanta, already beginning to slur his words. "We never get together anymore." Kenji resisted the urge to correct *anymore*.

The rain was still falling, so they entered the club, both dripping rain all over the floor. The Chinese headwaiter smiled, showing none of the disgust he felt for them, and had a servant take Kenji's poncho and bring them dry towels.

Kanta led Kenji to his table where two of his flunkies, who were quite well along in drink, stood to receive them. They were all seated and Kanta, who was never at a loss for words, began his boisterous assault on the ears. The contributions of his entourage were ready-canned laughter and encouragement for anything and everything Kanta was able to slur out.

"Two more bottles here," yelled Kanta to the headwaiter. "To the great Lieutenant Kenji Watanabe," he said while raising an almost-empty bottle of *sake* and pouring unsteadily for everyone. After he had poured, some in glasses and some lost to gravity on the table, he raised his glass high.

"*Kanpai*, to our good friend Kenji!" he toasted.

"*Kanpai*," joined the puppets. Kenji tried to hide his contempt. He thought of how he might be able to turn the subject to the children before they were too drunk to be of any assistance.

"What's the matter, Kenji? Oh, I get it. You can't drink to yourself. That would be boasting, wouldn't it? You're too good for that. Let's drink to the Watanabe family then, shall we? To the great and noble Watanabe name – *Kanpai!*" he shouted raising his glass. The two nimrods had begun to follow the direction of the cajoling and hit the *Kanpai* in stride with their leader. Again, they all drank while Kenji sat staring.

Feigning surprise, Kanta stopped again with a quizzical expression and turned from Kenji to his minions and back to Kenji again. "Why, it's alright to drink to your family, isn't it?"

"You said you had someone I might want to see," said Kenji.

"He is *so* humble that he will not even drink to his own fucking family," he said to his companions, clearly putting on a show.

What Kenji didn't understand, however, was that Kanta's drunkenness was part of an act. He was as sober as Kenji. He was toasting so Kenji would drink.

The waiter came and placed a bottle of *sake* on the table and turned to leave. Kanta slammed his fist down and yelled, "I ordered two you miserable cockroach." The waiter ran for the kitchen, but that didn't slow Kanta's tirade. "No wonder it's so damn easy to beat these fucking Chinks, they can't follow instructions." He had risen to his feet as he cursed and swayed unsteadily while still holding the bottle in the air.

"This is terribly entertaining, Kanta, but I do have business to attend to tonight. Is there someone you want me to meet here, or not?"

"No, no, no, Kenji. When I said here," he pointed to the floor, "I didn't mean here at the club. I meant here in the area, ole buddy. I know you're married to a beautiful woman," Kanta said as he sat down, looking all around as if he were checking for spies, "but if I were to tell you that my men had hit the jackpot today, would you be interested?" The waiter had come back into the room but froze when he heard the comment.

"What kind of jackpot?" asked Kenji.

Another glance around the room before he leaned closer to Kenji. Then, in a whisper, he said, "Some young ladies, and I do not mean whores."

"Young ladies? What are you talking about?" The waiter moved closer in hopes of discovering the location so he could relay it to his superiors. "Kenji, I'm sure whatever business you have can wait until tomorrow," Kanta said with a wink.

An idea came to mind – a diversion would work to help speed him along to finding out where they were and get rid of the sidekicks at the same time.

"How could I have been so rude to you, Kanta?" said Kenji. "You have invited me to join this fine group, brought me the best of Japanese *sake*, toasted me and my family, and I have shown nothing but ingratitude." He reached down and picked up his glass and raised it high. "To the Fujii family – *Kanpai*!" Kenji turned up his glass and drank, and the sycophants, who stood on instinct at the mention of their master's name, shouted "*Kanpai*!" and downed their drinks. Kenji seized the opportunity and called out for more *sake* as he filled all the glasses, splashing just a drop into his own. "To our motherland – Japan – the country of our birth." With this patriotic oath, the small group stood at attention again. After he believed he had made enough of a scene to get their minds occupied, Kenji had everyone sit back down so he could direct the conversation where he needed it to go.

Thinking that the trio was not far from complete incapacitation, Kenji ordered beer and began an onslaught of toasting in which Kanta and his two friends were all too eager to join. First, he got the family names of the flunkies and toasted to their health; then to the Imperial Japanese Army; then to the company commander; then to their involuntary host China, all of which would soon be part of the Japanese Empire.

Then more beer, please.

He toasted to each of their mothers; then to the waiter's mother; then to women and girls in general; then to fat women, like the one who had just arrived to deliver beer with her husband. This last toast had brought the room's occupants, even some of the Chinese waiters and staff, to their knees. Kanta was lying on the table with tears in his eyes. One of the nimrods fell over backward in his chair and smashed into the floor, which caused the uproar to gain even more momentum. The other slid off his chair and rolled about on the floor, howling and pointing. Even the butt of the joke, who hadn't heard the toast in her honor and had no idea that everyone was laughing at her expense, got caught in the mood and began to laugh. Everyone had started to calm down after a few minutes, but when they noticed the fat woman laughing, which caused her girth to jiggle, a new wave of hysteria swept through the room, and every time someone came up for air, one more look at the fat woman was all that was needed to fuel another burst. After several minutes of this, the lady and her husband left, and the room returned to normal with everyone clutching their sides and trying to stand upright.

The quarry was now set.

Kenji leaned over to Kanta and said, "Now how about we look in on those girls you were talking about?"

"Are you serious, Kenji? You actually *want* to have a little fun? I thought you might frown on this as a newly married man."

It was distasteful to Kenji to act as though he was an actual friend of this wretch, but it was a necessary evil under the circumstances.

"I'm a man, Kanta. How long do you think I can go without a little satisfaction?"

"Well, well. Even the self-righteous Kenji Watanabe likes to dip his wick once in a while."

"Of course," said Kenji. "Are these new girls upstairs?"

"You guys take care of the tab," Kanta said to his men. "We have some business to tend to."

The headwaiter handed Kenji his poncho on the way out, and Kanta led him to his car where a driver was waiting.

"To The Ranch we go," said Kanta.

Kenji looked back and saw Gang's car lurching and halting. There was no way he was going to be able to follow them. The rain was still pouring, and lightning continued to flash across the night sky as they drove off.

"What is this Ranch?" asked Kenji.

"Just a little place for the top brass to visit. They don't like screwing the same whores as us mortals."

Kenji noticed Kanta wasn't nearly as drunk as he had thought but didn't pay it any further attention. His focus was on the children, and things were going well except for the fact that he was on his own. But he hadn't done anything wrong yet – just a soldier out on the town drinking. How perfectly normal was that?

"How much farther?" asked Kenji.

"Impatient aren't we, Watanabe? You really have surprised me tonight."

Kenji tried to make mental notes of where they were going as they left the city. They emerged from a forest into a broad track of open land, and Kanta told the driver to pull over and stop.

"There she is," said Kanta, pointing to a farmhouse standing tall behind a row of trees quite a way off.

"Why are we stopping here?" asked Kenji.

"We don't want to spook the old fogies. They might be in the middle of something special. Have fun, Watanabe."

"You're not coming?"

"We have to pick up some other guests, but we'll be back."

"What do I say when I get there?"

"What do you say? You say you're fucking Lieutenant Kenji Watanabe, and you want to have some fun. Just tell them you're with me. Believe me, nobody's going to stop you, my friend. You have my word on that."

"And you are coming back?"

"Of course. Thirty minutes – an hour tops. Enough time for you to have a couple of goes if you like."

Kenji got out, stood in the pouring rain with his poncho hood over his head, and watched the car turn around and leave. He began toward the house, mulling over his options. He glanced back to the road where they had emerged, and it looked as though there would be no help coming from Gang. All he could do was find out where they were and let Wei know when he got back.

As he approached, he could see that there was a line of thick cedars about ten meters from the house. He stopped when he reached them and looked between the branches to get an idea of what was happening. It was a two-story house, and there were four windows on both the first and second floors. There were no lights on in the upper level. On the first floor, it was dark in the two rooms to the right. He could see lights coming from the two windows on the left, however, and he thought that was probably the front of the house as he saw two cars parked in that direction. He had no idea how many people were in the house, and he couldn't make out what was going on inside.

According to Kanta, there would be no problem with him entering the house, but he wasn't at all sure that he wanted to lose his anonymity just yet. At the moment, only Kanta and his driver knew he was in the area, and he hoped to keep it that way until he had a plan.

He decided to surveil the perimeter. The strong wind and rain would help him move about unnoticed, he thought. He moved to his right toward the rear where the line of cedars turned, crossing along behind the property.

On the back of the house, he could see that there were two windows on the first floor and two on the second directly above. Only the light in the second-floor window to the right was on. As he moved closer to that side of the house, he heard the voice of a girl protesting and crying, apparently in pain.

There was a wide-trunked oak in the backyard between the house and hedge. He slid through the thick, wet foliage of the cedars, and ran beside it. As he stood peering through the branches for a better look, the light went out. Over the sound of the heavy rain, he heard a girl crying and pleading in Chinese. While he was unable to understand what she said, it was clear that she was begging someone to stop.

What am I doing here? he thought. These things went on every day all over the world, and there was no way he could stop every act of evil. Why should he put his life and career on the line for strangers who were being harmed by other strangers? He was an officer in the Imperial Japanese Army, yet he was spying on a fellow soldier. He should get back to his barracks and forget all about these people – never go to Lu's again.

But then he wondered if cowardice was fueling his thoughts. Wouldn't his superiors, all the way up to the Emperor of Japan, want him to help these children if they were who Wei said they were?

Lights shone through the trees from the direction of the road where Kanta had let him out, so he moved back behind the cedars at the rear of the yard. The girl in the room cried out again, and then he heard sounds of a struggle.

He moved to the side of the house away from the approaching car, the side to which he had not yet been. There were four windows on both levels of the house on this side as well. The lights on the second floor were out. The light in the room nearest the backyard, below the room where he had heard the girl crying was out, but when he looked to the window to the right of that, he was startled. The light was on, and he saw the clear silhouette of a young girl standing at the window looking out. He glanced forward and saw that the lights were on in the two rooms at the front of the house.

The car pulled up out front, so he moved up to have a look. A man got out of the car and ran into the house. He wore an overcoat and carried an umbrella, so Kenji was unable to get a look at the man's face. He could only see vaguely through the front windows, but it looked and sounded as if the room at the front was some type of parlor or living room. The rooms to the back and upstairs were probably bedrooms. When he walked back, the little girl was no longer at the window.

He decided to have a look, so he moved through the cedars, ran over, and crouched low under the window. He turned to face the house and raised his head until he was able to see inside.

The first thing he saw was a candle on a chest of drawers. As he cautiously moved his head to take in more, he saw the bedroom door. It was shut with a thin ray of light coming in at the bottom. Moving his head a bit further, he found what he was looking for, at least partially. It was the same young lady he had seen by the pond in a red dress, another young lady in a plain gown, and a young girl and boy in ordinary peasant dress, all with their hands bound behind their backs leaning against the wall to his left.

He heard laughter and voices in the front room, the officers no doubt drinking. These were definitely the children Wei and his men wanted to find. However, he did not see the young lady who had captivated his attention by the pond, and he feared she might have been the girl he heard upstairs.

The door swung open and Kenji ducked out of sight. He heard one of the young ladies pleading and peeked back in to see a man standing in the center of the room looking down at the children and was surprised to see it was the doctor who had let the Chinese girl die at the hospital. Kenji leaned back so that he couldn't be seen and listened. One of the older girls, most likely the spy Chang had put with them, volunteered to go with the man in Japanese.

There was a long silence. Kenji couldn't resist the temptation to look in again. He ducked down and moved to the other side of the window in order to see the children without being seen by the doctor. When he peeked back in, the terror on the face of the young boy caught his attention. It was painful to watch without taking action. Kenji was sure the doctor would take the girl who had offered to go freely, but a desperate pandemonium erupted when he reached down and grabbed the youngest girl by the arm. Kenji's right hand impulsively went for his gun, but he steadied himself and tried to reason. The girl couldn't be ten years old. The doctor pulled her out of the room as the others screamed and tried to stand. The door slammed shut, and the girls attempted in vain to back up to the door and open it with their bound hands.

The door was locked, and the little girl was gone.

CHAPTER 27

Thursday, July 15ᵗʰ, 1943: Late Night
The Ranch – Ai

The first time was supposed to be something special. In every culture, every country, throughout history, it was supposed to be a time to be treasured.

That had not been the case for Ai.

She had been given no say in the matter. It had been done against her will. It wasn't even a man she would have found remotely interesting under any circumstances. It was an old man. And to make matters even worse, if that were possible, he was a soldier in an army that she considered to be her enemy.

It had been excruciating. It had been degrading. *Humans should not treat other people this way*, she had thought as the man was on top of her. She had tried to plead with him, but he had seemed to gain more satisfaction the more she had protested. She had struggled as long as she could, but he was too powerful in the end.

She begged.

He smiled and slapped her.

There came a time when she had given up. The man had already violated her, and she had just wanted it to be over as quickly as possible.

She would never, ever forget his face.

The only way she was able to calm herself was to make a vow. While he went on and on, she repeated it over and over, speaking in a low, deranged voice. Her oath. Her promise to herself.

"Someday, I will watch you die."

CHAPTER 28

Thursday, July 15th, 1943: Late Night
The Ranch – Kenji

The time to make a decision had come. Kenji knew he could be in the living room drying off in a matter of seconds. When Kanta returned, he could demand to be taken back to the barracks. Better yet, he could walk home. It might take all night, but he wouldn't have to worry about court-martial or any of the things going on in this house. This wasn't his concern – not his children. Chang was probably dead.

What does any of this have to do with me?

There was a noise from the back of the house, from the room that had been dark earlier. He crept in that direction and saw there was a light in the first-floor corner room now. He looked in and saw the little girl sitting on the floor near the rear window as the doctor placed a candle on a table and began taking off his shirt. The girl's hands were still behind her back, but he was amazed to see that she had a very calm expression. She was the only one who hadn't shed a tear or screamed when she was taken by this monster. She had to be terrified, he thought, but she sat and stared in cold silence.

Kenji continued to wrestle with his thoughts: whether he had any duty to rescue these children, whether all this was any of his concern, but he had to decide now. All of this was for children he didn't even know, for some odd Chinese man that he barely knew. Were they worth the risk to his life and career? Would they even appreciate his sacrifice?

Make up your mind dammit.

He ran to the backyard, behind the oak tree, almost ready to give up and go in the house. As he stood thinking, he saw that a light was on again in the same room where he had heard the girl pleading upstairs and saw a man smoking by the window. The man was partially obscured by leaves and the rain, so he crept forward enough to get a clear view. The man opened the window and threw out his cigar.

Unbelievable, he thought. *It can't be.*

But it was. It was his father.

Kenji was paralyzed.

The thoughts began to take shape. Eventually, it started to make sense. This was why Kanta had brought him here. This was all planned. The bastard knew his father was here and brought Kenji to drag him into the mud along with the rest of them.

And then there was his father.

"Dammit," he said aloud.

This changed everything. Kenji tried to settle on a clear course, but he could only condemn himself for being so fainthearted as he stood, wavering in the intense, obfuscating rain. The general shut the window and moved out of view.

Kenji ran through his options. Go through the front door, use his real name, and demand that the children be set free – hopeless. Laughable. Break the window and beat the doctor – court-martial.

The walk-home-and-forget-all-about-it option was looking better every second, but he was compelled to walk to the window at the back of the house and have one last look.

The doctor was loosening the rope that bound her hands. She sat perfectly still. After her hands were free, he began pulling her top over her head. Kenji pulled away and started to run. He couldn't watch this happen. He ran through the cedars and out into the open field. He ran as fast as he could in the driving rain.

But then he stopped.

He couldn't run away from this. The decision he was desperate to find had finally come.

He ran back, trying to decide the best way to carry out the plan. He returned to the window, making sure his face was under the hood of his poncho. Then he reached with his right hand, unsheathed his knife, and tapped on the glass with his left.

The doctor was startled. Both he and the girl stared at the figure, a shrouded shadow outside the window, obscured by darkness and streaks of rain.

"Sorry to interrupt you, sir, but I need to ask you something," said Kenji. It was probably not completely intelligible through the closed window and over the sound of the rain, but Kenji was pretty sure that the doctor would know that he was a Japanese soldier.

It worked.

The doctor stood and opened the window.

"What the hell do you mean interrupting me like this soldier? Do you have a death wish?" he said over the sounds of the wind and falling rain.

"Sorry, sir," said Kenji. "Just checking on your safety. You see, my partner's been shot," he said pointing. The doctor leaned his head out the window and followed the indicated path where he saw nothing but a puddle. His head spun back to Kenji – the same malevolent, angry face Kenji remembered from the hospital. The essence of evil.

And then it just happened. Something primal. Something paternal. Kenji couldn't stop it. The blade shot out from under the rain poncho. Fast as lightning. Right through the neck. Slicing the jugular.

Warm, viscous blood oozed over Kenji's hand. He pulled the knife out, dropped to his knees, and retched. As he did so, the body of the doctor tumbled out of the window and fell in front of him. The sight of the dead man's eyes made him vomit again.

It was the first man he had ever killed.

It was the only man he would kill in his lifetime.

Kenji held the knife out into the rain to wash the blood away, but it held stubbornly to the blade.

He started when he heard a voice. The little girl was standing in the window saying something to him. Kenji didn't know how to say 'be quiet' in Chinese, so he just held his hand over his mouth. He went to the puddle where he had pointed earlier and washed his hands and knife clean, then slid it back into its sheath. The girl watched patiently without saying another word. He gestured for her to sit down and to stay quiet. Then he lowered the window and left her to make his entrance.

CHAPTER 29

Thursday, July 15th, 1943: Late Night
Hsinking, Manchuria (Changchun, China) – Kanta

Just like clockwork, thought Kanta. It had all fallen into place better than he could have imagined. Kenji was drunk, and, if he hadn't already, would soon see what a philandering counterfeit his father really is. The prude had even wanted to partake himself. It was too good to be true.

Now he just needed to gather a couple more men to go and witness the spectacle. As he sat in the barracks waiting for his driver to return, he had another look at the letter.

> *Kanta,*
> *General Watanabe has decided to pay a little surprise visit on Thursday, July 15th to see how his darling little son is doing and inspect the troops. Whatever you do, don't let the sniveling brat know. If you can line up a few girls, I'm sure the old geezer would be appreciative. Let me know if you can cause any trouble.*
> *Lt. Gen. Fujii*

When his father learned how well he had used that little note, he would be a happy man. Both the general *and* his son snared. How awkwardly beautiful this was going to be.

CHAPTER 30

Thursday, July 15th, 1943: Late Night
The Ranch – Kenji

Kenji walked up the steps of the covered front porch and into the house where two privates sat smoking cigarettes by the front door. They stood and saluted as he removed his rain poncho. There were a few high-level officers present, but they paid him very little attention, not realizing he was General Watanabe's son. They were all on the right side of the room where two tables had been set up for cards and *shogi*.

An older Japanese woman dressed formally in a kimono came and took his poncho and handed him a towel. A Japanese private rushed down the stairs, also on his right, and began cleaning his boots. Other than the woman and the three privates, he could see no other staff in the house. There was a full bar straight ahead and a couple of empty tables on the left where the woman guided him and pulled out a chair. The warm lights around the room and soft music playing on the phonograph were meant to set everyone at ease, but Kenji was anything but.

He had just killed a man.

"What can I get for you, sir?" said the woman. He asked for a glass of beer.

How exactly does one ask for a girl under these circumstances? he thought. He knew he had to move quickly because he didn't want to see his father and needed to get to the room with the children before anyone else. There was no way of knowing when Kanta might reappear. He motioned for the private who had been upstairs to come over and asked discreetly about having a companion.

"Yes sir. Right this way, sir," he said. He began toward the staircase across the room.

"Wait a minute," said Kenji, trying to draw as little notice as possible. He motioned him back and quietly asked, "Where are you going?"

"To show you the girls, sir. We have several to choose from upstairs."

"Uh, well, I thought – don't you have any down here?"

The private could see Kenji was uneasy and was doing his best to use discerning etiquette. A direct no, or the inability to provide what was wanted, was abhorrent in their culture.

"Those," said the young man, "are, how can I say...reserved, sir."

Kenji thought for a moment.

"You see, my name is Lieutenant Watanabe. Lieutenant Fujii said I was welcome to the girl of my choice."

The young man bowed deeply and apologized for his rudeness. There were two hallways on either side of the house, and the young soldier led Kenji to the one on the left. They passed through a privacy curtain at the entrance to the hallway, and then the private stopped and pulled a ring of keys from his pocket in front of the room where Kenji had seen the children. He opened the door and stood aside for Kenji to enter.

The first thing Kenji noticed was the boy. He was lying on his side crying, hands still bound behind his back. The girl in the red dress glared hatefully, but the other smiled and spoke in Japanese.

"I go with you," she said.

"Lieutenant Fujii said there were four girls," Kenji said to the private.

"Yes sir, the other two are engaged at the moment. They will be available in a little while if none of these suit you, sir."

"No, she'll do just fine," said Kenji pointing to the girl who had spoken, feeling sick at playing the part of such a perverted character.

The soldier raised her delicately and led them out the door and toward the back of the house. Kenji noted that they were passing the room where the little girl was hopefully waiting quietly, then they moved along a back hallway to the other side of the house. The private opened a door for them and lit a candle. He used his knife to cut the restraints from the girl's hands, asked Kenji if there was anything else he could do for him, and then left.

After the door was shut, Kenji waited a moment and then whispered, "I'm here to help. Wei said you work for Chang."

"I do," said Ju. "Are they outside?"

"No. I don't think they followed me here."

"Do you have any transportation?"

"Nothing," said Kenji. "Do you know where we are?"

"Yes. If you can get us out, I can hide the children until Wei can get help to us. We are at the old Tan farm north of Changchun. If we get away, make sure to tell Wei that, and that I will take the children to the Kiang coal mines until they arrive. Do you have a plan to get us out?" she asked.

"I think so. We need to move right away. The young girl is in the back corner, beside the room where they are holding all of you."

"Yes, I know. She's with a major. We may have to leave her behind. The first priority is the boy."

"The major is dead," said Kenji. "I think we can use him to our advantage."

"Good," she said, without wasting a second to find out who had killed him or how. Irrelevant. Kenji could see the girl was good at what she did. "The eldest girl is with a general," she said. "I have no idea where they are, but, again, we have to focus first on the boy."

"She's on the second floor – corner room above the little girl," said Kenji. He saw lights flash through the room from the direction where Kanta had dropped him off. He looked out the window and saw a car coming. "We have to move soon. If he binds your hands again, can you get the restraints off?"

"Not a problem," she replied.

"Once you're back in the room, get the restraints off the others as well and be ready to move. I'll divert everyone to the south for as long as I can, then come to the window for you and the children. You take them in the opposite direction – to the north. After that, you're on your own. I'll tell Wei what you said."

"Tan farm - north of town," she said to confirm the relevant information. "Waiting at Kiang coal mines. He knows the area well. Call for the private now," she said.

"But we haven't had time to..."

"Make an excuse. Tell him I'm too ugly – that you've changed your mind and want to wait for one of the others."

Kenji opened the door and called for the private.

"This one's not for me," said Kenji to the young man hustling down the hallway.

"Very sorry, sir," he said. "Your beer is on the table." Kenji followed the private back through the halls and watched as he put restraints on Ju's hands and locked the room. Kenji then returned to his table just as Kanta and two colonels were coming through the front door.

The grandstanding bootlicker ignored him at first, walking over and kowtowing before the brass. After a sufficient period of fawning, he made his excuses and walked over to Kenji's table. The woman brought out a bottle of *sake* for the colonels who sat across the room. Kenji knew Kanta had certainly blabbed to them about his triumph in securing some young girls, so Kenji wanted to get to work before any more of the children were dispersed throughout the house.

Kenji said, "I need to talk to you about something."

"Please do, my friend," said Kanta, in an unusually reserved voice.

"Let's step outside," said Kenji, leading the way. The rain had stopped, and the clouds began to part, allowing some light into the night sky. Kenji pulled out some cigarettes and offered one to Kanta.

"Did you have a chance to sample the new talent?" said Kanta, slapping him on the back once they were out of sight of the others.

"Yeah. Boy it's been a while," said Kenji, taking his first drag and leading Kanta off the porch and around the side of the building. "I needed that."

"I never knew you had it in you, Watanabe."

The two walked casually, Kanta thinking about the dirty trick he was playing on Kenji, and Kenji thinking about how best to use Kanta to pull off the upcoming deception. Two men side by side, pretending to be best friends, plotting separate frauds.

"Who is this person you said you wanted me to meet here?" said Kenji as they passed the window of the children's room.

"You'll see soon. Don't worry."

As they approached the corner, Kenji lagged a step behind to allow Kanta to make the turn first. He tried to keep the conversation going.

"Oh, come on. You can give me..."

"*Son of a bitch!*" exclaimed Kanta as he backed into Kenji. "What the hell is that?"

Kenji went around and knelt on the ground beside the doctor. He felt for a pulse and informed Kanta that the man was dead. He told Kanta to go order the privates to come out at once. Within seconds, the soldiers, followed by Kanta, were running back and dropping to their knees beside Kenji.

"Who is this man?" shouted Kenji at the shocked young soldiers.

"It's the major, sir," said the private in charge of the girls and children. "He went into a room a short while ago. This room, sir," he said, pointing to the window.

"Tell everyone to get out here," said Kenji. The privates ran off to the front of the building.

"What do you think happened?" said Kanta.

"Obviously it's the work of rebels," said Kenji.

Kenji stepped back to the corner so he would be able to see them coming. The officers swept around the corner following the privates, many with their pistols drawn.

"Over there," yelled Kenji as they all ran toward him. "I saw men running over there," he shouted, pointing toward a section of forest across the field to the south.

"Rebels," shouted Kanta, believing that he had seen something also. "Those rebels killed the major!"

They ran through the line of cedars out into the field to the south after the phantom insurgents.

"Kanta, get your car and go. Use the headlamps." Kanta took off toward his car as instructed and told his driver to light the way.

Kenji carried the dead man inside to occupy the old woman's attention. If anyone found the major's blood on him now, it would be obvious how it got there.

As he entered and placed the major on the floor, he saw his father coming down the stairs, pistol in hand, demanding to know what was happening. The old woman cried out that a man had been killed. It was at that point the general recognized his son.

"Kenji, what on earth are you doing here?"

"No time for that. We've got to catch the killers," he said, taking his father by the arm and leading him outside. "They ran that way," said Kenji, pointing to the group of men spreading out across the field. "You follow them, and I'll check around the house this way." The old man moved off at a brisk walk waving his pistol and shouting orders.

Kenji ran to the children's bedroom window on the other side of the house and tapped lightly. Ju opened it and lifted the boy through, then helped Lin out before jumping to the ground herself.

"This way," he said to them, leading them around the corner to the room where the little girl was waiting patiently. He raised the window and Fan crawled out. When he felt her petite frame in his arms, pressed close, and she hugged his neck tightly, he knew it was worth it. He had made the right decision.

"What shall we do about Ai?" said Ju.

"Who?" asked Kenji.

"Ai – their big sister."

Kenji had never heard her name. He looked up to the second-floor window. Ju looked out into the field to the south – a clear sign that she was anxious to leave.

"Give me one minute," said Kenji.

Leaving the children at the corner of the house, he ran around to the front door where the woman was cleaning the blood from the major's neck. As he ran past her, she asked if they had found the murderers.

"Not yet," he said, bounding up the steps three at a time. The room at the corner was unlocked, and he went in to find the girl clothed, sitting in a corner with her knees to her chest. He shut the door and quickly moved beside her.

"Ai, you've got to get out of here," he said in Japanese. "I'm going to help you." She couldn't understand Japanese, but in her current state, she wouldn't have heard him in any language. She was catatonic.

She stared through him as if he wasn't there, trembling, a faint humming sound escaping her lips. Kenji opened the window and then reached over to help her up. She screamed and slapped his hand away. Kenji knew the men would be returning soon. The woman downstairs might come to see what was happening. He had to get her out of the window without delay.

He leaned out the window and asked Ju what the children's names were. She told him.

He moved back to Ai and took her by the shoulders. He put his face directly in her line of vision.

"Listen to me Ai. You have to go. Shou. Fan," he said. "Shou. Fan."

The tears finally came.

She tried to stand but vomited on his pants. He leaned out the window and saw some of the officers walking back across the field.

"Listen, I'm going to lower her out and you two try to break the fall," he said to Ju.

Ju pulled Lin into position below as Kenji helped Ai through the window frame. His shoulder was giving him fits, but it had to be done. He took her hands, helped her into position, and then pushed her off the sill with his chest while still holding her hands. He lowered her until his arms were fully extended and let go.

"*Arigato*," said Ju.

"Go," said Kenji. "Don't let them see you."

Ju took Shou and Fan by the hands and ran through the line of cedars to the north, using the house as a shield from the returning soldiers. Lin put her arms around Ai, pulling her along to keep pace with the others.

Kenji left the window open, walked out, closed the door and ran down the stairs. He went out the door and to the side of the house where the children had fled. He peered out into the darkness and saw small specks of movement. To make it look as if he had been involved in the search, he ran out past the back of the house into the fields, then turned toward the direction of the approaching men. He spotted his father near the front and ran to join him.

Once they had all returned to the house, Kenji was careful not to let the private return to the back rooms. He detained him in the parlor with questions about the major who had been murdered. All the other officers had joined in the questioning, the old woman pouring coffee as fast as she could make it. The guards had notified the military police who arrived and began looking over the house and grounds. It was almost an hour later, when the police began asking about the girl who had been with the major when he had last been seen, that the discovery was made of the missing children. None of the officers, most notably Lieutenant Kanta Fujii, appeared to want to talk much about these children or where they had come from. There was no mad rush to discover what had become of them.

"Let's get out of here," Kenji said to Kanta.

No one objected when the lieutenants wearily shuffled out the front door at 2:00 a.m.

CHAPTER 31

Friday, July 16th, 1943: Afternoon
Hsinking, Manchuria (Changchun, China) – Kenji and Wei

The view from the front of Lu's Place was somehow different today. Life was different. Kenji thought he could never understand or trust people the way he had in the past. Not after yesterday. Everything would be different now.

Wei came out and placed two beers on the table, sat down beside him and said, "We have to take care of our best customer."

"I thought you had a rule against sitting with me," Kenji said.

"That was before Kenji became my hero."

Wei could see that Kenji was far off in thought. He tried to give him room, let him think in peace.

"I tried my best, Wei. I just didn't make it in time."

"You did everything you could – far more than we could have ever asked or expected. There's no need for regret. Ai is strong. She's thankful for what you've done for her and her family. We all are."

"I just wish..." started Kenji, and then shook his head. They spent a few minutes sitting quietly, watching people go by.

"Life isn't perfect for any of us, you know," said Wei. "Think about me. I had this done," he said, motioning to his groin, "when I was just five years old because my family was poor and needed money. I had no say in the matter."

Kenji continued to shake his head as he sipped at his beer.

"You haven't mentioned Chang," said Kenji.

"How do you say...Duty is heavier than a mountain; death is lighter than a feather. Just like your great samurai warriors, Kenji, if you die for a good cause, you die with honor. Chang died with honor, and that is a great thing to say about a man."

Kenji nodded in agreement. He had only known Chang for a day or two, but the man had made an enormous impact on his life in that short time.

"Ai's father, the Emperor, would like to give you a little something."

"I want nothing," said Kenji.

"I suppose it would be problematical to have gifts from the Emperor at this time, but we won't forget once the war is over."

"You don't understand. I want nothing today, tomorrow, forever. You don't know what I did, Wei. You don't know the whole story."

"I'm afraid I do," said Wei. "We've debriefed Ju and Ai, and all of our other people in Changchun, and put all the pieces together now. I will not speak names because I don't want to cause you any embarrassment, but we know who was in the old Tan farm last night."

"Then you can understand why I don't want a damn thing for what I did."

"Yes, I can," said the Manchurian.

After another long silence Kenji said, "Wei, don't ever tell Ai who did that to her."

"I'm sorry I can't do that for you, Kenji, after all you've done for us. She already knows. She's a very strong-minded young lady, but, as I said, she will forever be deeply grateful for what you've done."

They watched children playing in the street for a long while. Both men had lost their appetites to discuss Asian history, at least for one day.

"So what happened to Mrs. Wang?" asked Kenji.

Wei took a sip of beer and wiped his mouth with the back of his hand.

"One day, when the children went out to play, she took a knife from the kitchen, went out into the woods, and cut her own her throat," said Wei. "You see, her honor had been compromised. She couldn't live with that."

Kenji nodded, still watching the children.

There was nothing left to say.

EPILOGUE

The police would be coming soon – could be on the way now. If he was going to avoid them, he would have to get out of the house pronto.

As this day had long been anticipated, very little additional thought was required to set his final earthly plan into motion. He wanted to be sure his death would not be viewed as suicide. To that end, he convinced himself that he wouldn't go through with it. While that could be done honorably in certain circumstances, he didn't want anyone to believe he had killed himself to avoid the detective's questions. If he ended up being careless in the woods today and died, that would just be an unfortunate accident – an old man routinely battling gout, lost in the forest.

The forecast called for snow and temperatures below freezing tonight. As a sign that this was just an ordinary day, he decided to call Ami's mobile using his cell phone, knowing that of all the people he could phone to leave a message, she would be the least likely to pick up. He hoped to call, get no answer, and then leave an ambiguous message about his day's itinerary.

She answered on the first ring. "Kenji, where are you?"

"Good morning. Is something wrong?" he asked.

"Haven't you heard? Detective Miyabe called and said he had new information about your father's murder, and that it was urgent that he speak with you immediately."

"Calm down, Ami. What could be so urgent after all these years?"

"He said he *knows* who killed your father and why. All he needs is confirmation and a few facts from you and the case can be solved."

"Even if he solves it," replied Kenji calmly, "he can't do anything. The statute of limitations ran out a long time ago."

"But we'd know, after all these years we would know. Don't you care anymore, Kenji?"

"Did you tell him where I am?"

"Of course. Is that a problem?"

"No. No problem at all. It's just that I'm not actually at the house right now. I hope they're not wasting a trip there."

"He wouldn't tell me any details. Can you call him and call me back?"

"I'll call when I get back home this afternoon. By the way, have you left yet?"

"I'm leaving now. I'll be there in a few hours."

"I left you a note on the coffee table."

"I don't care about that. Did you hear me? He knows who killed your father. Call him right away, Kenji. I want to know what he's found out."

"Listen, you're breaking up. I'll call you later."

He hung up, grabbed a sheet of paper and pencil and wrote:

Ami,
I'm going for a short hike. Maybe Mount Hanare.
May go for a bath at the hot spring.
Will be home this afternoon.
Kenji

After putting the note on the coffee table, he dressed as he normally would for a hike – long underwear, warm socks, hiking pants, and a flannel shirt. Then he went to the liquor cabinet and pulled out a large bottle of vodka and put it in his backpack along with a pack of Luckies. After putting on a down jacket, wool cap, and hiking boots, he grabbed his bag, had a last look around the house he would never see again, and left.

It took longer to reach the trails at this age than it had as a younger man, and as he neared the first path away from the road, a police car flew past in the direction of his house. He had left the door unlocked on purpose. They might wait for Ami to arrive, or they might decide to go in uninvited, but either way, the note would lead them to places he wouldn't be going.

Once safely off the road and into the forest, his mind began to roam. He had always imagined he would be sad if this time came; that he would change his mind and return home to give the police a full disclosure, but he felt surprisingly at peace and comfortable with his decision. He was eighty years old now. There couldn't be that many healthy years left. Perhaps it would have been harder if the discovery had come sooner.

Some memories that came to him seemed perfectly natural at such a time: the first time in the grass with Naomi – how nothing had ever matched that feeling; his children and grandson – how they would mourn his loss and try to make sense of what happened.

But other memories seemed to come from nowhere. Aberrations. The fight he had had with Taro when he was fourteen because he didn't want his younger brother to follow him to the lake. The guilt he had felt at Mrs. Ishii's funeral and, again, a few months later at Kazu's.

Deep in the forest, he ran across a young couple taking pictures of each other and decided to use the opportunity to be noticed. He approached and asked if they would like him to take their picture together, and they happily said they would. He made a point to introduce himself and let them know his foot was aching because of a nagging battle with gout. Although the couple insisted on helping him get back, he assured them that he would be fine after he took the medication in his pocket. He watched as they walked away, engrossed in love, almost immediately forgetting about the old man and his infirmities.

His cell phone rang, and he saw that it was Yoshi. Although not sure at first whether it would be wise to answer, he was overtaken by the desire to speak to his son one last time.

"Hello."

"Hey, Dad. Where are you?"

"Taking a little hike."

"Without the cigarettes, I hope. We'll be leaving Tokyo this evening when I finish work. We should get there before midnight hopefully."

"Great. Can't wait to see you and my grandson."

"Yeah, he can't wait to see you either. He's got a special surprise for you. He can't shut up about it. 'Gotta show Grandpa,' he keeps saying. 'Don't tell him what it is,' he says. He's really excited, so act surprised, okay?"

"Sure. Tell Koji I love him."

"Whoa. Is this my dad? Getting sappy in your old age, aren't you? You tell him that yourself tonight. Gotta go. See ya."

"Yoshi, wait a minute. Don't hang up." But it was too late. The line went dead.

The sky was gray; the forecast snow beginning to fall. The path was frozen in places, and the dead leaves swirled in the cold wind. Kenji thought about all the days of his life which he hadn't enjoyed as he should have. As he moved deeper and deeper into the forest, his old bones aching, he pondered if it had all been worth it. All of the stress and troubles seemed so meaningless and petty now.

There had been a Catholic priest, Father Jorge from Madrid, he remembered. They played golf together on Tuesdays for a while when he was in his sixties. He had taught Kenji some things about his faith. He recalled asking Father Jorge about that thing in the movies where people go into a little room and talk into a screen. *Confession. It's good for the soul,* he had said with his Spanish accent. Kenji had written it off as nonsense back then, but it actually sounded like a good idea now. Not much chance of finding one of those little rooms or a priest out here, though.

As evening approached, the snow began to fall harder, blowing sideways. Kenji stopped, pulled out a Lucky Strike, and lit up, taking special note of the burning object between his index and middle finger. "This one won't be taking any time off my life," he said out loud and took a long draw. He pulled out the vodka and took a shot. It was time to start moving off the trail.

There was a tragic story, he remembered, from his teenage years, of a man who had lost his way in Nagano during a fierce blizzard. He was found dead the next day, naked, fifty paces away from the warmth and comfort of his home. The newspaper had reported that some people who freeze to death, their minds start to play tricks on them, and they think it's hot – they take off their clothes. He hoped he wouldn't do that. The vodka should help there. Another shot.

With darkness came stronger wind and even heavier snow. The treetops bent to-and-fro, and it was getting harder to move as the snow piled higher. He found a fallen tree and decided that this would be as good a place as any.

He checked his phone.

Dead.

To move the process along, he removed his hat and jacket and sat against the decaying tree. He pulled out another cigarette and examined it before lighting up. He took a drag and turned the bottle of vodka straight up.

His mind was relaxing. Slow now.

The *Moonlight Sonata* played in his mind. He could listen to it for hours.

How many nights he had sat and thought as Ami played, drinking his wine and letting his mind roam.

They did it, he thought. Ai always said it had to be done at some point, but he never believed she would really go through with it.

He certainly had it coming.

Ai had never lied about it. She told him the truth immediately after – about creating the notes, copying Kenji's keys to his father's house, Shou breaking into the general's home in Tokyo to leave the note and steal the sword. They had waited all those years out of respect and appreciation for what Kenji had done, but they also had a family code of honor. And when they learned he was dying, they had to do it. He had to pay the price.

We all have to pay eventually.

Ai had gotten them the job working with the catering company. It had been no problem at all for them to sneak the sword into the tent while they were working that day. After they had finished, and everyone else left to work elsewhere around the island, they remained in the tent, hiding.

At six o'clock they reviewed the plan and made their final preparations. Shou was originally supposed to be the one to kill him, but Fan could see that he was having second thoughts. She decided to take on the role, and Shou was happy to let her. She took the war sword, and Shou took the short knife. Then they lay in wait in their hiding places in the tent, waiting for the general to arrive. If they had been forced to abort the plan at any time, they would have just left, claimed to have been workers not knowing where to go. They were supposed to be selling hot dogs anyway.

Ai was in the crowd, disguised as heavily as she could be without looking suspicious. She made sure to get to the lake early and get a good seat.

The general had arrived promptly at eight o'clock and started drinking whiskey. As soon as the fireworks began, they crept out and surprised him. Shou came up from behind and held the short knife to his throat. They guided him just outside the tent so Ai could watch from the banks of the lake while everyone else stared up into the sky at the fireworks. Shou and Fan had studied Japanese assiduously in the months leading up to the date of execution. Fan informed him of the date – Thursday, July 15th, 1943 – and nature of his crime before thrusting his own sword into his stomach as Shou let go. Shou dragged him into the water and returned to the tent. They decided to take the sheath with them at the last minute. Fan hid it under her clothes. When they were ready, they walked around the stage, passing Yumi who was on her way to the tent, and then past the rest of the Watanabe family. The guards on the bridge, who were watching the fireworks, let them pass. Their only focus was to check people coming onto the island.

They had met Ai at the gate and left.

Kenji took one final, long draw on the Lucky and buried it in the snow with his forefinger. He gazed upward through the leafless trees and longed to see the stars one last time.

He turned the bottle up and drank away the last.

He thought about his grandfather and the constellations. He heard Beethoven playing through the driving snow.

The bottle slid slowly, almost imperceptibly, and after a few minutes it escaped his grasp completely and rolled away. The snow covered his face, but he didn't move. His eyelids were closed. The stars still shone above the clouds, but not on Kenji.

The snow fell all night. The wind blew. The animals took shelter. And the Watanabe name survived.

•   •   •

Saturday, May 3rd, 2003 (Golden Week Holiday): Morning
Karuizawa – Village in Mountains of Nagano, Japan

Captain Miyabe parked on the street and walked up the same steps he had climbed back in 1967, only slower. He found Mrs. Watanabe sitting at a table on the front deck, still beautiful, he thought, but now with white hair.

"Pardon me for not standing, Captain Miyabe. Please sit down."

"Quite alright, Mrs. Watanabe," he said, taking the seat she proffered across from her. "I hope you're enjoying your holiday."

"I don't enjoy much these days, Captain."

"I'm very sorry for your loss, Mrs. Watanabe. Kenji was truly a good man."

Ami didn't comment. She looked out into the yard, lost in her own world.

"Mrs. Watanabe, I came here today because you asked me," he said cautiously, "but I'm not sure this is a good idea. I've been retired for many years now. The statute of limitations ran out over twenty years ago. Nothing can be done except to stir up more grief. What I'm saying is...are you sure you really want to dredge up the past? Without Kenji, all I can do is speculate."

"Captain Miyabe," she said without looking at him, "I was married to that man for sixty years, and sometimes I feel like I never knew him. I just want the truth."

"Well," he said, wringing his hands, "if you insist, I'll tell you what I know. But as I've said, Kenji was the only one who could have tied it all together. But then, of course, there was the tragic accident."

Ami smiled at the comment. "Is that what you think it was, Captain? Kenji out in the middle of nowhere, with a bottle of vodka, on the very day you want to speak with him?"

Miyabe regarded the woman with pity. The family had undoubtedly seen more than its fair share of tragedy.

"Last year," he began, "a book of memoirs was published in Los Angeles, California. The author was a man by the name of Shou Wang. He had not made them public in his lifetime, but after he died, his children realized they might have historical import and contacted a literary agent."

"In the book, in addition to claiming he was the son of the last Chinese Emperor, he also claimed to have avenged the rape of his eldest sister by a Japanese officer in Manchuria during World War II."

"As I'm sure you can imagine, the Chinese, specifically members of the Chinese Communist Party, were not amused with this. They believed they had finished dealing with such matters decades ago, but it was causing such a sensation that they felt they needed to at least inquire into the matter."

"Mr. Wang had not given the name of the Japanese officer in his memoirs, but it was determined that his eldest sister's name was a Ms. Ai Wang. Reporters and investigators digging into the story found her and asked Ms. Wang, who also lives in Los Angeles, about the allegations, but she refused to speak to them. It was discovered she had lived in Japan for many years after the war with a daughter. She has refused to answer any questions about her past or whether she even has a daughter."

"Eventually, the trail led to the Karuizawa Police Department, and a possible connection was discovered to General Watanabe's murder. As I mentioned earlier, I retired in 1990, but was asked to come back and have a look at the case."

"We have learned that a Ms. Ai Wang did live in Nagano from sometime in 1946 until October of 1967, when she moved to Los Angeles. During our investigation, we also learned your husband was in Hsinking, Manchuria, the area of China where Mr. Shou Wang wrote that his family lived during the war."

"Although I have been retired for a very long time, I remember General Watanabe's case like it happened yesterday. And with all these pieces of evidence pointing to the general's death, I thought we could finally solve the case and give your family closure. As we're blocked by the statute of limitations, and Ms. Wang refuses to cooperate, your husband was the only possible witness in the case who could put all the pieces together. But with his passing, I'm afraid our investigation is at an end unless Ms. Wang has a change of heart."

"Do you have a theory then?" asked Ami, without looking at him.

"Well, we know that Kenji was in Manchuria. We know that his father was there occasionally, also. If you look at Mr. Wang's story, his sister living here in Nagano after the war with a child, the claim of avenging a rape, the note on the general's door, and the man and woman who worked on the island the day the general was murdered – signed up by a woman with a foreign accent if you will recall – it makes for a very intriguing case don't you think?"

Ami continued to stare without any reaction to the question.

"If I could have just talked to your husband, I think we could have gotten the answers."

There was no conversation for several minutes, the detective waiting to see if Mrs. Watanabe had anything else to ask.

"Well, I suppose I should be going now," said Captain Miyabe. "Are you watching a movie?" he asked, looking into the house.

Ami turned to look at him, apparently not understanding his question, and saw that Miyabe was referring to sounds coming from the living room.

"That's Masa."

"Masa?" said Miyabe, surprised. "Alright if I go in and say hello?"

"Be my guest."

Miyabe walked into the house and saw Masa alone on a sofa in the living room, watching the television with all the lights out. Masa didn't look up or appear to notice his presence. Miyabe thought he looked far off. Sad.

"Long time no see," said Miyabe, but Masa continued to stare at the television.

"Bet you don't remember me," said Miyabe, trying one more time to make conversation.

"Captain Miyabe," said Masa, without taking his eyes off the screen.

Miyabe moved a little closer. "You and your brother have become quite famous, haven't you?" he said.

No response.

"Do both of you have families of your own now?"

There was a lengthy pause. Miyabe walked close enough to have a good look at Masa's face.

"Yoshi's married – got a son. Not me."

"I've kept up with you guys over the years. Successful lawyers and businessmen – keeping the family business going strong."

No reaction.

"What are you watching there?" asked the captain, stepping to where he could see the screen beside Masa.

"*Before We Were Lost.*"

"Say, I've heard of that. An American movie. The main character is a Japanese girl, right?"

"No," said Masa, dryly.

"Really? I thought she had a Japanese name."

"She does," replied Masa, without explanation.

"What is it?" asked the captain.

"She just goes by her first name. It's Kayo."

"Yeah, that's it."

Miyabe looked closely at Masa, thinking over the case back to when he had been a young man. He decided to leave him and his mother alone. It was obvious they had no desire to speak to him.

"Nice seeing you again," he said as he walked out.

He stepped out onto the deck and saw Ami still staring into the treetops and decided to leave without interrupting her any further.

"Have a nice day," he said quietly.

As he took the steps, he remembered his last visit so many years ago. He was happy that the family could finally move on now. Two sons, successful businessmen just like their father and grandfather, and a mother with more money than she could ever spend.

Captain Miyabe decided to pay his respects at the Watanabe *ohaka*, the family grave, one last time. It was on his way, and it would give him closure in the case he had worked so many years without resolution.

When he reached the temple where the family cemetery was located, he parked and began walking up the steep steps. The Watanabe stone monument was, of course, at the top, with a gorgeous view of nature.

As he was making the climb, he was surprised to see a woman kneeling at the Watanabe grave all alone. He did not recognize her as a family member but decided the polite thing to do would be to let her finish paying her respects in private.

·   ·   ·

It was ironic that she knelt before the final resting place of the man she admired above all others for his distinguished bravery and courage and, at the same time, before the man she hated most – so much so she had planned his execution. But she rarely thought about the latter these days.

"Thank you, Kenji," she said in Japanese, but with a delightful Chinese accent.

"I wish you had not done this, though."

She knew it was no accident from the moment she heard the story about Kenji Watanabe's death. When the police had started asking questions, she wanted to talk to him and tell him not to do anything foolish. When he hadn't called for days, she searched the news online.

But she already had a feeling. She knew Kenji Watanabe.

They said it was a terrible accident. She knew better.

"You could've moved away all those years ago and been happy. But you always had to think of everyone else, didn't you?"

The statement caused her to think back to the war – the day he saved her family. He was a hero. Other men in that position would have probably just run away, but not Kenji Watanabe.

She decided to talk about happier things.

"Kayo's doing great. A famous movie star – just like you said she'd be." She stood up, turned around, and looked at the view.

"It's so beautiful here."

The cemetery was surrounded with Japanese cherry trees abloom in their full glory on the sunny spring day.

"I will never tell anyone what happened, Kenji. I just wish everyone could know what a good man, a truly honorable man, you are. Spent your whole life protecting other people – taking care of other people's mistakes."

A gust of wind swept through and cherry blossoms filled the air above the many stone monuments of the cemetery. As she looked out at the beautiful sight, she noticed a man below furtively watching her. She turned back to face the grave, kissed her fingers, and placed them on the stone above Kenji's name.

"Goodbye, Kenji."

She walked down the steps, and when she neared the man he spoke to her.

"Good morning. How are you today?"

"Wonderful, and you?" she said.

Miyabe detected the foreign accent right away. "I don't believe we've met. I'm Captain Miyabe."

"Nice to meet you, Captain Miyabe."

"Would you happen to be Ms. Wang?"

"Why yes, I would."

"Would you mind if I ask you a few questions, Ai?" said Miyabe.

The woman gently shook her head. "I'm sorry, Captain. That will not be possible. You see, Ai passed away last week."

Miyabe was visibly stunned. "I'm so sorry," he managed to say. He tried to get a grip on his thoughts and proper decorum, but the detective in him pushed on.

"May I ask what happened?"

The woman looked up into the sky. "I'm no doctor, Captain Miyabe, so I really can't say for sure," she said, and then looked directly at the detective. "But my guess is that she died of a broken heart. Have a nice day, sir," the woman said as she walked by.

She stepped to the bottom where her taxi driver waited with his white hat with black brim and white gloves holding the door.

The captain was puzzled, trying to make sense of all the old and new clues of the case. "Pardon me, ma'am, but you are...?"

She stopped as she was entering the taxi and said, "Fan – it means lethal in Chinese." She sat down in the back seat, and the driver shut her door, climbed in, and drove away as Miyabe watched them through a sea of floating pink and white petals.

NOTE FROM THE AUTHOR

Word-of-mouth is crucial for any author to succeed. If you enjoyed the book, please leave a review online—anywhere you are able. Even if it's just a sentence or two. It would make all the difference and would be very much appreciated.

Thanks!
Sakura

ABOUT THE AUTHOR

Sakura Nobeyama is a student in the mountains of Japan. She studies English literature and history and enjoys horseback riding, mountain climbing, reading, and classical music. This is her first novel. You can leave her a message at https://www.bluesky-es.site/ or email her at scsm389@gmail.com

Thank you so much for reading one of our **Mystery Detective** novels.

If you enjoyed our book, please check out our recommended title for your next great read!

Bailey's Law by Meg Lelvis

"An intelligent, immersive police procedural that will leave you pining for another Jack Bailey novel." –*BEST THRILLERS*

View other Black Rose Writing titles at
www.blackrosewriting.com/books and use promo code
PRINT to receive a **20% discount** when purchasing.

Ingram Content Group UK Ltd.
Milton Keynes UK
UKHW041253230423
420639UK00001B/8